ONCE UPON A
Wish-mas

LAURA BARNARD

Laura Barnard

This book is dedicated to my amazing mum. Without her helping me in every way possible this book wouldn't have got done.

CHAPTER 1

Monday 25th November

Ruby

'Now.' She sighs, slapping her hands on her thighs. 'Mr Rothchester is not the easiest to get along with,' Mrs Dumfy, the housekeeper, explains, with a hard swallow and scratch of the neck.

I can't help but think of my favourite movie, *Mary Poppins*. *"Master is hard to get along with."* Well, he clearly just needs a Mary Poppins like me, a Nanny extraordinaire, to come in and help him look after his kiddies. I'll show him how easy life can be when you have the right help.

'I get on with most people,' I insist, adding a smile.

I guessed he was going to be a nightmare when I noticed on the ad it specified "no person with tattoos need apply".

I only have a small one, one that they'll never see, thank god. A stupid butterfly on my lower back. Sure, they call that area a tramp stamp now, but I was fifteen, drunk and it was oh so pretty.

'Oh, I don't doubt that.' Mrs Dumfy smiles warmly.

I liked her from the moment I walked into the Notting Hill townhouse. In her late fifties with brown hair tied back into a no-nonsense neat bun, she kind of gives me a Mrs Doubtfire vibe, but obviously without the whole being a secret man thing.

'It's just that he... doesn't.' She grimaces. 'Not since his wife died, I'm afraid.'

That's the only reason I bothered coming to the interview today. I've actually already been offered a placement in the South of France but when I heard their mother had died it broke my heart a little. Reminded me of when I was little and my dad died.

'May I ask... how long ago did she pass?'

Her eyes become glassy. They were clearly close. 'Two and a half years ago. The youngest was only a little baby, the poor love.' Her voice breaks a little and she quickly takes out a tissue from her sleeve and dabs at her eyes. It reminds me of my grandma. She always used to have a tissue up her sleeve in case of emergencies.

Poor little babies losing their mum. I smile back politely. The *poor* man. I can only imagine the grief he must have suffered, and while looking after two little girls. No wonder he needs help and comes across as unfriendly. He has every right to be angry with the world.

'So, I'm assuming the girls have had a nanny before? Can I

ask why she's leaving?' I ask the question that always tells me everything I need to know.

'Left.' The housekeeper purses her lips. 'She left. Just like all the others.'

'Others?' I balk. How many have they been through? How unfriendly is this guy?

She nods. 'Like I said, Mr Rothchester can be hard to get along with.'

'Right.' I nod in understanding; he's clearly a nightmare. 'So, you're basically warning me to have a thick skin if I get the job.'

'Exactly.' She nods with an optimistic smile and crinkle of her eyes.

He can't be that awful if she's stayed working for him. He must have a soft side underneath all that angst. I can't see her taking his bullshit. She's friendly and warm, but I can already tell she doesn't take fools gladly.

'And the job is yours if you want it.'

'Really?' I can't help but beam a smile back at her. Don't ask me why, but even with all these warnings, the place has a good vibe about it. 'Doesn't Mr Rothchester want to meet me first?'

She chuckles. 'Don't want him spoiling things before we've even got you moved in.'

She hands over a contract. I take a quick scan of it. On top of my healthy pay is a rent-free room in the basement of the townhouse, use of a chauffeur driven car and expenses. I read closer, noticing the lack of contracted hours being listed. That's strange.

'Sorry, but how many hours a week is the job? I can't see it on here.' It is possible it's just written in small print.

She bites her lip and avoids meeting my eye. 'Well, it's actually unlimited. Mr Rothchester is very busy with his work. We expect you to look after the girls from morning, through until the evening when you put them to bed. That does mean,' she hesitates, 'if one of them were to wake you'd have to deal with it.'

'Right.' I nod, wondering if they wake every night. 'But do I ever get a night off?' I force a laugh.

Don't get me wrong, I'm used to only one or two nights off a week, but the fact that it's not stated in black and white has me nervous.

'Yes, every Tuesday night I'll stay here so you can have a night out. If you'd like anymore nights off just ask me and I'll see if I can cover for you.'

Given how hard it sounds like I'll be working, I'll probably just want a pizza in bed.

'Wow, so it's quite a commitment?'

Not that the one in the South of France isn't. They want me to sign up for the next two years and the truth is that they're all just as demanding as each other. At least this one is being upfront about it.

'It is.' She nods. 'But that's why you're compensated so well. And remember, it's just looking after the kiddies. Marge will do all the cooking and I'll do the cleaning. I see that the house is run properly.'

Oh, that's not so bad. I'm used to doing both in my other jobs.

'If you'd like to think about it, by all means take the contract home. But I will continue to interview in case you change your mind.'

Wow, she's turning the screws. *Sneaky lady trying to lock me down.*

It's not like I can take it home to look at. I'm currently living in the nearest Premier Inn. When I'd realised I'd outgrown my old family and decided to leave, I knew I'd only be out of work a few days. Let's just say I know I'm good at my job.

My mum died the day after my eighteenth birthday. She was perfectly healthy but had never gotten over the death of my dad. The doctors said they thought it was broken heart syndrome; although they'd never known anyone to die from it ten years after losing their husband. It was as though she'd waited for me to turn eighteen. I already knew I wanted to work with kids. Nannying seemed like it solved both problems; gave me a home, a job, and a family.

Oh, what am I so worried about? It says here I only need to give one month's notice.

If I hate it, I can just leave.

Maybe they'll still take me back at the South of France job. I didn't actually need to start until January, and I hate the idea of twiddling my thumbs at the Premier Inn until then.

'No need.' I shake my head, grabbing the pen off her and signing my name. 'I'll take it.'

CHAPTER 2

Tuesday 26th November

Ruby

So, that's how I find myself moving my luggage into the rather large basement studio flat the next day. Some people might find it sad I can fit all my worldly possessions into three suitcases, but not me. I only ever keep what I need. Everyone knows important things, like your memories, are carried everywhere, all the time.

The house is a typical Victorian terraced townhouse over a whole four floors. It doesn't look that big when you look up at it on the street, but it goes way back. Probably cost a couple of million round here. Notting Hill is ridiculous money.

My room is a self-contained studio flat next to an enormous playroom which leads onto the garden via bi-folding doors. It was clearly done by the wife, as it's fabulous. One entire wall is blackboard painted with the girl's names, Jessica and Charlotte, in big bold pink and yellow. One corner is a set up as a little market with the kid's art hung with pegs on rope, another is a cute and cosy reading corner with fairy lights.

I've been to some fancy houses and playrooms in my time, but this one is Pinterest worthy. It's clear she loved her kids. Makes it all the more heart-breaking that she left them so soon.

My space is a complete contrast to the rest of the house. It's modern and practical, nothing has been done to look nice but just to serve a purpose. But saying that, once I make it my own, I know it'll be cosy. I've lived in far worse.

This Nanny game doesn't always guarantee good accommodation. I was once in a box bedroom barely bigger than a cupboard. In fact, it didn't have a window so I think it *could* have been a cupboard.

The rest of the house oozes glamour and somehow at the same time feels homely. It's decorated in warm browns, oak hardwood floors and original features like fireplaces and sash windows kept in place. I take myself up into the sage green open plan kitchen to meet the girls for the first time. Mrs Dumfy is there with them, waiting for me.

I smile and drop down to their level; the overwhelming urge to get them to like me strong. The six-year-old twirls some of her long blonde hair around her finger and chews on her lip.

'Hey, little lady. What's your name?' I ask, knowing full well. Mrs Dumfy has already given me a detailed brief of them.

'I'm Jessica.' She extends her hand out for me to shake. *Ooh, very formal.* I take her little hand and shake it, smiling at her.

'Lovely to meet you, Jessica.' She gives me a guarded smile. *Hmm, clear trust issues.* Understandable with a revolving door of nannies.

I pretend to look around. 'Now, I'm sure I was told you had a younger sister, but I can't see her anywhere?'

I look around everywhere, deliberately avoiding the little girl hiding behind Mrs Dumfy's leg, clinging to a bunny comforter. If only my drama teacher could see me now, and she'd said I'd amount to nothing.

'She's Lottie,' Jessica says. She smacks her forehead, dramatically. 'I mean, Charlotte. Daddy keeps telling me off for calling her Lottie.'

I wave towards the little girl with the dark blonde hair and chubby cheeks.

'Hi, baby. I'm Ruby. Do you prefer Charlotte or Lottie? That's all that matters.'

'Lottie,' she mumbles, her bunny pressed into her mouth. Oh, bless her.

'Okay, Lottie it is.' I look back at Jessica who giggles mischievously. 'Just don't tell Daddy.' I wink causing her to burst out laughing. I knew I'd win her over.

'Come say hi, Lottie,' Jessica instructs her, holding out her hand. Lottie dubiously takes it and walks towards me, chewing on her bunny's ears. Stunning hazel eyes take me in. She surprises me by throwing her little arms around my neck and snuggling into me.

I snort a laugh, almost falling backwards from the force, but wrap my arms around her little squishy body, breathing in the scent of baby lotion. They seriously need to make a room spray of this scent. It's my favourite.

'Nice to meet both of you. Now, what do you fancy doing?'

Jessica shrugs, her blue eyes bored. A six-year-old with no ideas on what to do? I'm not used to this. I'll have to come up with some options.

'You could help me unpack downstairs. We could have a picnic in the garden or... go swimming?'

'A picnic?' Jessica shouts, eyes wide, as if it's an outrageous idea. 'It's November. It's too cold for a picnic.'

'Picnic,' Lottie repeats, clapping her hands in glee. 'I want picnic.'

'It's never too cold.' I smile mischievously. 'We'll get all wrapped up and build a cosy fort.'

Their eyes light up in wonder. 'Picnic it is then.'

Two hours later, we're snuggled up with all the blankets we could find in the fort we've built in the small courtyard garden. Throwing the blankets over the garden chairs, it was easy to build. I've never understood people who buy houses as large as this one, but then have a pathetic little garden.

The girls are all wrapped up in their coats, hats, gloves and scarfs. We're just sipping out of the little teacups Jessica owns and drinking our hot chocolate Marge, their cook, made for us in a Thermos, when we hear the slam of what must be the back door.

Jessica's eyes widen and her body stiffens. 'Uh-oh. Daddy.'

I stare back at her in dismay. What kind of six-year-old has this kind of reaction to her daddy? That's not normal. I'm used to children leaping up and running towards them in excitement. Not looking fretful.

Footsteps thud towards us, causing my stomach to lurch violently. How bad is this guy? Before I know what's happening the top blanket is pulled off to reveal the person who I'm assuming is Daddy. We stare back at the man who looks at me in disgust, as if he just caught us in a crack den not a pretend tent made of blankets.

He's got a vein on the left side of his forehead which is so engorged it looks like it might burst. His square jaw is tense and his dark brown eyes murderous. They actually look black right now. They're the kind of eyes I think you'd see just before you're strangled to death.

'What the hell is going on here?' he thunders, his voice booming around the garden. *Jesus, man, the neighbours!*

'Sorry, Daddy,' Jessica says straight away, eyes downcast to the floor.

'Sorry for what?' I ask Jessica. Scrambling up from the floor I extend my hand to him. 'Hi. I'm assuming you're Mr Rothchester?'

He looks down at my hand in revulsion, like I've just tried to pass him a pineapple. Like it's just that random that I might want to shake his hand.

'And I'm *assuming* you're the new nanny who decided it would be a good idea to take my children out into the freezing cold garden in an attempt to get them ill?' he asks, his eyebrows drawn together and his nostrils flaring.

I balk. I've never been spoken to so rudely, and that's saying something. Nannies are often ignored or treated as if we're stupid, but I've never had someone look at me with such animosity.

I must remember that Mrs Dumfy warned me. And that he's lost his wife. It's only natural for him to protect his girls. Saying that, I don't appreciate his tone. *Quick discreet deep breath, Ruby.*

'I think you'll find, Mr Rothchester, that the girls are wrapped up very warmly and we've been having a great time enjoying our picnic.' I smile at the girls in encouragement.

'We have, Daddy.' Jessica nods, biting on her bottom lip, obviously scared of his reaction.

'Dada,' Lottie says, extending her arms to him.

Good idea, kid. *Distract him with your cuteness.* He bends down and scoops her up as if she weighs nothing. It's crazy to see someone look so hostile, also holding his daughter like she's the most precious thing in the world.

'Whatever,' he barks back at me.

I stop myself giggling. It's such a moody teenage boy response.

'I want the girls brought back inside and their routine adhered to.'

He carries Lottie back inside and curls his finger for Jessica to follow him. She smiles back at me, hesitating, before following him in.

Well, I've met some rude people in my time, but this guy takes the biscuit. In fact, I bet if there was a last digestive on a plate, he would shamelessly snatch it. And who says *'adhered to'* in real life? I roll my eyes. What a control freak.

I pack up our food and fold the blankets. Anything to give me a minute to calm down. My hands are actually shaking with rage, causing me to put the blankets into more of a roll.

How dare he speak to me like that... And in front of the girls. What a complete arsehole.

I'm fuming and I don't want the girls to see me like this, so I take a deep calming breath before heading back inside; ready to face the music. He's having a heated discussion with Mrs Dumfy. I cringe when I realise she's taking the flack because of me. They both stop talking and turn, making it pretty clear I'm the topic of discussion.

'Miss Campbell,' he snaps; his hands behind his back like an ancient headmaster. 'Can I have a private word with you, please?'

I'm surprised he's even bothered putting a please on there. It doesn't sound like he's giving me a choice.

'Of course.' I smile brightly, ignoring my quivering tongue. I won't give him the satisfaction of knowing I find him a tad scary. Okay, kind of terrifying.

Jessica's eyes widen and she starts chewing again on her bottom lip. To think only ten minutes ago we were enjoying a lovely picnic. I shoot her a quick reassuring wink.

I follow him upstairs, through the kitchen and into his office. It's far more traditional than the rest of the house. An old oak desk sits next to a library full of books. I try to make out some of the titles, but it's hard to take my eyes from his face.

His furious, but annoyingly handsome, face is staring at me as if I'm the devil. He'd really be gorgeous if he just dared to crack a smile. Something I doubt I'll ever see. He's got all the characteristics of a model; strong jaw covered with the smallest hint of stubble, olive skin and full lips.

He sighs and pulls his tie from his neck. Something I definitely should not find sexy. Why do I forever love a bad boy?

'Miss Campbell,' he starts, sitting down behind his desk in what is clearly a power move. Scratch the sexy. He obviously has a tiny penis.

'Ruby, please.' I smile. Kill 'em with kindness, that's my motto. I almost fire finger guns at him. Thankfully I stop myself just in time.

His nostrils flare, probably at me interrupting him, or maybe because I'm acting unaffected. He probably wants to be quivering in fear, maybe that's how he gets off.

I can't help but feel a smile tugging at my lips. I bite my tongue to stop it becoming a proper one. I don't want him to burst into actual flames.

'Miss Campbell,' he says again, his gaze sharpening, as if to reiterate that this is a business relationship and nothing personal. 'I would appreciate if in future you would check with me before deciding to take my children outside into the cold.'

I smile, wanting to challenge him. There's just something about someone being so unnecessary rude that makes me want to be a rebellious dick back.

'Okay,' I nod. 'But just to check, does that include their daily walk to school and back? Or a play in the park?' I can't help but be sarcastic. He's being ridiculous.

He smirks back at me, his eyes anything but amused. He's pissed off that I've called him out. 'Perhaps when I learn to trust you more, I won't be so full on and involved. But heaven help me if I don't think it strange you want to take my children out into the garden for a picnic in November on your first day. I don't want them getting ill just before the holidays.'

I hate how he's looking at me, like I'm some sort of uninformed idiot who didn't think twice about endangering his children.

'They were fully wrapped up and studies have proved that exposure to outside, regardless of the season, is good for a child's development. It builds confidence, promotes stimulation through creativity and imagination and also reduces stress and fatigue.'

His eyes widen. Obviously he's not got me down as someone who can read. He must think I'm some thick blonde bimbo who couldn't get a real career so instead decided to look after children. Quite the opposite. *Ha, take that.*

I always knew I wanted to work with children. I've taken every course available and even done an open university degree in childcare. After losing my own dad I realised how important a stable home is.

He ignores me and hands over a piece of paper. 'Here is the children's itinerary, which I expect you to stick to.'

I glance down at it. Wow, this guy is proper anal. He's got their movements planned for every hour; gymnastics, swimming, keyboard, tap dance, ballet. You name it, they're doing it.

He hands over a white box. 'This is your new phone. My PA has synced my diary up with yours so you can see my whereabouts.'

'Oh, thanks, but I already have a phone.' I mean, sure it's not as swanky as this new model, but it's fine for what I need.

He glares back at me; his eyes like red hot pokers burning through my skull. 'I expect you to carry this phone with you at all times and be available to take my calls checking in.'

Jesus, why doesn't he just put a tracker in my neck?

'Okay,' I shrug. It's better than my phone anyway.

He leans back in his chair; his anger having dissipated slightly. 'The holidays are a very stressful time for me, what with work and events.'

Mrs Dumfy did mention that he was in events planning. Plus, when you've lost someone the holidays are always hard.

'I'd appreciate it if I don't have to worry about you too.' He narrows his dark brown eyes. 'Do I make myself clear?'

No. Me dumb dumb. You speak slow, easy words for me to understand.

I sarcastically salute him. 'Yes, sir.' *You complete jackass.*

Turning on my heel, I go to walk out.

'Oh, and Miss Campbell?' he calls from over my shoulder

I turn to face him, plastering on a fake smile. 'Hmm?'

'Try not to let any of that sass rub off onto my daughters.'

CHAPTER 3

Monday 2nd December

Ruby

*T*he man is impossible. It's as simple as that. It's only been one week, but any fool can see that these girls are missing some fun and spontaneity in their lives. In the first week of looking after them I've managed to stay within his rigid routine, while also injecting a bit of fun and love into their lives.

I started with asking Marge, their cook, if I could make Jessica's school lunch. She refused, so I asked her if she'd ever made a bento lunch. She looked at me like I'd grown another head, so I introduced her to my pack of goodies, meaning Jessica's sandwiches and cucumber are now cut into stars and flowers. Her cheese and grapes now sit in brightly coloured silicone cups and

I make sure to include a different note every day telling her how fabulous I think she is.

She likes to pretend that she's very confident, but it doesn't take an expert to see that she's a bit insecure. The poor girl lost her mother when she was just three years old and has since been subjected to a revolving door of nannies. She needs someone to build her up and I've decided I'm the perfect person for the job. Seeing her smile when I pick her up from her posh prep school down the road is already making it all worth it.

Lottie goes to nursery every morning from nine until midday. I've volunteered to help with their reading and Lottie seems to love the idea of me being in there. She really is a bit of a clinger, but again, she's not had a mother's touch from six months old. Luckily, I'm not going anywhere. I don't care how bad Mr Rothchester is; I'm here for the girls and I intend to stay and be their stability.

They need someone. Their dad doesn't seem to be in the picture much. Some days he hasn't seen them at all. Others, it's a phone call or brief half hour spent with them while he's distractedly checking his phone. It makes me wonder if the guy cares at all.

When I pick up Jessica from school, I ask her how school was, wondering what else I can do for her to prove how special she is.

'It was okay,' she says, kicking a stone on the floor, her face glum.

I stop and kneel down to her level. 'What happened, honey?'

She shrugs, her eyes dropped to the pavement. 'Nothing.'

I raise my eyebrows, as if to say *pull the other one*. The idea of her sad has me feeling sick to my stomach.

She sighs, as if the weight of the world is on her shoulders. Life shouldn't be this hard at six-years-old. 'It's just that I want to be on the float.'

What the hell is she going on about?

'What float, sweetheart? Remember, you're going to have to be specific. I'm not used to this school yet.'

Her glassy eyes meet mine. I'll do anything to put a smile back on her face.

'There's a local parade just before Christmas. Our school has a float, but the only kids that get to be on it are the PTA kids.'

'PTA kids? What, so they get preferential treatment just because their mums are on the PTA?' *That can't be bloody right.*

'Yep.' She nods wistfully. 'And it looks so much fun. You get to dress up as Santa's elves and learn a dance.' The slutty dance from Mean Girls flashes through my head and I bite my tongue to stop from giggling.

Well, I have to put this right immediately.

'Do you know who the head of the PTA is, sweetie?'

'Yes,' she nods. 'It's Clementine.'

Of course, it is.

She points towards an immaculate blonde woman walking out of the gates with a young boy I recognise from Jessica's class.

'Right, well, let's go then.'

I march on over to her, dragging a resistant Jessica and a bemused Lottie with me.

'Clementine!' I shout, stopping her in her tracks. Oops, maybe it came out a bit more aggressive than I'd planned.

She turns around, a candy sweet, utterly insincere smile on her filler-full lips. 'Yes?' She does a quick disapproving glance over my clothes. Today had to be the day I'm wearing dungarees under my leopard print faux fur coat. I smile confidently regardless, imagining I'm in designer and this is so next season.

'Hi, I'm Ruby. I'm interested in joining the PTA.'

She blinks rapidly. I guess people don't normally dare talking directly to her.

'Sorry, *you* want to join the PTA?'

I look behind myself jokingly. 'Yep. Me.' *You stuck up bitch.*

She purses her trout pout. How women think that's attractive I'll never know.

'I'm afraid that nannies aren't allowed to join the PTA. It does, after all, stand for Parent, Teacher Association.' She smiles, as if I'm slow. 'Sorry.' She turns to walk away, but I'm quicker.

'I'm sure you'd be understanding to our situation.' I notion with my eyes towards the girls. She obviously knows they're motherless. 'Jessica would just love to go on the float with her friends.'

She snorts an unattractive laugh. Reminds me of a horse.

'I'm so sick of mothers suddenly wanting to join the PTA when there's a perk for their child. Us active mothers put in a lot of work throughout the year.'

What the fuck ever, bitch. Grow a heart.

'Well, I'd be more than willing to put in the work.' I beam back at her, refusing to back down.

She looks me over, her lips twisted in concentration, assessing me. I'm desperate to roll my eyes and lean on one hip but I force myself to appear friendly, even if it is through gritted teeth.

'Look, I'd really like to give you a chance...' She looks like she'd like to do *anything* but. 'But the official rules state that you must be a mother. Sorry.'

This bitch. She turns to walk away.

'You will be sorry,' I say loud enough for her to hear me.

She scoffs, hand to her chest, as she spins to face me. 'I beg your pardon?' Her eyes shoot lasers, warning me not to cross her. She might as well have said, *"what the fuck did you say?"*

This isn't the first stuck up PTA mother I've had to deal with. They're at every school.

I fake a sad smile. 'It's just that I'm sure the headmistress will be very sad when I inform her that you've refused to let me join the PTA. After all, it is about us all working together for the good of the children.' I smile back at her, just as insincerely.

She glares at me, arms crossed over her medically enhanced chest. She must have a very rich husband.

'Especially when she finds out that only the children of those parents are selected to ride the float. Seems a bit unfair to me.'

Her nostrils flare with rage. Ha! *Take that bitch.* I've had my fair bit of practise with bitchy mothers. I'm a veteran.

'Fine,' she snaps. 'You can join. First meeting is Friday 6th December. Bring a notebook. You'll have a *lot* of work to do.' She turns, flicking her long blonde locks in my face. The bitch smells of baby prostitute.

I just hope Jessica appreciates going on the float, because I have a feeling I might regret this.

CHAPTER 4

Ruby

As soon as we're home after gymnastics, I tell the girls it's time to write their letters to Santa. Anything to distract us from that heinous bitch Clementine and her vapid existence.

'Aren't we too late?' Jessica asks, her nose scrunched up.

'Of course not, honey.' I smooth her hair down her neck.

She shrugs. 'It's just that the girls at school sent them months ago.' I'm sure they did. Spoilt little madams.

'And you didn't?' I can't help but ask. Whatever Nanny was looking after her should be ashamed of herself. Probably too busy being shit scared of Mr Rothchester. I can imagine them scuttling around whenever he was near.

She smiles, but it's small and pulls at my heartstrings. 'What's the point? I never get what I want.'

I find it shocking that someone as anal as Mr Rothchester fails to get her the right present. What the hell is up with that?

'Well, have you ever sent a letter before?' I ask her, hands on my hip.

She looks to Lottie, already scribbling out a list in crayons. She pulls me to the side so she can't overhear.

'Ruby, you don't have to lie to me. Daddy's already told me Santa isn't real.'

I clutch my stomach, as if I've been shot. My heart nearly stops. The guy told her Santa isn't real? What kind of monster are we dealing with here?

'What are you talking about?' I gasp, finding it difficult to get my words out. 'Santa is one hundred percent real,' I state with certainty.

She sighs. 'I used to think that when Mummy was alive, but since then I never got what I wanted at Christmas. I asked Daddy about it last year and he told me it was because Santa isn't real.'

'Well, your daddy is wrong.' *And an insensitive dickhead.* Never before have I wanted to head-butt someone so strongly.

She balks, obviously shocked. 'Daddy's never wrong.'

I scoff a laugh. Yeah, he'd like her to think that.

'Well he's wrong about this. I don't know what kind of twisted information your father got, but Santa is real.'

Her little forehead wrinkles. 'How do you know?'

'Because I've always got what I wanted from Santa,' I say firmly. 'So, have all the boys and girls I've looked after, and do you know why?'

She looks up at me, chewing on her lip, as if not sure to believe me. 'Why?'

'Because we all wrote letters. I bet since your mummy passed you stopped writing letters and that's where Santa has got confused.'

'Really?' she asks, her eyes glancing from side to side if she's trying to figure it out. 'I suppose we *did* stop writing letters. We were all too sad. Daddy doesn't like Christmas anymore.'

'Yes,' I nod encouragingly. 'Santa needs to hear from you, hear that you've been a good girl. He probably just assumes you've been too busy being naughty.' She gasps at the very idea.

'So why doesn't Daddy believe in him?' she asks, chewing on her bottom lip.

'Well... I bet your daddy wasn't a good boy when he was little and...'

Her blue eyes nearly burst out of her skull. 'He was on the *naughty list?*' she shrieks in horror.

I nod my head, stifling a giggle. 'I mean, that's what I'm guessing. But your daddy probably didn't want to admit that to you, or even himself. That's why he's convinced Santa isn't real.'

'That makes sense.' She nods. Yeah it does, especially with him being so rude all the time. 'Wow, so Santa is real! That's so cool.'

She hugs me and runs off to join her sister who's still writing her list.

I can't believe Mr Rothchester told her that. What kind of devil spirited man is he? Jesus, trust me to move into Scrooge's house. I don't care what I have to do, but these girls are going to have a magical Christmas one way or the other. I make a silent vow to the girls and send a wish up to the Christmas fairies.

I've bathed the girls, Jessica's read us her story book, put them to bed and am just cleaning up the playroom when I sense a presence behind me. I turn, hoping to god it's not the ghost of Mrs Rothchester, to instead find Mr Rothchester leaning against the doorframe, his tie pulled down in that way he seems to like. It's annoying how sexy it makes him look. *Sexy idiot that doesn't believe in Santa.*

'I've missed the girls again?' he asks in defeat, as if already knowing the answer. It's nice to know he actually wants to see them. I haven't been sure up until now.

'Yep.' I smile sadly. 'Can't be loosening up their very tight schedule, I'm afraid. The boss would kill me.' I chance a cheeky smile.

His face softens, just slightly, and I can't help but notice the darkness around his eyes.

'I've heard he's a real dick,' he says, with an almost smile.

I burst out a laugh. Wow, turns out he does have a sense of humour. 'Oh, he's not that bad. I don't even see him much.'

He sighs as his phone goes off in his pocket. 'Right, well I'll try and make it back for them tomorrow.' He turns to check his phone and walk away.

'Have you got the pictures I've been sending?' I can't help but ask. I don't know why I've bothered asking. The blue double tick at the bottom of the messages tells me he *has* seen the pictures of the girls. Not that's he's ever replied or said thank you.

'Yes,' he says, with his back turned to me. 'Thank you.'

Now a thank you. I must be dreaming.

'There's something else I want to talk to you about,' I quickly add before he has the chance to walk away.

He begrudgingly turns around, one eyebrow raised. It pisses me off, as if raising both eyebrows is too much effort for him. Like I'm not worth both of them.

'Yes?' he presses, obviously annoyed by my deliberate silence.

'You...told Jessica that Santa isn't real?' I phrase it like a question, when I already know the answer.

He shrugs as if he hasn't gone around breaking years of tradition. 'And?'

I can't help but sneer. '*And* did you think it through before you broke that little girls' heart?'

He glares at me, his eyes icy. 'That little girls' heart broke when her mother died. I told her night after night that her mum would be okay. After all that I just didn't want to lie to her anymore.'

Wow. Well that kind of breaks my heart. I can see how his loss has made his heart hard.

'But don't you think that the magic of Christmas can help to heal her heart? Every kid needs to believe in Santa Claus.'

He glares back at me. 'Why? It's a terrible tradition. Lying to your children about a strange man breaking in through the fireplace and leaving them a present. It's creepy.'

'It is not creepy!' I shout. Okay, maybe I'm a *bit* more into

Christmas that I realised. But damn it, he's disrespecting the big man. Definitely on the naughty list.

'It's an honoured tradition, giving children the belief and faith in a mythical being who's only job is to make them happy on Christmas day. She deserves that in her life.' *After what she's been through, she deserves the world.*

'Whatever.' He shrugs, looking towards his phone.

'Which is why I told her that you were wrong.'

'I'm sorry?' He sounds anything but sorry. He eyeballs me, daring me to explain myself.

'I told her that you were wrong, and that Santa is real.' I shrug unapologetically. I can be as blasé as him.

'Well, it wasn't your place to tell her that.'

'It wasn't your place to tell her either!' I retort back. Okay, so apparently, I'm a lot angrier than I thought.

He steels his jaw, clenching it tight with his teeth. 'I'm her father and it's up to me how I plan on raising my girls. Please remember who's writing your pay cheques.'

I raise my eyes at the arsehole. Who the hell writes pay cheques anymore? *Get with the programme, Grandad.*

'You can't fire me for telling your daughter Santa is real.' I square my shoulders up at him, ready for a fight.

I think I'm going to get one too, until he sighs and drops his shoulders.

'Well, if you're going to play Christmas elf make sure to find out what they've asked for so I can get it right.'

Wow. He backed down. He must really be shattered tonight. A weird urge to give him a cuddle comes over me. To tuck him into bed, just like I did with the girls.

Then, before I can say anything back, he walks away.

What a very strange man. It's funny to think that if I saw him on the street, I'd think what a yummy looking guy he is, without knowing what a complex weirdo he really is.

My head barely hits the pillow before I'm asleep.

Barclay

The woman infuriates me. Imagine telling Jessica that Santa *does* exist after all. I don't want to join the millions of parents lying to their children. I prefer to tell mine the truth, thank you very much. My parents told me at a young age and I far preferred it; laughing at the kids talking about what Santa was going to bring them. I loved knowing they were stupid enough to believe it.

I can't imagine telling the kids that a magical man breaks into our house in the middle of the night and is watching us all year. Jessica would probably tell me to call the police!

Still, it seems like she's going along with her way of doing things, regardless of my opinion. I've let it slide this time, purely because I'm too exhausted to argue with her.

Dad is putting major pressure on me at the firm to become official partner. The truth is that I don't feel like I deserve it. I'm already Managing Director of event planning and I'm happy where I am. If I suddenly became partner everyone would be rolling their eyes and whispering about how I only got it because my dad owns the company. And they'd be right.

Plus, I don't see the girl's half as much as I'd like to already, becoming partner would only add more pressure onto my plate. Not that Dad is listening to me. Keeps brushing off my refusal, telling me how lucky I am to be in such a privileged position. I know I am, but that doesn't mean I have to turn into him.

I never saw him when I was growing up. He only ever turned up to tell me what he expected from me. What a disappointment I am. Well, I've had enough. He either lets it go or I'll have to look for another company to work for. That would really piss him off.

The same thought about Ruby, I mean Miss Campbell, keeps running to the front of my brain.

Did you see the arse on her?

What the hell is wrong with me? Perving on my own children's nanny. I don't care how good her arse is, if she keeps going on like this she'll be fired before Christmas.

CHAPTER 5

Tuesday 3rd December

Ruby

I'm woken up in the darkness by something wriggling under my duvet. I freeze. Oh my god, have they got a cat or a dog I don't know about? Or even worse... a snake? If they're a reptile family I'm grabbing my purse and running.

'Hello?' I ask into the darkness; my voice shaky with fear.

I lift the duvet, ready to come head to head with anaconda, but instead find Lottie crawling up my legs; her eyes red and puffy.

'I had bad dream,' she says on a sniff.

'Oh, poor baby.' I let her lie next to me while I rub her back in reassuring circles. She snuggles into me, her little hand holding onto my vest top, while still clinging onto her little bunny.

I let my heavy eyelids close for a second, knowing I have to make the two flights of stairs to tuck her back in.

Ruby

Next thing I know I'm woken up by someone shouting in the distance. I'm still in bed, with Lottie snuggled up beside me, as if she hasn't moved an inch. She's all warm and toasty. I press my cheek against hers before checking my phone to see its only six a.m. Who the hell is shouting at this hour?

Probably Sir Know-it-all shouting at someone. Maybe Marge didn't make his organic pancakes the way he likes them. Ridiculous pompous toff.

I throw the duvet back over my head, making sure not to cover Lottie. I don't want to suffocate her. It works to muffle the sound. Doesn't he know that normal people don't have to be up for at least an hour?

My door suddenly bangs open and my eyes widen as he shouts, 'Charlotte?'

I pull the duvet from over my face and open one eye to stare at him; my eyes still crusted over with sleep. He's in just work trousers, his top half completely bare, showing off broad muscled shoulders and a bronzed six pack. Damn, he must lift.

'Have you seen...?' He spots her sleeping next to me mid-sentence. 'Charlotte? She's HERE?' he booms.

Jesus, anyone shouting before coffee deserves to be shot. Thank God once again I don't own a shot gun. *Saved myself another twenty five years to life.*

Lottie stirs, rubbing at her eyes.

'Shush!' I hiss, jumping out of bed and pushing him out of my room and towards the playroom. 'Let her sleep.'

'What the fuck is going on?' he roars, running his hands through his hair. Visions of me doing that exact same thing flash into my mind. *Damn it. I must still be asleep.* 'I thought she'd been abducted. I was close to calling the police.'

Is this guy for real? Someone give him a crown so he can be a full blown drama queen.

'No, she just had a nightmare.' I yawn shamelessly in his face. I don't get paid enough for this shit. And as for bursting into my room when I could have been sleeping naked; well, I'll bring that up when he's less murdery.

He balls his fists by his sides. It reminds me of a toddler that hasn't got his way. It almost makes me want to laugh, but the murdery vibe he's got going on stops me.

'So, you decided to bring her into your bed and completely destroy her routine?' he howls, like it's the end of the world.

Here he goes again with the "routine". I huff, crossing my arms over my chest. My chest with no bra, my nipples remind me all too pertly.

'Jesus, what is it with you and this bloody routine? She came and found *me*. She had a bad dream. It's not my fault she wanted comfort from me and not her own father.'

As soon the words leave my mouth, I regret it. Especially as his face falls.

He takes a sharp intake of breath. 'She needs to learn to sleep in her own bed,' he reiterates, his voice low and controlled. It's possibly scarier than when he was yelling.

'She's three years old, for gods' sakes,' I snap back through gritted teeth. If he wants a fight before coffee so be it.

'So what? I don't want your hippy influence un-doing all the hard work I've put into her. She needs to learn to sleep in her own bed like a big girl.'

'Hippy influence?' I scoff. 'Are you for real? She's not a big girl yet, she's a little three-year-old that wanted comfort because she was afraid. She's not a pet project you put a lot of work into.'

The vein on his forehead bulges. 'She's *my* daughter. It's *my* rules. Don't let it happen again.'

'I'm sorry.' I stop him, just as he's about to walk away. 'But my care and interest here is to the children. Yes, I'll stick to your rigid routine, but I refuse to put the feelings of these children second behind what you want.'

'Excuse me?' He towers over me. Jeepers, he can be a scary fucker when he wants to be.

I swallow down the fear creeping over me and square my shoulders.

'I said, that I will be putting the needs of your children first and foremost. If you don't agree with that, then you should just go ahead and fire me.'

His chest rising and falling so dramatically I wouldn't be surprised if he started to breathe fire. I await my firing with defiant eyes. Until, just like that, he turns and walks away.

Phew. Safe. For now.

Barclay

I can't believe that Charlotte went to her. She's only known her for just over a week and she went to find her, all the way in the basement. She's always come to me when she's had a bad dream. We have a routine for when it happens. I soothe her, calm her down and then pop her back into her bed with a story. She's soon off back to sleep back in her own bed. Just like all the books tell you to.

She's probably sensed that Miss Campbell is a soft touch and would let her sleep with her. It's little surprise to me that she did. When I didn't find her in her bed my heart stopped. Bile crept up my throat. I just can't lose another person. I wouldn't survive it.

All these years I've been trying so hard to build up a safe wall around my girls. A wall that stops me falling unbelievably and deeply in love with them. I've only allowed myself to love them eighty five percent. That way if something were to, god forbid, happen to them, it wouldn't gut me as much as it did with Claire. I could live through it.

I was completely useless when she passed. For six months I just slept, barely eating. Mrs Dumfy and Marge kept me and the girls alive. But one day I just knew it had to end. I was getting nowhere crying into my pillow. I needed to get up, go back to work and earn a living for my girls. Sure, I could never let myself love them as much as I did Claire, but I could at least provide a good life for them.

But seeing her bed empty this morning scared the shit out of me. It turns out, with all my trying, those girls have still managed to sneak into my heart and get the whole thing. Which means I'm in trouble.

If only I can find a nanny who does what I want.

CHAPTER 6

Wednesday 4th December

Ruby

Yesterday my whole day was off track, thanks to that complete arse. How a man can be so un-connected to his children I don't know. I've always worked for busy parents, but they've always made sure that if they only spend five minutes with their kids, they were precious moments. They were one hundred percent committed to them in that moment. Not distractedly checking their phone.

So today after kids' yoga I've decided to talk to Jessica about happier times with her mummy. I've noticed there are no photos of her around the house. Not that this place feels much of a home. We spend most of our time in the playroom, which to be fair, is about the size of an average house.

It's definitely missing a woman's touch and I can't help but wonder if that's because his wife was a minimalist or because he took down anything that reminded him of her. I suppose I'm just looking for something to explain why he's such a cold-hearted arsehole.

So, while we're having a tea party, I broach the subject with Jessica.

'Jessica, do you remember your mummy?'

She smiles sadly. 'Not really. I know it makes me sad when I think of her. I miss having a mummy.'

I rub her soothingly on the back, my throat prickling with emotion. 'I bet you do, baby.'

You forget how grateful you are to have had a mum raise you until you hear how others have to cope without one. Mine might have only made it to my eighteenth, but for those eighteen years I was blessed with the best mum ever.

'But I do remember that she loved Christmas.' Her little face lights up at the memory. 'We used to dance around to Christmas songs and decorate the house. Apart from that, I don't remember much.'

I must google whether children can remember such early memories at this age.

'And Daddy doesn't decorate for Christmas anymore?' I ask, glancing around at the bland house. We always did it as soon as it hit 1st December, but then I did drive my parents mad. It's my favourite time of the year, even now as a thirty-year-old.

She shrugs. 'Not since Mummy died. It's okay. Some of my friends are Ewish so they don't decorate either.'

ONCE UPON A WISH MAS

'Do you mean Jewish, honey?' I bite my lip so as not to laugh.

She shrugs again. 'I don't know. They celebrate something called Anneka.'

I stifle another laugh. 'I think you mean Hanukkah.'

She laughs and covers her mouth with her hand. 'Oops.'

I look to Lottie, concentrating hard on spoon feeding her bunny imaginary food. She insisted on having a messy bun today so she could be just like me. How adorable.

I can't have them living in this sterile house, with no decorations at Christmas. It's unimaginably cruel. Barbaric even. Even prisons decorate for Christmas.

'Girls, would you like to decorate this year?'

Lottie starts clapping her hands together. 'Yes! Decorate!'

'I think Daddy would love that,' Jessica says with an excited smile.

I smile back at them, wanting nothing more than to scoop them both in my arms and kiss them all over their face. To tell them that I'll always be there for them to get their needs met.

'Then, that's exactly what we'll do.'

We head up to their storage room on the fourth floor, next to Mr Rothchester's bedroom, and start rifling through boxes until we find the ones marked Christmas. They're dusty and it's clear they haven't been used in years. It's bad enough these poor girls have been deprived a mother, let alone missed out on Christmas the last three years.

We take them downstairs, with the help of Marge who warns me that Mr Rothchester won't like this idea. I tell her to

39

chill out. Surely anything done by his children can't be seen as something to be angry about? We're celebrating a holiday, not worshipping the devil.

Just in case he doesn't see the fun side, we decide to decorate minimally in the main house and to really go to town in the playroom. He can't be too cross with that, right?

Three hours later and we're almost done. We've gone a bit more over the top in the main house than I'd originally planned, but the decorations they had were just amazing. Their mum obviously adored Christmas.

We've put a wreath on the front door and lined the staircases with fairy lights. The playroom is where we let ourselves go mad, with fairy lights adorning every wall, a large plastic Christmas tree in the corner with multi coloured lights. We're just putting baubles on the tree when I hear footsteps thunder down the stairs.

'Please don't leave,' Jessica says, clinging to my arm.

I frown back at her. 'Jessica, why would I leave?'

Her lip trembles. 'Because they all do. Daddy scares them.'

Poor child. Doesn't he realise what he's doing to his own children? If he carries on like this, they're going to be in therapy by the time they're teenagers.

I crouch down until I'm at her eye line. 'Well, your daddy doesn't scare me.' I wink reassuringly. She smiles back, her eyes still unsure.

The door to the playroom bursts open and in walks Mr

Rothchester, his nostrils flaring, his face red. I smile as confidently as I can. *Remember, Ruby, all you've done is decorate his house, you haven't let squatters move in.*

'What the hell is this?' he shouts, pointing at the lights in disgust.

'They're called Christmas decorations,' I say with a sarcastic smile.

He looks down at the bauble in my hand, his eyes ablaze with rage. 'Put. That. Down.'

'I was just about to,' I say as calmly as I can, hanging it on the tree. It annoys me that my hand is trembling. I don't want him to know he scares me in the slightest. Big bully.

He opens his mouth and it's clear to everyone that he's about to go off on one.

'Can I just stop you right there?' I interrupt quickly. 'Perhaps if you have something to discuss we should go to your study, and not worry the children with it?'

He stops himself, taking a deep breath. I can see on his face he hates that he is agreeing with me. 'Can I see you in my office a moment?' It's nothing more than a demand.

I smile politely. 'Of course, Mr Rothchester.'

He spins on his heel and practically runs ahead. I follow him out of the room, glancing back at the girls. They've clung together. It's obvious they think I'm leaving tonight.

I give them a reassuring thumbs up and follow him up the stairs, trying and failing to avoid checking out his arse and glutes in those trousers. God knows how they don't split. We walk along to his office and I close the door behind me.

My stomach is in my knickers and sweat is trickling down the back of my neck; not that I let it show. The sadistic bastard wants that. I lean on one hip in what I hope is a defiant stance. I hate that he makes me this jittery.

'What the fuck is this?' he shouts from behind his desk. 'Who the hell do you think you are? Decorating my house?'

I sigh, stopping myself from eye rolling. 'I spoke to the girls and they said that you never decorate and that they'd like to.'

'I don't decorate for a reason,' he practically spits. His whole face is red and blotchy, his neck muscles tensed. He needs a lavender wheat bag to the neck. 'I would have thought you'd have respected that.'

'Why? I know you haven't decorated since your wife died, but Jessica remembers her mummy loving Christmas and them decorating together. So, what's the big deal?'

His nostrils flare. He reminds me of a rhino.

'And you thought you could just walk in and try to replace those memories? Touch my wives' things?'

I get that he could be upset with me, a mere mortal, touching his wives' things, but can't he see I'm doing this for the girls?

'Don't you get it? Those memories will fade if you don't continue to talk about your wife. By just ignoring her you're ruining her memory. Do you really think she'd want it like this?'

He slams his hand down on the desk so hard I flinch.

'How *dare* you think you have any idea of what my wife would have wanted. She can't want anything, because she's dead!' I blanch, as if he's slapped me. 'Yes, she loved Christmas, but Christmas is also when she died.'

Oh. I didn't know that. Well now I can maybe understand why he's so pissed. Turns out *I'm* the insensitive arsehole.

'Look, I'm sorry if I upset you,' I say in a calmer, more controlled, voice. 'But I was just trying to make the girls happy. That's all I ever try to do.'

The vein on his forehead throbs. 'Well, I've had enough of you trying to take control of my children. You're fired.'

I bark a laugh. Who the fuck does he think he is?

'Oh, don't for one second think I'm going anywhere,' I retort, my chest heaving with outrage.

He stares back, blankly. 'I just told you, you're fired. Get out.' He attempts to shoo me away. *Arrogant tosser.*

I scoff. 'I just told you, I'm not going anywhere. These girls have no stability in their lives. They have a constant stream of nannies. I'm going to stay here for the holidays. I'll go in the new year and that, Mr Rothchester, is final.'

The look on his face is priceless.

Barclay

The woman is certifiable. I fired her, for goodness sakes. She should be packing her bags and fucking off back to where she came from. But insisting she's going to stay for Christmas... like she's doing me a favour...? It's infuriating.

I still can't believe she touched all of Claire's Christmas decorations. Of course I don't decorate at Christmas. Claire died at Christmas. It doesn't matter how many decorations you have surrounding you; when your wife passes nothing can cheer you up.

Claire really did love Christmas. She was one of those annoying people that got excited about it in July. I used to tease her relentlessly about it, but I actually found it adorable. She came from a very modest household where they couldn't afford a real tree or good decorations. I remember when we were teenagers, she'd tell me she dreamed of a big house that she could decorate exactly as she wanted.

She got those wishes, but who cares about them if then you have your life taken from you? God, just thinking of how cruel and unjust it all is makes me mad again. If someone needed to be taken it should have been me. The girls could have lived without me easily, but without their mother's loving touch? I don't know.

Maybe it's good that Ruby is staying for Christmas. God knows it would be a nightmare to recruit a nanny so close to the holidays. Probably be fobbed off with agency staff. I just worry that the girls will bond with her before then. They probably will —she lets them get away with murder.

When she was back-chatting me, I got to really glare at her, face to face. I never noticed before how beautiful she is. So far, she's always struck me as kind of a mess, with her messy top bun, skinny jeans and baggy jumpers, like she's been put together in a whirlwind, but her face is actually pretty striking.

She's got the most unusual coloured eyes. They're the palest sea green with a dark brown outer rim, making them seem almost hazel. They really are remarkable.

I like the fact that she isn't like those over botoxed women you see every day. She has a natural beauty, only enhanced by the freckles all over her face.

Well, regardless of how enchanting I find her face, the fact remains that she's still a pain in the arse. And still fired. I just have to deal with her a few more weeks and then I'll never have to clap eyes on her again. Thank god.

CHAPTER 7

Thursday 5th December

Ruby

The girls were really clingy at bedtime. They kept asking if I was going away. I reassured them that everything was fine and that I wasn't going anywhere. Which is kind of a lie, seen as I'll be leaving in the new year, but for now I want them to have a great Christmas. I can't have them worrying over the holidays. Little people shouldn't have so much on their shoulders, especially at Christmas time. I distracted them by teaching them the entire *"see you later"* song and braiding their hair. I can't believe they've only heard of the first two verses.

Today is Jessica's school nativity. We've been working hard on her lines and the songs at home. She's an innkeeper's wife.

She's over the moon she can tell Mary and Jesus, "Sorry, no room at the inn." Such an epic line.

Who wants to be Mary anyway? She's boring. Much more fun to be the lady turning her away. After all, would it have been such an epic story if they gave birth in a regular old inn? I don't think so. The innkeeper's wife changed history.

It's taking place at two o'clock, so I haven't held my breath over Mr Rothchester turning up. Even though it's a total milestone in my mind. I would have been devastated if my dad hadn't shown up to my school nativity. Luckily my dad was at every single assembly, well, up until the day he died.

I could hardly ask Mr Rotchester this morning if he was coming, what with him firing me last night. I'm sure he still despises me.

I'm sat with Lottie on my lap when Clementine walks over, a smug smile on her face. Oh shit, what has she got in store for me?

'Ah, Ruby! Just the person. I need your email address.'

'Okay, but...why?'

'To send over the PTA meeting itinerary of course.' She laughs, almost cruelly. She reminds me of Cruella D'ville. 'Don't forget that your first meeting is tomorrow night at Lucinda's house. 8pm. Don't be late. We'd hate for you to get a reputation as being sloppy from day one.' She looks disapprovingly down at my skinny jeans and baggy jumper.

I force a smile through gritted teeth. 'I'll be there.' I salute her, as if I were in her army. *Hitler like bitch.*

The lights go down as soon as she walks away, as if she knows the lighting guy. Probably black mailing him too.

The excited chatter of the parents teeters off as we all sit with nervous anticipation.

I cross my fingers. Please God, let everything go well. If she fluffs her lines, I'll die for her. Those kinds of embarrassing moments can define a kid's future. Something they later realise in therapy was the catalyst for them becoming a crack whore.

'Excuse me,' I hear to my right. I turn to see who's turning up this late. To my complete shock it's Mr Rothchester. He made it. Wow. I stare at him aghast.

He sits down beside me on my coat I'd put holding his space with just in case. No need to pick it up, you arse hat. Just crush it with your bottom.

'You made it,' I whisper towards him. I can't keep the surprise out of my voice.

He smiles. It's so brief that I wonder whether I imagined it. You know how they say a smile can light up a room? Well his is like the flicker of a candle in a dark room. I'm drawn to it; begging for more.

'Dada!' Lottie says, crawling into his arms.

The curtains pull open and there's Jessica singing with her class. She looks absolutely beautiful in the little outfit I sewed for her. Once again, I'm glad my mum taught me. She's the most fashionable inn keeper's wife that'll ever be seen. She's wearing a headband round her hair which makes her look like a glorious hippy.

She spots me and smiles, but then does a double take when she spots her daddy. Her mouth drops open, before beaming back at him, unashamedly waving.

It warms my heart. Before I consider what I'm doing I'm

squeezing his arm. His bicep to be more specific. It was meant to be an encouraging gesture, but the way he looks down at my hand makes me feel like I've just crossed a line. Like I'm some sort of dirty whore nanny who's trying to get in his pants.

I quickly take it back and sit on my hands to stop myself doing something ridiculous. But damn, that man has muscles. When the hell does he find the time to work out? Or is that just his wanking hand? I stifle a giggle. God, I'm immature.

I practically hold my breath until it's Jessica's line. She says it with so much spunk and sass that everyone in the audience laughs. She looks back at me, wondering if she's done something silly, because of their reaction. I give her a thumbs up and actually fist pump the air in excitement. I glance at Mr Rothchester and he's beaming back at her, rolling his eyes at me; God forbid anyone shows emotion.

When it finally finishes, I realise that I've been singing along to everything, keeping eye contact with Jessica, in case she was to forget anything we've practised. Mr Rothchester's been filming it on his phone.

We all stand to applause.

'Wasn't she amazing!' I beam at him. I'm so overwhelmingly proud of her I could cry.

He nods, amusement dancing in his eyes. 'Of course, she was. She's a Rothchester.'

I roll my eyes but continue to clap. 'I hope you didn't get me singing on there,' I say, pointing towards his phone.

'Oh, plenty.' He grins. *Now I get a grin.* What is going on here? Probably just ecstatic that I'm leaving.

He checks his phone, frowning. 'I have to go.'

And just like that, the Christmas magic is over.

'Can't you stay to tell her how fantastic she was? I know she'd love to hear it in person.'

He takes Lottie's arms from around his neck and hands her over to me.

'Afraid not. I've barely made it out to see her. But tell her I'll see her tonight.'

'You'll make it back before bed time?' I ask hopefully.

He grimaces. 'I can't promise.' Of course, he can't.

I sigh. 'Okay, fine.'

'Daddy!' Lottie cries, reaching out for him with grabby hands as he makes his way through the crowd and disappears. Every woman stops to watch him. He is some serious man candy around here. Not that he notices; too busy on his phone.

'Don't worry, Lottie, we'll see Daddy later.' She sobs onto my shoulder. Poor little mite. 'Come on. We need to dry our tears so we can tell Jessica what a good job she did.'

'Okay,' she agrees, wiping her nose with the back of her hand.

We make our way towards the front of the classroom, where all the parents are already queuing up.

'Hi,' a man in jeans and a ridiculous Christmas jumper says to me. I think I've seen him before at pick up. He's got a toddler on his hip.

'Hi,' I nod politely. I smile over at Juliette, the only friendly mum to have introduced herself to me.

'You're the new nanny for Jessica, right?' he asks, with a friendly smile. He's not bad looking with mousey brown hair and pale green eyes. If I had a couple of pinots in me, I'd find him *very* sexy.

'That's me. I'm Ruby.' I awkwardly wave.

Why do I always clam up and act like a buffoon in front of men? Sometimes I wonder how I ever lost my virginity.

'I'm Jared, Verity's nanny. Or Manny, as they like to call me.' He laughs nervously. 'I noticed that you were new to the area and I wondered if you fancied meeting up for coffee one day. Let me fill you in on the nanny circuit.'

Oh, is he asking me out? Romantic styles? Or just being friendly? I wish I knew more about dating and men sometimes.

'That would be lovely, thanks.'

God knows it's hard to have any kind of relationship when you're in this line of work. If he's in the same boat he'll understand. At the very least, I'll gain a friend. It's not like they're banging my door down.

'Great.' He hands over his phone. 'Put your number in that and I'll text you to find out your schedule.'

I put the number in with fumbling fingers and hand it back to him, not sure if I actually want him to message me.

One by one, the children are changed and released over. I'm hoping Jessica will come out soon. There's nothing worse than when someone's asked you out and you've accepted but then you're forced to stand in weird silence together. This is why I hardly date. It's so difficult and embarrassing.

Thankfully Jessica comes practically skipping out at that very moment. Her little smile fades when she realises Mr Rothchester is no longer here.

'You were amazing!' I screech, hugging her close to me.

Well, as close as I can with Lottie on my hip. The girl never wants to be put down, clingy little koala bear that she is.

'Daddy had to go?' she asks, her eyes drop, her bottom lip wobbling.

I pull her away from everyone. 'Yes, sweetie, but he filmed it on his phone and was so damn proud of you. He's over the moon with how good you were. I think you should start writing your Oscars speech.'

Her face scrunches up. 'What's an Oscar?'

I scoff a laugh. 'An award for being an amazing actress.'

She sighs, resigned. 'Okay, let's go home.'

I can't have her being this glum. Especially after her trying so hard and performing so well.

'Well, actually. Daddy suggested we do something special to celebrate.'

Her face lights up. 'Really? He did?'

'Yep! I think we should go for doughnuts and babychinos.'

'What's a babychino?' Lottie asks, her eyes wide. 'I'm not a baby.'

'Oh, I know you aren't sweetness. It's just the name of the nicest hot chocolate in the whole of London!'

'With marshmallows?' Jessica asks excitedly, clapping her hands together.

'Soooo many marshmallows.' I nod with a giggle.

'What are we waiting for?' she shrieks, grabbing my hand. 'Let's go!'

Barclay

I'm only shortly back at work from the nativity when there's a knock on my door. I know those three raps, it's my mother.

'Hi, darling!' she sings, floating in without waiting for me to answer. 'How was my little granddaughter's performance? Is she going to be a thespian like her Grandma?'

Please, the woman was in her high school production of Romeo and Juliet and now she fancies herself a thespian.

'She was brilliant, of course,' I answer, looking back to my computer. Hopefully she'll see how busy I am and leave.

'And the nanny?'

I flinch at the mention of her. I still can't believe she grasped my arm like that. At first, I thought she was attempting to try it on with me, but then I realised that she was just genuinely over the moon at Jessica's performance. It almost made me chuckle. She was like a child herself. She really is invested in my girls.

'She's fine,' I answer quickly, when I realise Mum is staring at me.

'Really?' she asks with raised eyebrows. Dammit, did Mrs Dumfy tell her I've already fired her? Not that I've told her, it would be Ruby spilling the beans.

'Really,' I nod. 'I mean, the woman is infuriating, but she'll do until after the holidays.'

'Oh, Barclay,' she sighs, her shoulders drooping dramatically. 'I do wish you'd let the girl's bond properly to a nanny. Goodness knows they deserve someone to stick around longer. When will you just accept that no nanny you ever have will be Claire?'

I take it like a bullet to the heart. She thinks I'm trying to replace Claire?

'No-one and I mean *no-one* will ever be able to replace Claire,' I growl. 'I'm horrified you've even said that.'

She sits down across from me.

'I know that, darling, but you don't have to find someone one hundred percent perfect. People are flawed, but the right one, the girls will love anyway.'

'Hmm,' I muse, already deciding to ignore her advice. She lucked out with getting the perfect nanny for me. I doubt much thought went into it at all.

There's no time for flawed people helping to raise my children. They deserve the very best, especially with the bad hand they've been dealt.

'Just promise me you'll try, darling?'

I look up to see her eyebrows raised in such hope. She's always been an optimist.

'Fine,' I huff. 'I'll try.'

CHAPTER 8

Barclay

I let myself in at 7pm. I'd hoped to be home sooner so I could tell Jessica how proud of her I am today but work just got away with me. With it being Christmas every single company on our books is having at least one Christmas event and each thinks they're more important than the other.

I notice the quietness of the house immediately. Where are the girls?

I run into the kitchen where Marge is covering four plates of dinner in tin foil.

'Where are the girls?' I ask her, already feeling frantic. They're always here when I get home.

'I was hoping you'd tell me, Mr Rothchester, she says, her jaw tense. 'I've called and left several messages asking them what time they'd be back for dinner, but I've heard nothing.'

Shit. Where the hell are they?

I pull my phone out and call Ruby's number. No answer. *For fucks sakes, Ruby.* My biggest bug bear is people not answering their phones. I call Mrs Dumfy next.

'Have you seen the girls?' I ask, before she's even finished saying hello.

'No, Barclay.' I hear her moving around. 'They're not back yet? That does seem late for them.'

'Doesn't it just,' I grunt. 'I'm sick of Ruby not sticking to the rules. Now I have no idea where my children are at this time of night.'

'I'll keep trying to call her myself,' she tries to reassure. 'But I really wouldn't worry.'

'Ok thanks.' I'm about to hang up when I remember my mum. 'Oh, you didn't tell my mother anything did you?'

'Like what?' she asks, sounding like she doesn't know anything.

'Oh, nothing.' I hang up. I don't want her knowing I've fired her this early on and have all of them judging me and calling me unreasonable.

I start pacing in the hallway, watching every second on the clock. It's getting to the point now where I think I'm going to have to call the police. Get a search party going. For all I know Ruby is a complete unhinged nutcase and me firing her has sent her over the edge. She could have thrown them in the Thames just to spite me for all I know.

That's it. I'm calling them.

Ruby

We had the most amazing afternoon eating beautiful glazed doughnuts from Hole of Glory. A bit inappropriately named if you ask me, but they've decorated it so beautifully for Christmas. It's got so many Christmas lights and so much fake snow it's like a Santa's grotto.

The girls loved it and they even got to decorate their own babychinos. They of course chose not only just marshmallows, but also whipped cream, chocolate sauce, smarties and chocolate chips.

I tried to encourage them away from the smarties, but hey, it was a celebration! We had so much fun, with Jessica chatting about her classmates. It was nice to finally put faces to the names. We talked about how Fenston has a crush on Figgy, but how she likes Titus. How Wigbert picks his nose and eats it and how Tansy likes to dress up as boys. Honestly, some of the names are ridiculous. I was half expecting her to mention an apple or netarine.

Even the walk home feels beautiful with all of the houses lit up with fairy lights in the darkness. It would be easy to mistake it for midnight instead of quarter to eight. The girls are giddy at having been spoilt and out so late; their cheeks rosy from the cold.

A quick bath, story and bed for these two, I think.

'One more time,' Jessica begs, pulling on my arm.

I roll my eyes, but my cheeks are sore from smiling and laughing with these beautiful girls.

'Okay,' I relent easily. 'See you later, alligator.'

'In a while, crocodile,' Jessica says back with a huge grin.

'Bye bye, butterfly,' Lottie sings. We both giggle.

'Be sweet, parakeet,' I say through a chuckle.

Jessica's giggles are so loud we're actually causing a public nuisance. I'm half expecting someone to turn a light on and shout out for us to shut up.

'Give a hug, ladybug.' She says it with so much sass that I crease up over again.

'See you soon, racoon,' Lottie says, clearly delighted at herself for remembering so much of it.

'Amazing! Well done girls. Only five more verses to learn. I'm so impressed you've got it nailed so quickly.'

We open the door to home, but our giggles taper off as we immediately know there's something wrong. The atmosphere seeps out. I try to ignore it for the sake of the girls, but then I hear his thudding footsteps.

'Ruby? Is that you?'

Well, he's finally on first name terms with me. Although I was hoping the first time he said my name it wouldn't be with so much rage and contempt.

'Yes, it's us,' I shout back, taking the girls coats off.

He skids into the main hall, his tie pulled down in that annoyingly sexy way he does.

'Sorry, false alarm,' he says into his phone before hanging up. 'Where the hell have you been?' he cries, bending down to check the girls, as if expecting them to have been damaged while in my care.

'We went for hot chocolate and doughnuts, Daddy,' Jessica says with a smile.

'Just like you suggested, *remember*,' I say to him, with a wink. 'To celebrate Jessica's success in her nativity.'

He seems to cotton on quickly, but that doesn't stop him and his rage.

'I assumed you wouldn't be staying out until nearly 8pm on a school night.' He says it like its eleven pm. 'They've missed their dinner. You should have told someone.'

I sigh. No matter what I do he'll always find a problem with it. We're just so different.

I take a discreet deep breath to calm myself. 'Sorry, but you said you probably wouldn't make it home tonight anyway. I didn't feel like we should bother rushing.'

'Well, you should have told Marge,' he retorts sharply. 'And you should have answered your phone.'

I take it from my bag to see fifteen missed calls from him, seven from Marge and five from Mrs Dumfy.

I grimace. 'Ah. It must still be on silent from the nativity. But I did message Marge and tell her we wouldn't be back for dinner.'

I check the message, but it's only as I go to present it to him that it suddenly gets a second tick. 'Ah, it mustn't have gone through.'

He bends down to the girls, ignoring me. 'Don't worry girls. Marge kept you some dinner.'

'We're full of doughnuts,' Lottie says with a grin. 'And smarties.'

Oh God, way to rat me out Lottie.

His nostrils flare as he sucks in an angered breath. 'How on earth is filling them up on sugar before bed time a good idea?'

God, was this guy *ever* a kid?

I shrug. 'Sometimes you just have to throw out the rule book.'

His eyes shoot daggers at me as if I just told him we snorted some cocaine.

'I want to be informed of any changes to their routines. Understood?'

I salute him again. 'Yes, sir,' I say sarcastically.

He falls to his knees to talk to the girls. 'Did you have a good time?' he asks, a tiny bit cheerier.

'The best time, Daddy!' Jessica babbles; filling him in on all our silly adventure.

'And you're sure you're not hungry for dinner?' he presses, sliding me an evil side eye.

'Sleepy,' Lottie says, rubbing her eyes.

'Okay, well then, quick bath and bed I think.'

Just like I was going to do before he threw a tantrum. Honestly, it's like looking after *three* kids.

Jessica's eyes light up. 'Are you giving us a bath and putting us to bed?'

His eyes look pained for a second, before he pulls it back and puts his impassive mask back on. What the hell is his deal?

'Afraid I can't sweetheart,' he admits with a grimace. 'I have to get ready for a work event. But Ruby will help you.'

My heart falls at exactly the same time as the girls do. I put on a smile and take them up to do our normal routine.

When I'm tucking Jessica in, she looks serious, her little forehead puckered with lines.

'What's on your mind, kitten?'

She smiles sleepily. 'I'm not a kitten.'

I stroke her cheek. 'I know you're not. You don't have any whiskers. Now, your teacher Mrs Engleton. She could be a kitty.'

She bursts out laughing. *What?* The woman has a ridiculous amount of facial hair!

'But tell me, what are you worrying about?' I smooth her blonde locks off her forehead.

She chews on her bottom lip. 'I'm just worried Daddy is going to drive you away.'

Oh God, my heart. Little does she know he already has.

'Do you think I look scared of that man?' I make a funny face, which makes her giggle.

'No, but he doesn't like you.' She says it so matter of factly. She doesn't mean to hurt my feelings; she's just being perceptive.

I scoff a laugh. 'Well, luckily he doesn't have to like me for me to do my job. And even luckier is that my job is to look after you beautiful girls. Can you even believe they pay me to do this?' I cuddle her up in her duvet, kissing her cheek.

She grins. 'Are you sure? All of the others went.' She looks so hopeful.

'Well, all of the others weren't me, were they?'

I feel awful lying to her, but I can't have her worrying about this. She's too young for this type of responsibility.

She giggles. 'Okay.'

'Why don't I teach you those last few lines of the song, to take your mind off it?'

She grins back up at me, her eyes full of excitement.

'So, the next bits go;
"out the door, dinosaur,
take care, polar bear,
so long, king kong,
blow a kiss, goldfish,
toodle-loo, kangaroo."
What do you think?'

She beams back at me. 'I love it.' But there's something more she wants to say. I can tell by the way she's twiddling with the leg of her teddy bear.

'What is it, sweetheart?'

'Well, I was wondering if you could find something for me?' She looks down shyly at her hands.

'Of course, honey. What?' I'd give this girl the world if I could. I've already joined the bloody PTA for her. Clementine's been sending me emails practically every twenty minutes.

'A picture of my mummy.'

Oh, my heart. My eyes sting with the tears I want to shed for her.

'I can't remember what she looks like and that makes me sad. I'd like a picture of her I could put next to my bed.'

The poor little mite. I wish I could take all her heartache away and bear it as my own.

'Of course. I'll do my very best.'

'Thanks. Night night, Ruby.' She smiles dreamily.

'Night, night, baby. Love you.'

And in that moment, I realise that I do. I do love her.

I close the door, the tears already falling silently down my cheek. I'm in big trouble.

CHAPTER 9

Friday 6th December

Ruby

Okay, so I need to find a picture of their mum. The next day I'm on it as soon as the girls are at school. Well, as soon as I've finished reading through the bloody PTA itinerary for tonight. God, if it's any indication of how the groups going to run, I'm bloody terrified.

I've quizzed Marge about a photo, but she's said she has no idea. Apparently, she was hired after she had passed. Their mum used to do all the cooking. I like her already. Every time I think of her missing out on the girl's lives, I want to just break down and cry.

So that's how I find myself speaking to Mrs Dumfy. I don't know why, but I'm more uneasy asking her.

'Why do you want it?' she asks, eyeing me suspiciously.

'It's not me, it's for Jessica.'

She sighs, checks no one is around us and pulls me to one side. 'Mr Rothchester doesn't like pictures of her up around the house.'

I knew it.

'Why not?'

'Too painful for him.' She purses her lips. 'Her face is a constant reminder of the life he used to have that can no longer continue. I think it breaks his heart.'

Who knew the beast has a heart after all? Mrs Dumfy seems to know him so well.

'I can understand that, but he can't stop his daughters, surely?'

She sighs. 'I think he considers them better off not feeling the same sadness and loss that he has. Thinks they'd be better off to carry on without her. That they'll be better off that way, not remembering.'

'But that's bloody ridiculous!' I can't help but shriek. These girls can't just forget she ever existed.

She rolls her eyes in agreement. 'You're telling me. I've worked for the family for several years and it breaks my heart. Mrs Rothchester was such a loving, warm lady. I really think it's a shame for her memory not to live on.'

I think for a second about his loss. I can't even begin to imagine finding the love of your life only then to lose them. I saw how much it broke my mum when my dad died. She never truly recovered and if I'm honest with myself, it's the reason I've never been in a long-term relationship. I like to blame the job, but the truth is that handing over that kind of power to someone scares the hell out of me. The power to break me to a point of no return.

'Okay, so tell me where her photos are, and I'll be the one that gets in trouble. That's if he even finds it. He spends so little time with the girls.'

'I don't know where the photos are,' she admits with a sigh. 'You could check in the storage room, but something makes me think he'd have kept it closer and safer than that.' She winks conspiratorially, a twinkle in her eye.

'His office!' I run off towards it. 'Thanks, Mrs Dumfy!' I shout back.

I burst into his office, already wondering where I can rummage, when I realise, he's sat behind the bloody desk.

'Oh!' Shit. My heart nearly leaps out and smacks him in the face.

'Jesus, Ruby. What the hell's wrong?' He stands up, his eyes wide. 'Is it the girls?'

Well, how do I style *this* out?

'Oh no, I just...I wanted to know...' Think Ruby, *think*. Engage your brain.

He stares at me intently. It's making me panic more. My mind is blank.

'If... you're allergic to milk,' I randomly blurt out. Milk? Is that the best you could come up with? *Come on, Ruby.*

His lips quirk up on the right. Is he trying to hide a smile?

'You want to know if I'm allergic to milk?' he repeats bemused. God, I'm an idiot. 'Why didn't you just ask Marge?'

'Ah, what a good idea!' I giggle, like a complete and utter bimbo. Way to gain his respect.

'And dare I ask why you need to know that information?' he questions, a rare grin spreading. 'Not attempting to poison me, are you?' He looks back down at his papers, but I can tell he's entertained at the idea.

It pisses me off. *Mate, if I wanted to kill you, you wouldn't see it coming.* You'd be clutching at your throat and foaming at the mouth before you even cottoned on.

'Oh just... something me and the girls have planned.'

Crap, now I have to plan something with milk. Must put that on my to do list.

'Well, any surprise will have to wait until tomorrow. I'm out at a work event tonight.'

Ah, so his office will be empty. Nice. That's when I'll have a root through.

With him being out tonight it would have been perfect for me to rummage through his office, but I forgot I've got to be at the bloody PTA meeting at Lucinda's house. I let the girls stay up later than normal to watch Elf and then after putting them to bed I stupidly pour myself a glass of wine and sit down. Big mistake.

I wake up to my phone alarm going off. Shit. I must have dozed off. Thank God I had the foresight to set it.

I get an uber round there, trying to make my hair more presentable in the rear view mirror. Oh well, they're going to judge me anyway. I might as well look as much of a mess as I feel.

Lucinda's house is just as big as Barclay's. She opens the door clutching a huge glass of wine. More like a small vase.

'Hi, I'm Ruby. I'm here for the PTA thing,' I mumble, fumbling with my hands, feeling like a fool.

'Ah, yes, the nanny.' *Ouch*. 'Come on in,' she says, actually appearing half friendly.

I follow her down the stairs into their basement kitchen. It's the entire floor; so bloody enormous. All chrome and black gloss. It's not to my taste, but even I can admire it.

'Would you like a glass of pinot?' she offers, already going for the fridge.

'Yes please.' Looking around at the others who are glancing at me with distaste, it seems I'm going to need it.

That's when I spot Juliette; the friendly mum. I didn't know she was on the PTA. She waves over at me.

I take the glass, thank her and begrudgingly move to where the others have congregated in the sitting room area. I wave a meek hello at them.

'Right,' Clementine says, clapping her perfectly manicured hands together. 'Let's start, shall we?'

Everyone starts sitting around the enormous table and chairs. There must be fifteen women here but there's chairs for all of us. That's how big the room is.

'First of all,' Clementine says, seeming sweet as candy, 'I'd like to welcome Ruby.'

I wave awkwardly at them. Juliette really is the only friendly one here.

'Ruby has volunteered to take the notes tonight.'

I look up at her. 'Huh?' She smiles smugly. 'I mean, of course.' Oh crap, I forgot my notebook. 'Only...I forgot my notebook.' I grimace.

She looks at me in disgust, as if to say, *"you can't even remember a notebook and you want to be part of our clique?"*

Luckily one of the mums, Amanda, lends me hers and then I'm desperately rattling down the notes. *Damn these bitches talk fast.* I should have brought a Dictaphone with me.

Two hours later, I'm sure I've developed carpel tunnel syndrome.

'Oh, Ruby, I forgot to tell you,' Clementine says with a cruel smile. This isn't going to be good, whatever it is. 'We've decided that as you're new, your house can be where we host our monthly wine and cheese evening.'

Wine and cheese evening? God, could these people get anymore middle class?

'Well, it's not really my house, so I don't think we'd be able to do it there.' I fake a sad smile.

'I'm sorry, Ruby,' she scoffs, looking anything but sorry. 'But you insisted on being a part of the PTA. Part of being on the PTA is hosting these evenings. I'm sure you can persuade Barclay.' She smiles mischievously. Ah, so that's her angle.

'I...' I start but get quickly interrupted.

'It's pretty simple, Ruby. Either host the evening or leave the PTA.'

Well...I guess I'm hosting the evening then.

Barclay

This work event is boring as shit. Queenie, my work colleague, has insisted we mingle with everyone. Cringey if you ask me. I abhor small talk. I just want to get down to the nitty gritty. But I hate the whole smooze of socialising but I suppose you do need some of that in this business.

To get through the evening I've been chucking back plenty of free champagne. I don't even like the stuff, but I have far too much stuff on my mind right now which I need to escape from.

Dad let himself into my office today and told me I only had two choices left; take the partnership or leave the company. I already knew they were my only options, but to have him lay them out so clearly, and coldly, shocked me. He might be offering me good work opportunities, but apart from that, the man doesn't act like I'm his son at all. No compassion; just accept it or get the hell out. No empathy for me or his grandchildren.

I'm sure it's because he thinks I'm going to crumble and accept. I know then I'll be exactly where he wants me. Part of me wonders if I should just accept it. I don't know if I have the mental strength to move to a completely different company. I'd have to be friendly to everyone and make new friends. At least here everyone knows I'm a miserable bastard. They also know about my loss. I'd have to explain that all over again at a new company.

Maybe I'd be more willing to do it if the girls were settled at home with a remarkable nanny. Instead all I can see is them doting on the fluky and unreliable Ruby. Each day she stays they're liking her more and more. It worries me. God knows I don't want to break their heart, but I also can't have their routine disrupted like she is.

By the end of the night I find myself in a dark corner with Queenie. She's pushing her boobs against me and biting my ear. We fool around drunkenly from time to time. She knows the deal, I'm not interested in absolutely anything, but she always seems to find me when I'm feeling the most vulnerable.

'Shall we get out of here?' she purrs.

Fuck it, why not.

CHAPTER 10

Ruby

By the end of the night I have seventeen pages of barely legible scribbles. Apparently, I also volunteered to type them up and email them to everyone by the weekend. Oh, and don't forget the costumes I have to sew for the float. The only advantage is that it means I can make sure Jessica's outfit is extra awesome.

I get home absolutely shattered at around midnight. It's quiet up there. I wonder if Barclay's still out. I could rummage for the photos. This might be my only opportunity. I run upstairs and peer into his office. No sign of him.

I don't dare turn the light on, instead using my phone as a torch. I feel like a sexy spy. Now that's a career I should have looked into. Probably less stressful than working for Mr Rothchester.

I rifle through his drawers, careful to replace everything as neatly as I found it. I've nearly given up when I see that he has a small locked drawer on his desk hidden away. It's got to be in there!

Where would the key be? I rifle around his paperclips and find it hidden within them. Yes! So predictable. I unlock and slowly open it.

Inside are a whole load of printed photos. I sit down on his leather chair and flick through them. It starts with Mr Rothchester and her together as a young couple. She's got long brunette hair and the most stunning pale blue eyes. The same eyes as Jessica's.

It seems they were school sweethearts. There's pictures of them together very young at what looks like a school ski trip.

Then photos of university, holidays, her holding up her engagement ring to the camera; their wedding day. They look so unbelievably happy. My chest feels tight at the thought of him losing all of this. I can almost not blame him for being so cold, when he's had his heart ripped out like he has. A tear falls down my cheek.

The photos continue to her sporting a large bump, getting the keys to this house, installing a new kitchen, having Jessica. More family pictures of the three of them before Lottie came along. Then the photos are further apart until she starts looking ill; her face gaunt, her hair thin.

The last picture is of the four of them on a hospital bed. She's as pale as a ghost, dark rings under her eyes, but she's putting on a brave smile for her girls. Jessica is looking up at her adoringly while Mr Rothchester helps her hold baby Lottie. I put the photo down, the tears running quickly now down my cheek. I don't want to ruin them with my tears.

No wonder he doesn't want to re-live this. In that last picture you can see the raw pain in his eyes. The disbelief, the anger; his fear. It's all there in those dark brown eyes attempting to put on a brave face for his girls. I allow myself to have a good sob, my heart hurting for the entire family. How can life be so cruel?

I eventually manage to pull myself together enough to pick out a gorgeous photo of her on the beach during a family holiday. She looks free and relaxed. Happy with a blue sky behind her. How I imagine she would be up in heaven.

I take it and lock the rest of the photos away safely. I get up to leave when suddenly the door spills open slightly, light from the hallway filling the room. Giggles of a woman filter through to where I'm stood. What the hell?

I immediately drop to the floor as the light is flicked on. Shit. The last thing I need is to be found snooping in here. He'll kill me.

I peer around the desk to see the back of him and the front of a woman in an evening gown snogging his face off. Oh Jesus, he just had to leave early with this woman!

I crawl around to the side of the desk as he's backed up against it by the woman. My heart beats erratically in my chest. I can't be found in here. There is no explanation of why I'd be in here, by myself, in the dark.

I peer around at them. Perfect, he's distracted; busy eating face. I get down onto my stomach and army crawl my arse out of there. I've almost made it to the door when I hear him.

'Ruby!'

Oh crap. I'm done for.

I roll onto my back to I face him. 'Oh, hi!' I say, as if I *too* am surprised to see him.

'What the hell are you doing in my office?' He quickly attempts to wipe the smudged red lipstick from his lips, realising I've caught him in quite the scandalous position.

The woman glares at me. She's not even pretty. She looks like a horse.

I look around, as if seeing it for the first time. 'Wait, this is your office? This isn't my bedroom! I must have been sleep crawling again. So sorry, my bad.' I jump up and start rubbing my eyes with a fake yawn.

He doesn't look convinced. He looks pissed off and embarrassed, his cheeks pink. To be found with this whore no doubt, as he bloody should be. There he is acting all high and mighty, busy with his work, when really, he's just drinking and having women throw themselves at him.

'Who is she?' the woman asks with disdain in a ridiculously posh rara voice. 'Your maid?'

God, who is this middle-class bitch looking down her nose at me? No-one has maids anymore. Do they?

'Actually, I'm his sex slave,' I say with a wink. 'But don't worry, I don't mind sharing.'

'RUBY!' he roars, his face bright red, that vein looking like it's going to burst, covering us all in his hot-red anger blood.

'Who is she?' the woman asks him again, hitting him on the arm. 'Answer me, Barclay!'

He sighs, pulling at his hair. 'She's my nanny. Well, my kids' nanny,' he quickly corrects.

I turn to walk out of the office, hoping he's distracted enough.

'Stop right there!' he yells. I begrudgingly turn around. 'And what is that in your hand?'

I put it behind my back. 'What hand?'

He rolls his eyes and pinches the bridge of his nose. 'Jesus, it's like dealing with a child.'

Takes one to know one, buddy. Like he'd even know. He's never here.

He walks to me, takes my arm and removes the photograph from my hand. When he sees who's on it his face drops and his eyes find mine. I'm shocked to see betrayal in them.

'Why do you have this?' he asks, in a completely different tone. A quiet tone. It's actually scarier—far scarier.

I look back over at the woman who's trying to tuck her large boob back in. I don't want to talk about it with her here. It's too intimate and private.

'Look, we'll talk tomorrow. In private.'

He sighs. 'Queenie, you need to go.'

She's called Queenie? *Jesus.*

She flings her hands to her chest. '*Me* go?' she asks, outraged.

I can't help but smile smugly back at her. *Bye bitch,* I say with my eyes. *Go back to the stables.*

She grabs her purse and hightails it out of there, but not before shooting him a look that says, *you're making a huge mistake.*

The sudden silence in the room is deafening. I look to the floor, dreading how he's going to go off on me now that there's no witnesses of my death.

He sits down behind his desk and pours himself a whiskey. 'You went into my private office, broke into my drawer...'

'Unlocked your drawer,' I interrupt.

He raises an eyebrow as if to say *really?* 'And took out a picture of my dead wife.' He crosses his arms over himself. 'Can you explain yourself?'

Well, obviously, it sounds terrible when you put it like that.

'Yes, actually.' I sit down opposite him, gulping down the panic. 'Jessica asked for a picture of her.'

His eyes find the desk, his jaw tense. 'And you didn't ask me...why?'

I snort. 'Isn't it obvious? You're never here and when you are, you're barking orders and telling me what I've done wrong. There's not one picture of her in the whole house. I figured there was a reason for that, but the girls deserve to have a picture of her. You can't just delete her from their memories.'

He sneers. 'And you'd know this from spending less than two weeks with my children?'

'It's more than you've spent with them the last six months, I'm guessing,' I snap back.

His eyes blaze. Way to go, Ruby. *Poke the bear.*

'Look, I don't have to explain myself to you. You can give Jessica the picture. That'll be all.'

Oh my God, this man riles me.

'That'll be all? Really?' I can't help but demand. He stares back at me blankly. 'I don't work in your office. And I'm not one of your whores. You can't tell me what to do.'

He stands up and comes over, placing his hands on both arms of my chair, pinning me in. My lady parts tingle in excitement. Bloody traitors. This guy is a dick, trust them to get excited.

'You would do well to remember who is employing you. Or...'

'Or, what?' I interrupt, my eyes raised in challenge. 'You'll fire me? Been there, done that.'

He glares back at me, his chest rising and falling dramatically. 'You are just so...

'Beautiful?' I joke. 'Charming? Intelligent?'

'Infuriating,' he finishes for me; his brown eyes intense.

Having him this close to me allows me to smell him. And oh, what a glorious smell he has; a mix of whiskey and spice. It's intoxicating.

He stares at me with indignation while I stare back, ready for a fight. Ready for whatever is going to come my way. Only... only, his face changes ever so slightly. It's as if he keeps glancing down to my lips. Now he's licking his. Shit, is he going to kiss me? Do I want him to? Am I going to let him?

Just as I'm starting to come around to the idea, he suddenly pulls back, pressing his body back against the wall and crossing his arms.

'Goodnight, Ruby.'

I clear my throat, get up onto like jelly legs and walk out, more bewildered than ever.

CHAPTER 11

Saturday 7th December

Barclay

I cannot believe her! Breaking into my office and going through my personal and precious possessions. And not just that but peeking into mine and Claire's lives. Those precious photos and memories are mine, they feel intimate to me and knowing she's not only put her grubby little hands all over them but stole one. Well, it's too much to bear all at once.

Truthfully the thing that's gutted me the most is being told that the girls wanted a photo of her. I've deliberately kept those photos from them. I just think it's better that they forget. Rather that, than continue with their heartbreak. But knowing they asked Ruby, someone they've only known a few weeks, to get a picture. Well, it makes me think they haven't forgotten her at all. Have I been doing it wrong all along? According to Ruby, yes.

I don't know if I'm madder at that or the fact that she caught me making out with Queenie. I hate being caught vulnerable and that really was not me at my best. Snogging someone I don't even like.

In a way I suppose it's a blessing in disguise. I had a feeling Queenie wasn't going to accept no as an answer last night. Yeah, we make out and have a quick grope now and again, but there's no way I'm actually having sex with her. The thought of sharing a bed with anyone but Claire repulses me. I still wear my wedding ring for God's sakes.

I can only think it was the alcohol, but for some reason I felt sexually attracted to Ruby last night. I don't know why, she still had her hair in that stupid top knot with no make-up on, but... well when she pretended to be my sex slave, I was both outraged and impressed. It's so unusual for someone, anyone in fact, to stand up to me. To not fear shocking me. To call me out on my bullshit.

Looking back, I obviously fired her too soon. Now she has all the control and that annoys the hell out of me. Or apparently turns me on. I'm seriously fucked up.

I want to do everything in my power to ensure my precious girls don't grow up messed up like me. I thought I was doing it all right, but Ruby's got me questioning everything. Damn that Ruby Campbell, coming in our lives and turning everything upside down.

Ruby

Things were weird this morning. Mr Rothchester made himself a quick slice of toast, never making eye contact with me, and then claimed he needed to go to the office. On a Saturday for God's sakes. He also said to plan something fun for tomorrow as he's going to be working. *Again.*

Not an ideal time to ask him to host a wine and cheese evening.

So, to distract ourselves before swimming class we're making a gingerbread house in the kitchen. I've told Marge to leave us to it. She's such a perfectionist that she finds it hard to watch.

I hear the front door close. Is Mr Rothchester back already? A lady walks into the kitchen. I'm just about to ask her who the hell she is when the girls run up to her. 'Grandma!' they coo, embracing her.

Now that I look at her properly, she's dressed quite well to do with a twin set lavender cardigan, navy slacks and a pearl necklace. Her hair is still brown but looking at her hands, that are wrapped around the girls, I'd say she's older than she looks. She must be. That's a serious amount of Botox or work she's had done making her seem mid-forties at first glance, when she must be at least early sixties.

She kisses the tops of their heads and then turns her focus to me.

'And you must be, Ruby.'

I can't help but be stunned. I was so ready for her to address me as *"the nanny"*. I'm so used to being referenced to like that it's almost normal. The fact she bothered to learn my name astounds me. She must be the late Mrs Rothchester's mum. She can't possibly be related to Mr Rothchester.

'Yes, that's me.' I smile shyly, feeling like an intruder in a private family moment.

She leans forward and extends her hand for me to shake. 'I'm Freda. Barclay's mother. Lovely to meet you.'

Wow. How can this woman have produced the same Mr Rothchester that barks almost every word?

'Lovely to meet you too.' I tuck some hair self-consciously behind my ear. Should I leave them to it?

'What are you girls up to, then?' she asks them. She has the same brown eyes as Barclay, except where his are cold hers are warm.

'We're making a gingerbread house,' Jessica explains proudly, presenting all the sweets laid out waiting to be used.

'Marvellous.' She smiles. 'Do me a favour girls and go and find Marge. I fancy one of her delicious teas.'

'Oh, I can make you one?' I offer, reaching for the kettle.

She winks at me. 'No, I fancy one of Marge's, but thank you.'

The girls skip off to find her where she'd no doubt having a cheeky smoke in the garden. I've caught her a few times already.

I steel myself, knowing she wants to talk to me about something away from the prying ears of the girls. Barclay must have told her what a nightmare I am. I hope she's not here to berate me.

As soon as they're out of ear shot, she turns to me, her eyes still warm.

'I wanted to know how my inhospitable son has been treating you?'

I bark out a laugh, but quickly correct myself. I must remember he is her son. She's probably just being polite.

'Oh, it's been fine.' I busy myself with wiping down the side.

'Now, now, Ruby,' she warns with an amused smile. 'I'd like you to be honest with me. I'm on your side here.'

My side? Not her sons? Well that's bloody strange. I look her over. She doesn't seem to be trying to catch me out and she's got nothing but good vibes coming from her. What have I got to lose anyway? I'm already fired.

'Well... okay we have had a *few* disagreements already,' I begrudgingly admit.

She grins mischievously. 'I thought so. There's something in his eyes when he talks about you. Something I haven't seen before.'

'Pure irritation?' I can't help but ask with a laugh.

'Oh yes.' She nods. 'Don't get me wrong, he's always complaining. If not about you then it will be something else. He's always been cantankerous, but I liked the sound of you. You sound spunky and it's clear the girls adore you.'

I find myself blushing. How can he have such a charming mother? His dad must be a pig.

She places her hand over mine. 'I just wanted to let you know that Barclay isn't a bad man. Sure, he can seem impossible at times, but his heart's in the right place.'

I smile and shrug. 'I get it. They're his kids.'

'Well, just remember that I'm on your side. If you ever feel like he's taken things too far I'd like you to call me.' She slides over her business card. 'It's not good for the girls to have a constant stream of nannies. I want you to stay.'

I smile. Shit, how can I tell her that he's already fired me?

'Thanks. It means a lot to me.'

She smiles back at me with a crinkled nose, like she's keeping a secret. 'Something tells me you'll be the one that sticks around.'

Oh, how little she knows.

Sunday 8th December

Ruby

Freda didn't stay long yesterday. She helped us build the ginger-bread house but then made her excuses. I decided to book a day at the local ski centre for today. They're doing a Christmas grotto for the holidays which sounds perfectly festive. This way the girls are guaranteed to play with the white stuff even if we don't have a white Christmas this year.

We arrive at around three pm, after having a lazy morning in our pyjamas before attending tap class, but it already seems packed, kids screaming with excitement.

They pass me a form where I basically sign away our lives, stating that any accident we have is our own fault and we can't sue them. I've seen these forms handed out at birthday parties. Some parents are mental.

'She is four, right?' the young lad asks me, pointing to Lottie, clinging on my hip. She looks adorable, still insisting on the messy bun every day.

'Err, of course.' I nod, not wanting to exclude her from anything. 'Why?'

He shrugs. 'Just that's our minimum age for the snow tunnel.'

'Ah.' Lottie smiles up at me. I doubt she'll want to go on it anyway. She's such a Cautious Cathy.

We hire our snow suits, waterproof gloves, boots and helmets and then we're led into the play area. Kids are doing snow angels and building snowmen while Mariah Carey's "*All I Want for Christmas*" blasts from the speakers. This is what I'm talking about. Finally, some Christmas cheer.

We get to work building our own snowman, using the props of plastic buttons and fake carrot they've given us. It's crap because they don't stay in place, but the girls are happy, their little pink cheeks raised in glee. That's all that matters.

'Can we go on the Ride the Ringo now?' Jessica asks, visibly shaking with excitement.

She's so adorable with her little rosy nose. I couldn't deny her even if I wanted to.

I roll my eyes playfully. 'Okay, we can go now.'

We que up for the slide and listen while an instructor tells us that you must hold onto the holdalls on the huge rubber rings. I assumed that Lottie won't want to go on it, but now she's seen the demonstration she's begged for us to go on together.

How can I say no to that face? These girls have me wrapped round their little fingers.

I'm just about to ask Jessica if she's nervous, but she's already jumping on the hoop and sliding off. It strikes me that her confidence has soared in these short few weeks. I love to think I've played a small part in that.

I can watch from here as she spins, slips and slides down the course. She makes it to the end safely and gets helped off by a member of staff. She gives me a big thumbs up, beaming with pride. Who knew she was so fearless?

'Right, our turn,' I say to Lottie, hoping she'll change her mind.

I go to sit in the ring and motion for Lottie to go on top of me, when a man stops us.

'Woah, only one person per rubber ring.'

I scrunch my nose up. 'What? Well, that's not safe. She's only thr...four,' I quickly correct. 'She wants to go down with me, don't you Lottie?'

She smiles shyly, nodding up at the man.

He bites his lip, mulling it over. 'Okay, but you have to hold onto your mummy.'

Lottie smiles secretly at me, her cheeks reddening, but neither of us correct him. I think she actually likes it, bless her. I get Lottie to climb on top of me so we're both star fishing the hoop.

'Hold on tight, baby,' I whisper into her ear as a fresh swoop of fear clutches at my stomach.

We're pushed down the slope and go under a small tunnel

lit with fairy lights, then we're out and sliding around a corner so fast we almost fall off. *Jesus, this is a kid's ride?*

We skid around a corner and then we're slung around another corner almost falling off again. This is fucking terrifying for a kid's ride. Forget Lottie being scared, I'm shitting a brick here. I see the end is near and I thank god. My stomach has fallen out somewhere back around the first bend.

We launch up towards the 'high five' board which is basically what stops us. I haven't had a chance to breathe a sigh of relief before Lottie is emitting an ear piercing scream. My heart feels like it stops, all blood draining from my face and pooling at my feet.

The man runs over and stops us. I lift Lottie up carefully before jumping up and immediately asking her what's wrong.

'My arm!' she cries, tears streaming down her cheeks. 'My arm!'

Her face is bright red, her eyes wide and panicked. I know it's bad instantly. *Real* bad.

'Shit. We need to see your first aider,' I shout loudly at the man, who I can't help but notice is no older than fourteen.

I grab Lottie and lift her up, careful not to touch her arm. Jessica joins us as we run towards the first aid room the boy is pointing at.

'Help!' I shout as soon as we're in the door, apparently scaring the teenage lad who's sat in there dunking biscuits in his tea. How is this little boy going to help? I probably know more first aid than him. 'She's hurt her arm.'

I look down at it and its swollen, quickly turning from red to purple and doubling in size.

'Lottie, can you move your fingers?' I ask.

She concentrates, her little eyes creasing at the corners. A pained sob escapes her mouth, deep from her throat.

'Right, I'm taking you straight to hospital,' I announce, already dragging them out of the room. I already know she needs it. I'm just praying to God it's just a sprain.

CHAPTER 12

Ruby

*I*t's not just a sprain. Her wrist is broken. The poor little darling. We've worked out that she must have reached out to high five the board and then had it crushed between it and the rubber ring. She's been given some pain killers which have taken the edge off and now we're waiting for it to be set in cast.

Every time I look at those gorgeous little chubby fingers, now surrounded by deep purple bruising I can't help but want to vomit. I caused this.

I'm going to have to call Mr Rothchester. My God, I feel sick to my stomach at the thought of it. If he hadn't fired me already, I know without a shadow of a doubt he would now.

I'm worried he's going to say I'm a danger to the girls and ask me to leave now. The thought of the girls having Christmas without me has a dull aching sadness attacking my heart I've never felt before. Maybe what I'm scared of is *me* being without *them*.

A nurse agrees to sit with the girls while I go outside to make the call. I swallow down the fear bubbling up my oesophagus. You can do this. It was an accident. You didn't do this on purpose. Not that he'll care. Tears prick at the back of my eyes. Be brave, Ruby, be brave.

It rings four times. I pray that he's in a meeting and I'll get to leave a voicemail.

'Hello?'

No such luck.

'Hi, Mr Rothchester,' I squeak. I don't even recognise my own voice. 'It's Ruby.'

'Yes?' he asks, obviously pissed I've disturbed him at work.

'It's... it's...' I clear my throat and pray for my tongue to stop wobbling. 'It's Lottie. I mean, Charlotte. She's... she's had an accident,' I stutter.

Silence greets me. 'Is she okay?' he asks on a pained whisper.

'She's broken her arm,' I blurt out, needing to tell the truth as quickly as possible. 'We're at the hospital now.'

He's quiet for a few moments, enough to wonder if he's putting out a hit on me.

'Jesus fucking Christ, Ruby,' he says, sounding more exhausted than angry. 'Which hospital?'

I give him the details and then he hangs up.

Well that went just as expected. Probably wants to wait until he sees me to fully berate me.

I go back in and hold Lottie's other hand while her arm is set in cast. She's so brave. Her little hazel eyes fill with tears, but she forces a smile at me. I try to stay strong in front of the girls, but a traitorous tear sneaks out. I quickly wipe it away, but not before Jessica's seen it.

'It's okay,' she says, like someone far older than her years, rubbing my shoulder. 'It wasn't your fault. It was an accident. Daddy will understand.' Even she doesn't sound convinced.

'I don't know if he will,' I admit, with a fake little laugh. 'But you don't need to worry about that.'

'I'll tell Daddy it was my fault,' Lottie says bravely. 'Don't worry, Ruby.'

What has it come to when the girls are comforting *me*?

We're ready a lot sooner than I thought we'd be.

'It looks like we're going to be home before Daddy,' I say as brightly as I can. I can't wait to get her home so I can look after her properly.

We're just walking out of the main doors when we spot him. He jumps out of the taxi and rushes in. He sees us straight away. His tie is dragged down and that vein on his forehead is throbbing. Never a good sign.

'Charlotte!' he calls, as if it physically hurts. He lands on his knees in front of her. 'How are you?' He looks at her cast arm, pushing back the hair from her face. 'My poor, baby.'

Is it possible for your throat to tremble in fear? Because I think mine is.

'It wasn't Ruby's fault,' Jessica says quickly, her eyes pleading.

He doesn't look at me. Instead he smiles tightly and says, 'We'll talk about it later.'

The girls seem happy that daddy isn't going off on one. They're not old enough to realise that he's so fuming he can't speak to me in a public place. He can't even look at me. I damaged one of his girls. Of course he's going to kill me. He just needs a quiet place with no witnesses.

In a way it's worse not knowing when he's going to turn and show his beastly rage. The anticipation is killing me.

We drive back to the house in silence. He ignores me, as I ignore him, getting the girls ready for bed and tucked in. I reassure the girls again that it'll all be fine before kissing them goodnight.

I take a deep breath as I close Jessica's bedroom door. Time to face the music. I walk downstairs, my body now physically shaking. I knock three raps on his office door.

'Come in,' he says sternly.

One more deep breath. It's going to be fine, Ruby. Yes, he'll be upset, but he'll get over it. Oh, who am I kidding?

He's sat behind his desk, no doubt a power play from him. I stand against the door, wanting as much distance between us as possible.

'What the hell happened, Ruby?' he asks, more exasperated than furious. It's scarier. Much scarier.

'We went on this ride at the snow centre. I think she must have reached out to touch the high five wall and it got crushed by the hoop.'

'Why the hell was she on a ride like that by herself?' he demands, his forehead marred with wrinkles.

'She wasn't. I was with her. Only... well, the guy did warn that it was only supposed to be one person at a time. Only...'

'Only...?' he encourages, his eyebrows raised, his full lips pursed.

I blow out a breath and flop down onto the spare chair across from him. I think it'll be safer.

'I'd lied. I said she was four so she could ride it in the first place. So yeah, it's basically completely my fault. I take full responsibility. But nothing you say to me will make me feel worse than I already do.'

He sighs. 'It's okay.'

My eyes dart from side to side. It's *okay*? Of all the things I was waiting for him to say it definitely wasn't *"okay"*. Is he playing with me?

'It's not okay,' I disagree, apparently wanting an argument. 'I broke your baby's arm. I'm a disgusting human being who shouldn't be allowed around children.'

He sighs and leans forward, clasping his hands together on the desk.

'Look, Ruby. I was furious when I first heard, but when I saw you, I realised that you felt just as sick about it as I did.'

I burst into tears, no longer able to contain my damn of emotions.

'I do feel sick about it,' I say between sobs. 'I can't believe it happened, that it's all my fault. I can't believe I was so reckless.'

He raises an eyebrow. 'Let's not be too dramatic. You were hardly letting her play in traffic. It was an accident.'

I sigh and shrug, wiping my weeping nose with the back of

my hand. 'Look, I'll be out of your hair by the new year. I think you're right. I'm not best suited to this position.'

He nods, his features serious. 'Fine.'

I stand up, dismissing myself. 'If you'll excuse me, I've got to go cry into my pillow or max out my credit card. Whichever comes first.' I turn to leave, wishing I could truly run away.

'Oh, and Ruby?'

I tense my shoulders and turn to hear his last words.

'You can call me Barclay.'

Huh?

'Really?' I shrill, a ridiculous giggle escaping my lips.

He smirks at me. 'It seems only fair, seeing as how I use your first name.'

God, he's weird.

Barclay

I can't believe my baby got harmed. When I first got the call from Ruby my whole world felt like it was falling apart. I was storming out when my mum spotted me and attempted to calm me down. Told me that she'd met Ruby and how she'd had her fair few scrapes with me when I was younger.

It just got me madder if I'm honest, but then the moment I laid eyes on Ruby in that hospital hallway I knew I couldn't make her feel any worse than she already did. Her eyes were red and puffy from crying. For all her craziness, she really does seem to genuinely care for my girls. Far more than any nanny before her.

I suppose whereas I think she's stubborn and pig headed to stay until after Christmas she thinks she just doing what's best for the girls. I'm starting to worry at their reaction of her leaving.

I mean, she broke Charlotte's wrist today and yet Charlotte still looks at her as if the sun shines out of her arse. Trust my girls to fall for someone with the exact opposite personality to their father.

I can't pretend it didn't hurt when she agreed she'd it best to leave by the new year.

I don't know what's come over me, whether it just be because she cried (I've never been good with crying women) or seeing my girls falling for her, but for a moment I actually wished she'd fight to stay.

CHAPTER 13

Monday 9th December

Ruby

Breakfast was tense, which seems to be a running theme in this house. Barclay—I'm not going to get used to that—ignored me when we saw each other in the kitchen. I tried my best to pretend I didn't notice. If I look into his eyes, I know I'll get another whole flash of guilt. It wasn't bad enough getting fired, now I've gone and fucked the reference too.

He can't hate me that much though, can he? *Of course he can. You maimed his child.* I barely slept a wink thinking about it. Either way, the girls seem happy that I'm still here.

After breakfast I decide to distract them from the horror that was yesterday by presenting them with the photo of their mum. I put it into an old frame of mine. Jessica was over the moon.

We decorated the frame together before school, spelling out Mum with buttons and pieces of fabric from my craft box. It was obviously a lot harder for poor little Lottie with her cast, but she's trying not to let it bother her; clearly for my sake.

The finished product is by no means perfect, but the girls are so happy with it.

'Mummy's so pretty,' Lottie says stroking the picture with her index finger.

'She was,' I agree. 'You both look like her so much.'

'Really?' Jessica asks hopefully.

'Of course,' I nod. 'She's looking down at you from heaven right now, so proud of you both.'

Jessica sighs. 'I just wish I could give her a cuddle.'

These girls are too young to know this sort of heartache. Why is life so bloody unfair?

'I know, baby. I bet she wishes the same. But I can cuddle you.' I open up my arms and they both step into it. I squeeze them tight, knowing there's only a limited amount of them left before I leave.

Jessica smiles up at me. 'You know I wished for you. A nanny that stayed. I think Mummy sent you to us.'

And I'm leaving her. My heart breaks into a million pieces.

Taking Lottie to nursery was mortifying with everyone asking about her wrist. You could see all the mothers looking at me with accusations. What kind of nanny lets a child be harmed in their care? I don't think I can ever work around Notting Hill again. Not that I'm sure I want to. With the internet these days this could follow me around and ruin my career I've worked so hard for.

So, to try and bring some joy to today I've organised a play date with one of the other mums from the school. Lottie can't do gymnastics because of her arm and Jessica was only too pleased to miss a week. Not that we'll tell Daddy. The only one who asked if I was okay, while the others whispered was Juliette, she seems like the most normal out of all of them. Least judgy.

There seem to be a few groups. One is the nannies, but they all seem to be from Eastern Europe and very hard to infiltrate. Whenever I've tried to go near them, they've started speaking another language, and you can hardly join in a conversation when it's in a language you don't know.

Then there's who I call the stereotypical Notting Hill mums, half of which seem to be on the PTA. The one's who do nothing but go for coffee or get their nails done after dropping off their little ones. They don't interest me at all.

I got chatting to Juliette because she appears relatively normal. She might be on the PTA but she's not like them. She was the only one this morning to tell me to ignore the whispers.

She has a son called Henry in the same class as Jessica and asked me round for coffee after I all but burst into tears at her kindness.

Her house is just as fabulous as the girls, but I try not to openly gawk too much. Makes me look too common.

'So…' she says with an excited grin. 'I saw the manny asked you out.'

'Oh God.' I cover my face with one hand. I hate that it's just another reason for them all to gossip about me. 'He's text me a few times but I've said I'm busy.'

'He could be good for you.' She nods, her brunette bob swinging. 'Such a nice guy.'

What a glowing reputation. Everyone knows a girl grows up looking to find a *nice* guy. Not. They want someone to sweep them off their feet. I really need to stop watching Cinderella. It's giving me unrealistic expectations.

I need to change the subject and quick.

'So, have you always lived in Notting Hill?' I ask her, as she serves the coffee, bouncing my clingy koala bear Lottie on my hip. The girl never wants to leave me. Even more so now that she has her broken wrist. My little soldier.

She cackles a laugh. 'God, no! I grew up in Putney.'

'Oh.' I can't help but be taken aback. You can't get further from Notting Hill society than Roehampton.

'So did James,' she explains. Ah, she's mentioned her husband is called James. 'We were in council houses down the same street.'

Oh my god. I did not see this coming. A rags to riches story where they end up in the snobbiest part of London? They should write a bloody inspirational book.

'Oh wow. You're so normal!' I can't help but blurt out, cringing when I realise how judgy I sound. 'How the hell did you end up in a house like this?'

Shit, I probably shouldn't have asked that. Me and my foot in mouth disease.

'Sorry.' I grimace. 'that's really nosey of me.'

'Don't be silly!' she chuckles. That's another reason why I like her. She proper belly laughs and throws her head back. Honest people do that. 'James got left some money by a distant uncle and he decided to start up his own company with it. It quickly went from strength to strength and then he sold it for a ridiculous amount of money. Started another one and he's still there as the CEO.'

'Wow, that's kind of amazing.' I've read those kinds of stories, but never I've met a real person living it.

'It is.' She nods with a frown. 'But it means we're mortgaged up to the hill with this place. I can't ever stop worrying about money. I think it's coming from none. Sometimes I wish we could just sell up and move to the country somewhere. Be mortgage free and not worry anymore.'

'I get that.' I nod.

My mum always taught me to live within my means. I'd probably be the same if I won the lottery. Not that I actually play. I'd rather buy a chocolate bar with the money. I actually have a healthy savings account though, and I got that discipline from my mum.

She leans across the breakfast bar. 'It's so refreshing to find someone normal. If I said that to the Notting Hill mums, they'd look at me as if I'd lost my mind. Their idea of leaving Notting Hill is to go to Dubai on holiday.'

I snort a laugh. 'Well, I feel the same way. It's always nice to have an ally in the same class as the kids. Especially now I've gone and broken a child's wrist.' I look down at little Lottie sucking her thumb.

'Do you mind if I ask what happened?' she smiles kindly.

'You mean you haven't heard already?' I ask with a forced laugh.

She grins. 'Oh, don't get me wrong, the rumours are rife. But I've heard everything from her being thrown from a moving car to falling down the stairs.'

'Jesus!' That's some imagination those mums have. I suppose the real story is a bit confusing and surreal anyway.'

I fill her in on what happened.

'You poor thing. You must have been distraught.' She smiles kindly. 'So where were you before this?' she asks, offering me a doughnut, which obviously I take.

And she eats carbs? New best friend, I think.

'I was with a family in Edinburgh. Two boys. They were eight and ten when I started and twelve and fourteen when I left.'

Her eyes widen. 'Wow, those are some really important years.'

'Yep.' I smile, feeling a bit teary whenever I think of them. 'They were the nicest family. They'd take me on all the family holidays. I felt more like a member of the family than a member of staff. I only left because the boys didn't need me anymore.' Not that they didn't beg me to stay.

'Ah.' she smiles, knowingly. 'I'm assuming Barclay hasn't been very accommodating?'

This guy clearly has a reputation. I must be careful here.

She's called him Barclay which means they're on first name terms. They could be besties for all I know.

'Um...' I look down at my sprinkled doughnut.

'Don't worry sweets.' She winks. 'This is between us.'

Hmm, I still can't help but be suspicious. I mean she *is* on the PTA. This could all be a set up by Clementine for all I know.

'How do you know Barclay?' I ask tentatively, stuffing a large bit of doughnut in my mouth so I can't speak.

She smiles sadly, her eyes glossing over. 'I used to be friends with Claire.'

'Claire?' I mumble through a full mouth. Oh, she must mean his wife. I quickly chew and force myself to swallow. 'Oh, Claire, as in his wife?'

'Yeah.' She smiles but it's small and half hearted. 'She was wonderful. Very warm and down to earth. She wasn't a Notting Hill born and bred either.'

'Oh really? Didn't they go to school together?' I know I'm being beyond nosy here and it really is none of my business, but I can't help but want to figure out Barclay.

She nods. 'She got in with a full scholarship. From a regular working class family in Watford.'

My jaw nearly drops the floor. 'Wow. I just assumed they were from the same worlds.'

Barclay is such a toff. I can't imagine him falling for a normal girl.

She shakes her head. 'I've seen Barclay go through quite a lot of nannies since she passed. He's grieved in... his own way.'

'Mmm.' I'm conscious of Lottie still on my lap. 'Baby, would you like to go and see Jessica and Henry?'

'No. Stay with you,' she says snuggling into my arm.

'Okay.' I turn back to Juliette. 'Well, I'm not going anywhere.'

Not until New Years anyway. I hate lying to everyone, but it's not like I can blurt out the truth with Lottie here.

The thing is, I'm already so attached to these girls. The thought of leaving them has my chest constricting.

Can I really consider giving up my life for these girls? I know the answer in an instant. Of course I can. The truth is that you don't have much of a life doing this job. You just slot into a family and do whatever is best for the kids. I've never minded before, but if I have to deal with Barclay having tantrums all over the place, well it'll really mean my life is over.

But giving it up for these girls, well it wouldn't feel like a sacrifice. I just need to convince Barclay that I'm worth keeping. For his own sake.

Barclay

My phone buzzes on the table. I look at it to see a message from Juliette. I worry immediately. Has something happened to the girls? I quickly grab it and open the message.

Met your new nanny today. She seems lovely. Pls try to be nice to this one!

Jesus, what is it with my reputation? Don't they see that it's not me being a nightmare, but the endless string of incompetent nannies?

What the hell is she doing chatting to Ruby anyway? I sigh, I know why she is. She was Claire's best friend, of course she wants to check in on how the girls are doing. The truth is that she's tried to be around a lot since Claire died, but I haven't let her. Seeing Juliette is just another reminder that she's gone.

Instead I've pushed her away. I suppose I've pushed everyone away. It's just better like this. I have more control. It's just the way it's got to be.

CHAPTER 14

Tuesday 10th December

Ruby

I have my date with the eager Manny tonight. He's sent me a ridiculous amount of texts and I've finally run out of excuses. *Way to play it cool, Manny.* I really must remember his name. So, I've decided to just get it over and done with tonight. You never know, I might actually like him. Stranger things have happened.

I managed to persuade him from a late-night coffee, to drinks. I'm always a better date with alcohol. I mean, isn't everyone?

I'm the first to arrive at the trendy bar I suggested around the corner. It's all dark mahogany and red velvet seats. I check out their cocktail list. Fifteen quid for a cocktail. Fuck a duck. I should have googled the nearest Wetherspoons.

'I'll have a house white wine please,' I say as quietly to the barman as possible. Don't want everyone overhearing what a cheap skate I am.

If in doubt, you always get more bang for your buck with wine. It's like loopy juice to me. If it's wet and alcoholic it'll do me just fine. It's still £12.50 for a glass of house white. Bloody joke.

I settle myself on a small candle lit table and check my watch. Just as I look up, there he is, in a smart gingham shirt and a beanie hat. God, why do men insist on wearing beanie hats at night time? Day time, in the winter, maybe it's acceptable. But anytime apart from that you just look like a stoner.

'Hi!' he says with an enthusiastic smile. That's the word I'd use to describe him. Enthusiastic. He points back towards the bar. 'I'll just go get a drink.'

I smile. Didn't offer me another one then. Tight bastard. But then I suppose we are both on Nanny wages and this is Notting Hill.

Money is never something that impresses me, but every girl will tell you that a tight man isn't an attractive one, no matter how much of a pretty a face he has. He's okay looking really.

He comes back with a bottle of Peroni. Barclay drinks those too. I've seen them in the fridge. Not that I'm thinking about Barclay. Of course not.

'So,' he starts, with a smile. Tell me a bit about yourself.'

Oh God, I hate when people say that. Like you're on a game

show and you have to sell yourself. *Well Matthew, my name's Ruby and I'm from Hertfordshire!'*

'Well, you obviously know I'm a nanny.' I force a grimaced smile and find myself nodding. 'What else would you like to know?'

He frowns, thinking for a second. 'Where did you grow up?'

'Oh, that was Tring. What about you?'

'We'll get to me in a minute.' He grins.

Okay....this feels weird. Get to him in a minute. Why?

'What made you want to be a nanny?' he presses, leaning so close to me I fear he'll lean in for a kiss. He does smell nice. Not as nice as Barclay. *Jesus, why is he in my head?*

What was he saying? Oh, that's right, being a nanny. God, I feel like I'm in an interview, not on a date.

I shrug, sweat forming on my upper lip. This is why I hate dating.

'I've just always loved kids. Always wanted to be a part of a family I suppose.'

His warm green eyes watch me appraisingly. 'I like that.'

I'm really not trying to impress you, manny. I can't even remember your name.

'So, what's your big story then?' I joke, taking a nervous gulp of wine. Okay, it *is* the best wine I've ever tasted.

He takes a deep breath, like he's about to impart an amazing story. I'm bored already. Unless he's going to tell me he used to be a woman. Then I'll be part interested and part planning my escape route.

'Well, when I was younger, I got myself into a bit of trouble.'

Oh God, this is not going well. He's got a sob story. I can't stand them on the X Factor, let alone on a date.

'I actually almost ended up in prison at one point.'

Jesus, I've found a right catch here.

'That's when I found myself at a real low point. I didn't know where to turn. My mum was never around, and I'd never known my dad.'

Wait for it. He's about to drop something weird. I can feel it in my waters.

'That's when I found Jesus.'

And there it is. Oh, for fucks sakes. I've got myself a bible basher.

'And since then my life has just been...blessed.' He looks up to the ceiling, as if he can actually see Jesus through it. I glance up myself, he's that convincing.

'Amazing,' I nod, already looking for my nearest exit.

Don't get me wrong, I'm not against God or anything. I wouldn't say I'm a strong Atheist, but I'm hardly a believer either. This is never going to work.

'So happy for you.'

'Thank you.' He grins, like he's the happiest person on the planet. 'It's so nice to share my happiness with someone.'

Time to change the subject.

'So... apart from that, your life is pretty normal, yeah? Any hobbies?'

He laughs. 'If you're asking if I touch the old monkey.' He grabs his balls through his tight jeans. 'Then no. I haven't touched that in five years.'

Jesus fucking Christ. I wasn't asking the man if he masturbates. But five years? That cannot be healthy. Blue balls city.

I have to sit through another two hours of him rambling on just to be seen as polite. I don't want him telling all the mums I'm some huge bitch. That wouldn't help my already battered reputation.

'Can I walk you home?' he offers after I've claimed a stomach ache.

I force a fake smile. 'Oh, thanks so much, but I think I'm just going to walk myself and have a nice early night.'

'Okay.' He smiles sadly. I give him a hug, careful not to press my boobs against him.

Now for the kicker. 'I'm so glad I have a friend like you.'

I feel him flinch. I might as well have just twisted a knife in his back, but it's easier to cut it off now. The way he's been talking about waiting for marriage, it would never work. I'm not a ho or anything, but I'm not marrying a guy before I've seen his penis. What if it was shaped like a banana?

I walk home past the fairy lit houses, already happy at the thought of my pyjamas. I'm much happier that way than being stuck in a tight bra with make up on.

I head into the main house and straight for the fridge. I need some chocolate to cheer myself up and I've got nothing in my mini fridge downstairs. I'm searching through the lettuce and avocados for something yummy when I hear a whistle.

I turn around and spot Barclay staring at me from the door, displaying a huge grin. His shirt is scrunched up to his elbows, his tie pulled down in disarray. Basically, sexy as sin.

'You're all dressed up for a date with the fridge,' he says, a playful glint in his eye.

I roll my eyes, hating that I can feel my cheeks blush. 'No, I had a date with a person. A man,' I quickly add. 'It just ended up being a disaster, as per usual.'

'Oh really?' He slides onto a chair, his olive toned arms extended out on the table in front of him.

Is he really interested? Maybe he just wants to laugh at what a loser I am. I can't blame him.

'Well, I've been out of the dating game a long time.' He grins, his eyes twinkling with mischief. I don't know about that. What about horse girl? 'Tell me, what was so terrible?'

I sigh, giving up my search, and slump down on the chair opposite. It's the first time he's talked to me since Lottie's broken arm. I have to take advantage while I can.

'He's a God botherer.'

He bursts out laughing, crinkles forming by his eyes. It's such a rare sight that I wish I could freeze time, go grab my phone and take a picture. Maybe frame it, place it by my bed and say goodnight to it every evening. *No Ruby, now you're being weird.*

'You're joking!' He chuckles, clutching at his sides.

'Nope.' I grimace. 'As if being a Manny wasn't bad enough.'

'No way? Stop!' His head shakes with laughter. 'How did you find this loser?'

Oh, you know, I have a magnet attached to my head that only attracts completely inappropriate people.

'At the school of course.' I shake my head. 'But he would have found me anyway. I'm like a beacon for losers like him.' I stand up again. 'Hence the search for the only thing I can depend on; chocolate.'

I boil the kettle, deciding I'll have to rely on hot chocolate for my fix instead. God, my life sucks right now. Really can't catch a break.

He stands up and walks slowly towards me, his eyes predatory. *What the hell is he doing?*

'You do know you can depend on some real humans too, right?'

I gulp. He stalks towards me, so close now that I push myself back against the cabinet in an attempt to escape him, but he follows me, his hot breath so close I feel it on my forehead. His delicious spicy scent envelops me. Is he going to kiss me?

The kettle boils noisily behind me. I look up and very almost lean in for a kiss I had no idea I wanted. Only...he opens the top cabinet above me and takes out a huge dairy milk bar.

He hands it over with a smug smile. 'Picked it up for a teacher's Christmas present the other day. It's all yours.'

I can't help but grin back at him, as if we have some weird inside joke. He knows I wouldn't have stopped him had he tried to kiss me. How embarrassing.

'My hero,' I mock, grabbing at it.

His eyes twinkle with mischief. 'See, not all of us are bad.'

Then, just like he always does, he turns and struts out.

'Looks like it's just me and you tonight,' I say to the chocolate.

CHAPTER 15

Wed 11th December

Ruby

*B*arclay's mum Freda is here again. She mustn't work. She comes across as bored, while also strangely being busy at the same time. She's always having to rush off to pick out china for an event, or a wall colour for a renovation of a room.

'So, Ruby,' she says as soon as the girls are out of ear shot and practising their moves from kids' yoga. 'Any improvements on getting on with my son?'

I smile with gritted teeth. *I'm finding him strangely sexy actually.*

'Well, the good news is that he's not here much.'

'That bad, huh?' she asks with a wicked grin. 'He's a workaholic, just like his father.'

'Was he always like this?' I can't help but ask her. 'I mean, did he work less when Claire was alive?'

She smiles sadly, her eyes turning teary. 'Honestly, everything changed when Claire passed. The minute he met her at school I knew he was in love. Had a stupid lovesick grin on his face whenever he talked about her.'

I can't imagine him being that over the moon in love. Nowadays he's so cold. Well, apart from last night. The more I think of last night the weirder it gets in my mind.

'She kept a light in Barclay that no-one else could. When she left this world that light went out and the darkness crept in.'

I put my hand on top of hers and give it a squeeze. It's clear she loved the woman too.

'Since you've been here, I've seen that light in the girls. I feel that Claire is with them again, in some small way.'

That's it. I can't lie to the poor woman anymore.

'Look, I don't want to mislead you.' I gulp, unsure of how she's going to react. 'Barclay's actually fired me already.'

She grins. 'Oh, I know, my dear. Mrs Dumfy told me.'

Mrs Dumfy? I'm shocked. I didn't tell her. I suppose Barclay must have told her to get my leaving papers ready.

'Oh, so you know I'll be leaving.' It's weird that she didn't mention it.

She waves me off, as if it's no big deal. 'He was always firing his own nannies as a child. It was a running joke in our family actually. Little Barclay and his temper.'

I can't help but laugh, imagining a bossy little boy with dark brown eyes.

I grimace. 'He meant it though.'

She rolls her eyes. 'Even if he did. Don't you want to stay for those girls?' She looks over at them, now getting snakes and ladders out on the carpet.

My heart squeezes at the thought of leaving them.

'Of course I do. But I can't change his mind. It's made up.'

'So.' She smiles mischievously. 'Make him change it back. Trust me, if I know Barclay like I think I do, he'll already be kicking himself for saying that in a moment of haste.'

He *was* different last night, but the more I think about it, the more I realise he must have been drunk.

I sigh. 'Something makes me think that Barclay means exactly what he says.'

She takes my hand in hers. 'Just promise you'll try, hmm?'

'Okay.' I nod, a wretched guilt beginning to grow inside me for letting the woman down. There's no way in hell he's changing his mind, but I can let her think he might.

Barclay

I can't stop laughing to myself whenever I think of Ruby's disastrous date last night. Honestly, the woman's a hot mess. *Emphasis on the hot,* my subconscious reminds me. I shake my head. She's not hot, she's an employee of mine.

It's just...well seeing her dressed up like that, it had some feelings that have been dormant for years come springing to the surface and most of those were worryingly in my dick.

I've decided that I enjoy teasing her. She really is easy to wind up. I love seeing her little angry face, the way she scrunches up her nose covered in freckles and steels her jaw. Its strangely adorable.

Jesus, what the hell is happening to me? I must really need to get some. This must just be my body's way of telling me its time, time to move on and have sex with someone else. Not Ruby, obviously. I suppose Queenie will do, although I'd far prefer a quick one-night stand with someone I don't need to see again. I know Queenie will turn on the cling factor no matter how straight up with her I am.

Anyway, I must stop thinking about Ruby. Except, well I'm on my way to the parent's evening where she's currently filling in for me. I can't help but feel bad that I had to get her to fill in so late and unprepared, but that's Ruby all over. Go with the flow, hippy dippy Ruby. And the weirdest thing of all? I can't wait to see her.

Ruby

Tonight, Mrs Dumfy is looking after the girls while I go to Jessica's parents evening. Barclay was supposed to be going but text me saying his meeting was going to run late. So that's how I find myself running into the classroom, late and dishevelled. I barely managed to get changed out of my pyjamas. What is it about having to get changed from pyjamas to skinny jeans that makes them feel all the skinnier.

'So, so sorry I'm late!' I apologise, seeing I'm already five minutes past our designated time.

'I assume you're the new nanny?' the woman in her early forties asks with a warm smile.

Ooh, she's friendly, thank god.

'That's me. I'm Ruby.' I awkwardly wave.

'I'm Mrs Engleton. Nice to meet you.'

She leads me into the classroom, and I sit down on a tiny child's chair across from her, trying desperately not to stare at her immense facial hair.

She shuffles her paperwork. 'Well, I must say that I've noticed a real difference in Jessica since you've come along.'

'Really?' I can't help but bluster, completely caught off guard.

'Yes.' She nods. 'I understand that the girls have suffered a carousel of nannies, none of them staying more than a few months. But you seem to have given Jessica some form of stability in merely a few weeks. She's more settled in class, less anxious. Whatever you're doing, please continue to do it.'

'Wow. I had no idea.'

I mean, I did, because I'm awesome. But still, to make such a noticeable difference in a few short weeks. That's why I accepted this job. I don't dare tell her I've already been fired and am leaving by New Years.

She talks briefly about how she's coming along in maths and English and where she'd ideally be by the end of the school year. We have to practise capital letters and full stops. Then I'm shaking her hand and walking out of the door, smiling as the next parent is called.

That's when I spot Barclay rushing down the corridor, iPhone in his hand. I'm starting to think its glued to him.

He stops when he sees me, out of breath.

'I'm assuming I'm too late?' he asks me, peering into the classroom where a parent is already deep in conversation.

'Yep.' I nod. 'Sadly, you missed her telling me how fantastic I am.'

'I'm sure.' He nods with a quirked lip, shaking his head ever so slightly. Obviously doesn't believe me.

'Don't worry, she went through everything with me. Was there something you wanted to know in particular?'

'Just...' he notices the other parents in close vicinity so takes my arm and starts leading me away. 'She was concerned about Jessica's behaviour last time. Said she needed more structure in her life. That's why I'm so regiment with their routine.'

Ah, so that's where it came from.

I scoff a laugh. 'She actually said she's massively improved since I've come along.'

'Seriously?' He raises his eyebrows, obviously un-convinced.

'Seriously.' I nod, a little pissed off he doesn't believe me. 'And I'm all about breaking those rigid rules.'

He scoffs. 'Well, trust my daughter to like a rebel.' He starts scrolling through his phone again. 'I should buy her a gift to congratulate her.'

I roll my eyes heavenwards. So typical of him.

'A gift? You seriously think your daughter wants a *gift*?'

He frowns. 'Well, don't you think she deserves it?'

I take a deep breath to stop myself getting angry. Remind myself he's just stupid, he's not going out of his way to hurt these girls.

'I think some time with you, and you telling her she's done well, will make her just as happy.'

He sighs and I suddenly notice the dark rings under his eyes. When was the last time he had a good night's sleep?

'Ruby, work is crazy right now. I don't have the time to spend.'

I think as we walk back towards his car. There must be something he can do to truly show how he cares for her.

I've got it!

'Okay, then I have something which might make her happy.'

'Oh yeah?' he asks, still scrolling down his phone, as if completely uninterested. 'Care to share?'

'I think we should buy her a real life Christmas tree.'

He stops in his tracks, his eyes jumping to mine.

'A Christmas tree? You've already set one up in their playroom.'

'Yes,' I roll my eyes, 'but I'm talking about a *real* one. Maybe put it in the living room or the kitchen. Then ask them to buy decorations for it.'

He seems to mull this over. 'Okay. A tree seems easy enough. Is there anything open at this time of night?'

I laugh. 'Barclay, this is London. Everything is always open somewhere. But I assumed you'd want to get at the weekend.'

He shrugs. 'No time like the present, Ruby. Besides, the evenings are the only time I have. Find me a place and we'll go now.'

'You want *me* to help you?' I can't help but sound taken aback. I just assumed he'd want to sort it himself. Control freak that he is.

He nods. 'I think so. I've never bought a Christmas tree before.'

My eyes nearly bulge out of their sockets.

'*Never?* Jesus, who were you brought up by? Scrooge?'

A smile plays on the edges of his lips. 'No, but we always had them brought in for us.'

'Ah, yes.' I nod. 'I keep forgetting you were brought up by the Royal Family.'

He rolls his eyes. 'Will you help me or not?'

'I will.'

CHAPTER 16

Barclay

It took us thirty minutes to drive to the place and a further hour for us to argue over which tree to get. The woman wanted the prettiest tree, not the most practical. We eventually agreed on a Norway Spruce.

'Great, now we just have to work out how to get it delivered,' she says, tapping a finger on her chin.

'Delivered?' I snort. 'I'll just tie it to the car.'

She barks a laugh. 'Yeah, like you'll be able to lift this enormous tree.'

Is she seriously insinuating that I'm some weak preppy shit that can't lift a bloody small Christmas tree?

I'll show her.

I lean forward and before she realises what's happening, I'm slinging her over my shoulder, fireman lift style. 'See.' I chuckle, so tempted to slap her on the arse. 'If I can lift you, I can lift a tree.'

I plonk her back down, smiling smugly at her. Her cheeks are burning. Have I embarrassed her? Or is it just all the blood rushing to her head.

'Are you saying I weigh the same as a tree?' she asks, weight on one hip. 'You're literally saying my thighs are tree trunks right now.'

Jesus, trust a woman to turn something into an issue about their weight. I can't help but glance down at them, wondering if they are in fact large. I've never noticed before. No, they're perfectly lean.

'All I'm saying is that I'm a strong guy.' I grin, feeling playful. She seems to bring that side out of me. 'I go to the gym.'

'When the hell do you go to the gym? How do you find the time for that?'

I feel my cheeks blush the slightest crimson. 'I go in my lunch break,' I admit, rocking on my heels. 'If I don't have meetings.'

She rolls her eyes disapprovingly, just as I knew she would. The truth is that I go more for my mind than my muscles.

'Fine,' she snaps, hands crossed against her chest. 'Carry the tree to the car.'

'Gladly.'

I bend down to try and pick it up but can't seem to do it without one end falling to the floor. Oh, for fucks sakes, just when I was feeling a cocky bastard, and now I can't even lift it! Way to bruise my own ego.

'Would you like some help to the car, sir?' the man that served us asks.

She smiles at me, awaiting my response. Damn, she's so bloody annoying; waiting for me to admit defeat.

I jut my chin out. 'No thanks, we're fine.'

'Shocking that a giant tree isn't the same weight as me.' She flicks her blonde hair in my face and walks towards the car. Sarcastic cow.

'Ruby!' I call after her. Dammit, I do need her help. I have a feeling she's going to make me beg for it.

She turns around with her hands on her hips.

'Yes?' she asks innocently, as if she has no idea what I'm about to ask.

'Come on.' I grin, hoping my boyish charms will win her over. 'You can help, can't you?'

'I thought you didn't need any help?' she retorts, inspecting her nails.

My jaw tenses. Why is she always calling me out? Making things difficult.

'Not from that stranger. I don't want him judging me for being too weak to carry it all,' I admit begrudgingly.

'Oh, but you'll be fine for me to judge you?' She smiles sweetly, her eyes telling me she's anything but.

'Please,' I scoff. 'You already judge me.'

She frowns as if genuinely shocked by my observation.

'I don't judge you,' she says, pretty affronted. It can't be a shock that I find her judgemental, can it?

My lips twist, trying to hold back a smile. 'Please, Ruby. I know you judge me for not spending enough time with my kids.'

She stares back, open mouthed. Well, I've got her there.

'I don't judge you, I just...' she searches for the right words, so as not to offend me further.

'You just think I should prioritise them over my work.'

She shrugs. 'Well, yeah. To be honest, the fact you even think that shows that you have your own guilt.'

My eyes turn sharp in an instant. Playful Barclay has gone.

'Hey, listen, you don't know me. You don't know what I've been through. So just mind your own business, okay. Something you seem to have a huge problem with.'

Her lip curls up in anger and that little freckled nose scrunches up.

'The only thing I have a problem with is you and how bloody rude you are. Damn, who raised you?'

'One of your kind, actually,' I snap, not recognising my own bitchy tone. She really brings out the worst in me. 'I saw my nanny more than I ever saw my parents.'

I watch as she thinks about it. Probably imagining some poor vulnerable little boy wanting love and only getting it from staff. It wasn't that bad; I had the best nanny in the world. No one will ever compare to her.

'Surely that made you not want to repeat history?'

I sigh, suddenly exhausted. 'Look, Ruby. Can you help me to the car with the tree or not?' I bark.

She rolls her eyes. 'Ugh, fine. If you're going to be a little bitch about it.'

I cannot believe she speaks to her boss this way. But what can I do? I've already fired her.

She grabs one end of the tree and starts dragging it behind her. I quickly pick up the other end. Together we drag/carry it towards the car. I'm surprised with how much strength she has in that small lithe body. She heaves it up to my roof, flinging it on top.

'Be careful, Ruby!' I snap, checking my car over. 'You're scratching my car.'

She rolls her eyes. 'Well how else do you expect to get it on here?' she shouts back; a sweaty mess from the exertion. She still manages to look cute, her freckled cheeks flushed pink.

After half an hour of us arguing over how best to tie it to the car we drive home. Well, after having to pull over twice and re-attach the loose tree.

Apparently, she told me to knot it well.

Remarked on how I've clearly never joined a local scouts.

Said I should at least have learnt it from some sort of posh yacht club or something.

Finally we untie it and heave it into the house, the sleet making it slippery. She falls. Twice. I help her up and insist I'm not laughing, but it's so hard to keep in. She's like bambi on ice. Hilarious.

'No wonder we had these brought in,' I huff, opening the door. 'This is a bloody nightmare.'

'Just think of the girls,' she says, grabbing the stand we bought and scrambling to put it together. 'They're going to love this.'

I bloody hope so. I push the tree into it, us both seeming to conclude that it's going to go in the hallway. Anywhere else is just too far. We stand back to admire it. She puffs out the branches.

'Not that I'll see it,' I gruff, thinking of my schedule the next few weeks.

'Yeah, what is the deal with that?' she asks. 'Honestly, is it work or is it because you don't like being at home?'

I stand up straight, astonished to find her asking such an honest question. I don't know why I'm surprised, she's excellent at overstepping the mark.

'You really want to know?' I ask, my shoulders slumping from that same exhaustion that came over me earlier. The exhaustion of being vulnerable. Or maybe just being around the ever challenging Ruby.

She leans on one hip. 'I wouldn't have asked if I didn't.'

I sigh and run my hand through my hair. Might as well be honest. Who better to be honest with, than a person leaving in two weeks?

'The horrible truth is that the girls remind me so much of my wife. Being around them, especially at this time of year, it just hurts too hard.'

Her eyes widen at my revelation. Yes, it's true. I'm a terrible human being.

'So, you think that by ignoring them you'll stop hurting. But what about them? You don't want them to lose their father too, do you?'

'Of course I don't,' I snap. 'But the girls need to learn that life is hard. They need to be tough. My wife was the most loving woman on the planet and look where that got her.' My heart squeezes just mentioning her.

'Life sadly isn't fair,' I continue. 'The sooner the girls learn that, the better for them in the long run.'

I turn and walk up the stairs, not saying a word more. Before she sees the first tear fall.

CHAPTER 17

Thursday 12th December

Ruby

$\mathcal{I}$'m so excited for the girls to see the real Christmas tree. There's really nothing like the real thing. My mum made sure we had one every year. Whenever I think of Christmas, I smell the pine needles. I'm so excited that I've set my alarm early and go to wake them up. I'm running so fast up the stairs that I almost don't notice it.

The tree is lined with fairy lights. We didn't put them up. It's six thirty in the morning. What time did he put those up? What a weirdo. A sweet weirdo, I guess.

I still can't believe he allowed himself to open up to me and be so vulnerable last night. Maybe it's one of those weird things, like after nine pm he becomes more human or something.

The girls seem dubious about why I'm so eager to bring them down for breakfast. Well, Charlotte does. She keeps asking if it's because I'm letting her have some Coco Pops. Not on her life.

We rush down the stairs and into the hallway. The girls halt to a stop when they see the enormous tree standing up proudly.

'A tree!' Lottie screams, eyes wide, hands up to her face.

'You got us a real tree?' Jessica asks me, her little face astonished.

I grin. 'No, *Daddy* got you a tree.'

'Daddy?' Lottie says, her eyes nearly completely squeezed closed with confusion.

'Yep.' I nod, unable to hide my enormous smile. 'Because you.' I hug Jessica's shoulders. 'Had such an amazing report from your teacher.'

'Really?' She actually sounds surprised.

I grin. 'Of course. Your teacher told us how well you were doing.'

'You went too?' she questions, her eyebrows narrowed.

Oops, I didn't want to let on that he'd been late and made me go. She deserves to think she's a priority.

'Err...Yep, your daddy wanted to show off to me what a good girl you are at school.'

'Wow.' She goes up and touches a bristle of the tree, like she's never seen a real one. I know she has from the photos I found, but maybe she doesn't remember. 'We need new decorations for this one.'

'Yep. I was thinking we could go buy some after school. What do you think?'

'Yes!' they both shout, jumping up and down excitedly.

'As long as I can have a go on the elephant,' Lottie demands. She means the Dumbo outside Waitrose.

'Well, we might go somewhere extra special to buy them. But if there's something like that, yes you can.'

'Somewhere extra special?' Jessica asks, eyes lit up in excitement. 'Like where?'

'Now, that, cheeky monkey.' I bop her on the nose with my index finger. 'Will be a surprise.'

Because I have to figure it out for myself first.

I've picked up the girls and just got off at our tube stop. They were excited enough with riding the tube. You'd think with living in London they'd be well used to it, but the pampered princesses have only ever been chauffeured about. The poor posh things.

It's already dark outside, the front of Harrods is lit up in majestic fairy lights. It's fabulous. I remember my mum taking me here once when I was eight years old, not long after my dad had died. It was the coolest thing I'd ever done.

The window display was themed as Cinderella. There was gold foliage all around the window frame with the most unimaginable diamond slippers that sparkled so much I had to shield my eyes. There was a mannequin in a couture dress sat on a pink chaise lounge. God, I would have done anything to have gone in and lived in that window display.

'We're going to Harrods?' Jessica asks, wrinkling her brow.

'Yep. I've heard they do the most beautiful baubles around.'

'Can we see Santa?' Lottie asks, tugging on my arm.

'Of course we can. We'll just have to que up.'

We rush in from the blistering cold and make our way up to the floor where they have their Christmas bits. It's beautiful, all arranged by colour theme. I hadn't even thought of a colour scheme.

'What colours are we looking at girls?'

'Pink!' Lottie shouts.

'Don't be silly, Lottie,' Jessica chastises with an eye roll. 'It's Christmas. It should be red and gold.'

Lottie sticks her tongue out. Thank God for Jessica. I can't see Barclay being pleased with a pink themed Christmas tree. In fact, I can imagine him ripping it all down and then throwing me out of his house.

'Well, we could always decorate half of the tree each? One pink side and one gold/red side.'

'But that'll look silly,' Jessica sulks. Perfectionist, just like her father.

'Well why don't you both have a think about it while we look around?'

We look at the decorations, each more beautiful than the last. We all fall in love with three baubles that are cream with London themed pictures hand painted on them. They have red ribbons around them and Lottie easily relents, agreeing with a red and gold theme.

We have so much fun picking out the most beautiful tree ornaments, some rich in colour and sewn in sequins, others glass and delicate. We've managed to find ones that mean something to the girls. An underground sign for our journey here, hot chocolate from our time at Hole of Glory, a gold glittery Harrods bag to remind us of this shopping trip. My favourite is the Christmas tree tied to a red car. It reminds me of mine and Barclay's trip home last night. He's going to love seeing the tree all done up.

They all seem so elegant, almost too elegant. If I smashed one of these on the floor I'd be gutted. But it's not like I'm spending my money on them. I'm using the money assigned to spend on the girls for the week. Not that these girls even need money, they just want what every kid wants, time.

We finally go to pick out something for the top of the tree. After another argument between the girls, Jessica lets Lottie win, as she got her colour scheme. So, a fairy is chosen.

The girls run over to the life-size bears dressed as a palace guard, policeman and fireman. I take a picture of them cuddling up to them. They look so happy, their little cheeks rosy from all the giggling. It makes my heart sad to think that their mum is missing this, but glad that I can bring them a bit of joy this time of year. Even if only for a small time.

We pick them out a bear each that has the year on its foot and take everything over to pay. The man rings everything up. I didn't pay too much attention to the prices while we were putting them in the basket, but now that I see one of them ring through at £107, I'm starting to sweat.

'That'll be £1,078 please madam.'

Fuck a duck! I should have been more sensible. Luckily Barclay gives me a ridiculous amount of money a week for the girls and I haven't spent much so far. I'm still a good couple of hundred over budget.

I hand over the credit card he gave me, praying to god it doesn't bounce. I tap my foot nervously, wondering what the hell I'll do if it's rejected. I see it go through. Thank God.

'Oh, and we'd like to queue up for Santa's grotto. Is it still open?'

His eyes widen and then he sneers. 'Sorry madam, I'm afraid that it's only for VIP members. Invitation only. Do you have a VIP card?' He looks down at my battered converse, already deciding I don't.

'Oh...' I look down at the girl's expectant faces. 'I don't.' Their shoulders droop.

He smiles, terrible at faking sympathy. Pompous arse. Whatever dude, you work behind the tills, you're not running the company.

'But maybe your daddy does?' I pick my phone out of my bag. 'Let me just call him.'

The man sighs, pissed off I'm holding up the queue.

'Please madam, if you could just give me the name and address, I can quickly check for you.' He looks behind me at the que forming, obviously wanting to dismiss me as soon as he can.

'Oh, that would be great. It's Barclay Rothchester. 40 Blenheim Cres—'

His eyes enlarge, like I've just shocked him. I don't get why.

'Oh of course, Mr Rothchester. His family have been VIP's for years.'

Look who suddenly turned friendly.

'Oh great.'

Who knew?

'We *have* been booked up since September I'm afraid.' He grimaces and this time it seems sincere. 'But hang on a moment, let me see if there's anything we can do.'

He wanders off, leaving everyone in the queue to give me filthy looks. Well, sorry for caring about the kids. It's amazing what a surname can do for you.

He comes back mere moments after with a smile. I don't know if that's good for us or bad.

'I'm happy to say that we're able to make special arrangements and accommodate you today.'

The girls beam back at me. For once their father has pulled through for them.

Barclay

Today has been rough. Dad's on my case again about this electronics event. I know it's just his way of saying why are you dealing with this shit when you can be partner? I'm so fucking tired. Not just from lack of sleep, but my soul is tired. After everything that's happened, planning parties for pompous dicks is not what I want to be doing.

I open the doors to squeals of laughter. It's such a difference to hear the girls this happy. No nanny has made them giggle like this. I suppose it's because there hasn't been a Ruby before now. She's definitely one of a kind.

I walk towards the noise and peek in to see that they've

dragged the tree into the kitchen and are decorating it in their elf pyjamas.

'Daddy!' Charlotte shouts when she spots me. She comes running over and jumps into my arms. I'm still careful of her, not wanting to touch her cast arm. Not that it seems to bother her.

'Hey baby.' I smell the top of her head. She always smells of her strawberry shampoo; it calms me like nothing else.

'Daddy!' Jessica squeals coming over to give me a squeeze around the waist.

Ruby looks on with a huge smile. 'Perfect timing. We're just finishing off the tree.'

'And Daddy, we went to Harrods!' Jessica says, her eyes lit up in excitement.

'And we saw Santa there!' Charlotte adds, bouncing in my arms.

'Wow.' I raise my eyebrows at Ruby. 'You *have* been busy.'

'Yeah,' she grimaces. 'There might be a huge charge on your credit card.'

It makes me laugh how she worries about money. It's quite cute.

'Ah, don't worry about that.' I turn back to the girls. 'I'll put you to bed tonight.'

They yelp in delight. This is what I need more of; my girls and their smiles. Not boardrooms and meetings.

I bring them up, read them a story, hear all about their afternoon and finally get them to bed.

I walk back down hoping Ruby will still be doing the tree. I don't know why, especially as the woman drives me insane, but I like being around her. Maybe it's just company I crave, after years of loneliness. I almost breathe a sigh of relief when I see her.

She smiles when she spots me. 'Marge had to leave early, but she's left your dinner in the oven on a low heat.'

I nod, grabbing a Peroni out of the fridge.

'You should have seen them earlier,' she gushes, her smile so wide I'm worried it's going to split her face open. 'Your name alone got them into the VIP, invite only, Santa's grotto. You wouldn't believe how amazing it was! It was themed like a gingerbread house. And there were these fairies.'

I can't help but smile. It's adorable how excited she is. I remember that grotto, every year when I was growing up. I suppose I never found it a big deal, but hearing it from her, it reminds me that I'm bloody privileged. My kids are too, even if they have lost their mother.

'Then we went on this sort of little train ride through a snowing tunnel. We got out at the end and the kids had to walk through a naughty or nice sort of thing. Like they have in airports. You should have seen Lottie's face. She was so nervous.'

It doesn't even bother me like it used to that she calls Charlotte Lottie. I know Jessica calls her it anyway.

'But they loved it.' She fiddles around with a tree branch. 'I was actually wondering... if I could photocopy some more pictures of your wife?'

The change of topic startles me.

'God, why?' I can't help but sound abrupt.

Her face drops. I've got to try and remember not to be such a miserable arsehole. I hate taking the smile off her face.

'I just...I bought some glass baubles that you can put photos in. I thought the girls would love it if they could have their mum on the tree. You know, like a way to include her.'

Fuck, how did she get this nice? Nothing bad must have ever happened to her in her entire life.

I take a deep breath, rubbing my temples. 'Yeah, I can find some for you.'

'Great.' She folds her arms. 'Oh, and don't forget Jessica's carol service tomorrow evening at the school.'

I nod, doubting I'll be able to make it.

'Oh and...' She looks at everything, but me. Jesus, what now?

'Spit it out, Ruby,' I snap, suddenly exhausted.

'Well, would I be able to host a wine and cheese night here?'

Is she serious?

'Sorry? You want to have a wine and cheese night *here?*'

She nods, chewing on her thumb nail. 'It's for the stupid PTA. I'd tell them to get stuffed, but I only joined so that Jessica can ride the float during the parade, and I've done too much now to screw it up for her.'

Jesus, her rambling drains me. 'Whatever. You organise it.'

'Thank you.' She beams back at me. 'Anyway, I should get going.' She walks backwards, clearly awkward. 'Night.'

I look back at her wanting nothing more than to give her a hug and thank her for everything she's doing for my girls. Instead I just nod.

'Night Ruby.'

CHAPTER 18

Friday 13th December

Ruby

*T*onight is Jessica's carol service at the school. It's ridiculously well organised by the notorious PTA. Although why they've chosen the unluckiest day of the year, Friday the 13th, I don't know.

I've been added to their What's App group, so I basically know exactly what's going to happen today and tomorrow at the school fair, hour by hour. I only managed to get out of volunteering on a stall because I'm still running behind on the costumes for the float.

Plus, now I have the added stress of organising this ridiculous wine and cheese night.

They hand out long skinny lit candles to us as we enter. I sit down in the darkness hoping Jessica, who I know is sick with nerves, is okay. Even though we've been practising night and day; I'll never tire of Christmas carols.

I look around, careful of Lottie getting hold of my candle. It does looks beautiful, if not a little dangerous. Each parent holds a candle, the flicker of light showcasing their proud and excited smiles. Everyone's parents seem to be here. All except for Barclay. With it being early evening, I actually thought he might make it.

The red curtains pull open to reveal them all lined up in their school uniforms. I find Jessica's eyes and smile, giving a thumbs up. I see her scan for her daddy and her little face falls ever so slightly. My heart breaks in two for her.

That stupid stubborn man is missing out on these perfect moments that you treasure in your heart forever. You just don't get this time back, but I get that he's busy.

They sing Silent Night and it speaks right to my soul. My dad used to sing it to me before bed, regardless of the month. My heart squeezes with how much I miss him, but I push it back down. I need to be here for Jessica, seen as he isn't.

They sing their parts beautifully, all of us looking on with tears in our eyes. The crowd erupts in a round of applause as soon as they're finished. We all spring up out of our seats to give them a standing ovation.

I'm clapping so hard, proud tears falling down my cheeks, that for a second I forget about the candle. I quickly zone back in on where it is, but it's gone slack in my hand. So slack in fact that it's lit the woman in front's hair on fire.

Fuck! *Fuck!*

Lottie's eyes nearly burst out from her head. 'Fire!' she shouts.

I hit the hair, and in doing so, the back of the woman. She turns around to confront me, but it just makes her realise that her hairs on fire. I slap her hair repeatedly until it goes out, my own hand burning. I barely notice, I'm so mortified.

'You lit my hair on fire!' she screams. 'You stupid nanny!'

Oh no, she didn't. She's played the nanny card, like a normal mother would never make such a mistake. We're all human lady.

A member of the PTA comes rushing in holding a fire extinguisher.

'No!' I shout. 'The fire's already—'

Too late. She sprays the white mist, covering the entire woman in it. I get some on my face too. Silence descends on the room as horrified parents look on at the scene I've somehow created. I look to the stage, expecting Jessica's eyes to have filled with tears from humiliation.

Instead I find them creased and then she lets out an explosion of giggles. She finds this funny? Before long all the kids are creased in laughter while the parents and the teachers glare at me.

'Ooops.'

Saturday 14th December

Ruby

I didn't see Barclay last night. He must have gone straight out from the office. It's weird but I actually wanted to tell him about the embarrassment that is "Fire Gate". The thing I miss most about having a mum is being able to call her and know she'll listen to me ramble on and still be interested. It just reminds me that I don't have any ride or die friends. Sure, I have mates wherever I go, but no-one I'd feel comfortable enough to just randomly ring. Definitely not if I had a dead body in my kitchen.

I texted Barclay again this morning while Jessica was swimming to remind him that today was her school Christmas fair. He's seen it but didn't reply. I'm not holding my breath. The man is impossible. Just when I think I'm getting somewhere with him he goes and lets the girls down again and doesn't even try to call them to apologise.

Plus, I could really do with the company. Everyone is still glaring at me after last night. I actually saw it trending on Twitter. I didn't have the guts to see if it was about me.

I've just treated myself to a mulled wine when I feel a presence behind me.

'Drinking on the job, I see.'

I spin round to see Barclay staring at me, only the tiniest hint of amusement on the corner of his lips.

I grimace. 'Just the one. Remember I've been here longer than you.'

He looks around at all the chaos, children screaming excitedly that they want to see Santa next.

He pouts his lips. 'True.'

A child runs past and knocks her hot chocolate over his jacket. I couldn't have timed it more perfectly.

'For fucks sakes,' he mutters under his breath through gritted teeth.

I get a tissue out of my bag and hand it over to him. He dabs at himself before realising it's a dry-cleaning job.

'I heard there was an incident with a mum setting someone's hair on fire last night.'

Oh shit, he knows. The PTA probably sent out a bloody newsletter.

'Was there?' I ask shrilly, my ridiculous voice giving me away.

He grins and raises one eyebrow. 'I know it was you, Ruby. I've already had the parents on the phone. I've promised to pay for replacement hair extensions.'

God, why do I always act like such an idiot?

'Oh... thank you.'

How easily you can fix things when you have money.

'Ladies and gentlemen, boys and girls!' The speakers boom.

We all quieten down and turn towards the stage, where the headmistress Mrs Langley is holding a microphone.

'Now, as you know, it's Abbots Hill school tradition for the parents to get involved in some of the fun. Now, can I please have a volunteer.'

Barclay raises his eyebrows, as if the whole thing is so below him. I've got just the idea to bring him crashing down to earth.

'Over here!' I shout, jumping up and down. 'Mr Rotch-ester would like to volunteer.'

His head snaps round at me, horror painted on his face.

'What the hell are you doing?' he hisses, pinching my elbow.

Jessica starts giggling.

'Excellent, Mr Rothchester!' Mrs Langley practically sings. 'If I could have you walk into the centre of the room please.'

'Oh no,' he says, his palms up in protest. 'Sorry, but no. I think someone else should do it.' His cheeks are actually turning pink. I love it.

'Rubbish!' I say loudly. 'He just needs some encouragement. Come on everyone. *Mr Rothchester! Mr Rothchester!*' I start chanting.

Everyone joins in. From the looks of it, the mums can't stop eye fucking him and the men want him to be embarrassed. God, private school is horrid.

He's still trying to protest when Jessica pulls on his jacket. 'Please, Daddy.'

He looks at her pleading face and something in him shifts, albeit begrudgingly.

'Fine,' he snaps, walking to the middle of the room with a roll of his eyes. I cannot wait for this.

'Now children,' Mrs Langley says. 'You know the drill.' She starts handing out toilet paper.

What the hell is going to happen here? By Barclay's face, I'm assuming he's never made it to a fair before, he seems equally bewildered.

'Now children,' Mrs Langley says, 'after three. One, two, *three!*'

Children descend on him with crazed excited eyes, wrapping him up with the toilet roll.

'Snowman!' they all laugh. They spin around him until he's basically zombied to within an inch of his life with Andrex. All that's left is his eyes which he's using to shoot me daggers. I shrug unapologetically, trying not to wet myself laughing.

'Excellent children!' Mrs Langley sings. 'Now for the accessories.'

Sticker bows are pressed down his front, a hat and scarf appear from someone and are placed on him.

'Now for the finishing touch.' She pulls a carrot from around her back. Barclay looks at it with wide eyed horror. 'Open up Mr Rothchester.'

His mouth falls open, but it's more from disbelief.

She slams the carrot into his mouth. 'There's his nose. Right, children, let's sing our song.'

The children break into *I'm a little snowman.*

Barclay's cheeks are getting so red I'm sure any minute he's going to burst into flames of rage. Or could it be embarrassment? To think, he's paying a ridiculous amount in tuition charges to get this humiliated.

As soon as the songs over he pulls everything off himself, smiling and trying to act like a good sport, when I can tell he's furious.

'Well done, Daddy!' Lottie says running up to him and hugging his leg. 'You're the best snow man.'

He smiles, despite the embarrassment, calmly walking up to me.

'I have to go back to work. In the meantime...' He leans

forward so he can whisper in my ear, 'Watch your back, Ruby. Paybacks a *bitch.*'

A thrill, as well as fear, runs up and down my spine. Images of him whipping me over his oak desk flash into my mind. Jesus, where the hell did that come from? How strong is this mulled wine?

I try to hide my blushes while he says his goodbyes to the girls.

'That was *so* funny,' Jessica says with a giggle.

'What next girls?' I ask, eyeing up the candle stall.

'Santa!' they both shriek at the same time.

Did they honestly not get enough Santa yesterday?

We queue up for thirty torturous minutes of kids whinging and crying that they want to see Santa next. We finally get in to see him. Wow, this isn't like the Santa's grotto they had at my school.

They've completely transformed a classroom so half of it is covered in what looks like cotton wool on the floor to simulate snow. The curtains are closed, the only light coming from the fairy lights dotted around the room. We round a corner and there the big man is, in his own little wooden room with an elf beside him. Lottie clings onto my leg, obviously unsure. Jessica is too but tries to brave it out.

'Come with me?' she asks, holding out her hand.

I don't care how many years I've been doing this, but when a child trusts and values you enough to want to hold your hand, it just feels like you've made it. It's the best feeling in the world.

'Okay, let's go see the big man.'

The dad is wearing a top-quality costume. Even his beard

looks freakishly real. I wonder if he grew it especially for today. That's some commitment.

'Ah, hello, Jessica. And this must be little Charlotte.'

That's weird, but I suppose if he's a dad he could know their names.

He smiles warmly. 'Come sit down and tell me what you'd like me to bring you this year.'

We sit down on the wooden sleigh covered in a fleecy blanket. It looks like this sleigh has been hand crafted. Absolutely amazing.

'What would you like?' he asks with a friendly smile.

I already know from the letter she wrote that she'd like a doll's house.

Jessica fidgets, looking everywhere but him as her cheeks redden.

'Don't worry, Jess,' I smile. 'It's just Santa. You can tell him anything.'

A thousand things rush through my head. Shit, is she being abused and she's choosing to tell Santa? Could it be a dad from the school? A teacher? Maybe it's this guy and that's why she looks so worried. Anger surges through my veins. I'll kill this guy with my own bare hands. By the time they drag me off he'll be nothing but a pair of eyes and bones.

'Well, my wish isn't for me. Well, not exactly,' she says shyly.

Oh... so she's not being abused. *Well, thank god for that.* I didn't fancy twenty years in prison.

'Whatever it is, Santa will help you. Right Santa,' I encourage with a wink.

He nods. 'Of course, Jessica. Just tell me what's on your mind.'

'Well...' She takes a deep breath. 'I'd quite like for my daddy to be happy again.'

Oh wow. I was not expecting that. Santa looks pretty taken aback too.

'Okay.' He nods. 'And how do you think he'll be happy again?'

'Well,' she fidgets, 'the last time I remember him happy was when my mummy was alive. I know you can't bring her back to life.'

Oh, my heart.

'But I was wondering if you could send someone for him to fall in love with. You know, like in Cinderella, except I don't want an awful step mother. I want her to be kind. But... but I suppose I could have her be a bit horrible, as long as she makes Daddy happy.'

How can one little girl have such a big heart? Mine is swelling and growing every day I get to look after these beautiful girls.

'Well...' Santa starts, looking to me for guidance.

I quickly brush a tear away.

'Jessie,' I take both of her small hands in mine. 'You are such a gorgeous girl to hope that for your daddy and I know that one day he will find someone who makes him happy. But in the meantime, don't for a second think he's not happy with you two girls. He loves you both to the moon and back. He just misses Mummy and wishes she could watch you grow up, like he is.'

'But she is,' Jessica says, matter of factly. 'From heaven.'

'Exactly.' I nod. I love children's unbreaking faith of heaven.

She throws herself into my arms for a cuddle. I squeeze her tight, promising with my hug to look after her forever. Except I'm leaving after Christmas. How can I leave her now?

'I want a hatchimal,' Lottie says over us. 'Please,' she adds with a cute cheeky smile.

CHAPTER 19

Sunday 15th December

Barclay

I'm just about to walk out the door in my tux for the latest company Christmas do when my phone starts ringing, Queenie's name flashing up. I roll my eyes instinctively. I can't help it. She annoys the hell out of me.

'Queenie, what's up?' Problems this early in the evening are a bad sign.

'I'm not coming.'

'Excuse me?' I scoff, completely caught off guard. What the hell is she playing at?

'I'm not coming tonight. To be frank, I really think you need to go to an event without me there to hold your hand. Maybe you'll realise that you miss me.'

Oh Jesus. Is she doing this because she thinks the absence will make my heart grow fonder? I've always been nothing but up front with her about not wanting a relationship. She knows we only snog when I'm tanked up.

'Well I'm very disappointed that you've let me down so last minute. Goodbye.' I hang up. There, that should tell her what I think of her. I am *so* not here for drama tactics from a crazy female. I get enough of that from Ruby.

Hmm, maybe I should invite Ruby to come in her place? No, Jesus, what am I even thinking? It's just...well, it will look bad if I arrive on my own. They always expect me to have dates to these things and Queenie's always been more than willing to fill in. If I sit next to an empty seat all night, it'll just get the gossip mongers chatting.

I know quite a few socialites will be going tonight. The only thing worse than bringing someone they don't already know is bringing no one at all. They'll see me as fair game and I'll have to have their surgically enhanced breasts stuffed in my face all night while they tell me how handsome I am. No thanks. Ruby it is then. Beggars can't be choosers.

Ruby

The girls are all tucked up in bed the next night when I'm wondering if I should tell Barclay what Jessica said yesterday. Maybe show him how they're sensing his mood and for him to try and at least *act* happier. But I know he'll tell me to mind my own business.

Plus, I should really work on the float costumes. It's in five days and I still haven't finished making them all, let alone tried them on the children or pinned and made alterations.

Still, I find I'm pacing the floor of my small kitchen area, trying to think of how to bring it up, eager for an excuse to see him. How pathetic is that. There's a knock at my door.

I frown. I thought the girls were down for the night. I open the door but look up to see Barclay in a dinner suit. Wowzas. That's some broad shoulders.

'Oh, hi.' My knees knock. *He's just so pretty.*

'Hi.' He's fidgeting with a button, a bit like how Jessica was yesterday talking to Santa. 'Sorry to interrupt you, but I'm in a bit of a bind.'

'Right?' I cross my arms over my chest, remembering I haven't got a bra on and I'm probably pointing at him. 'What's up?'

'I have a function tonight.' He checks his watch, as if he's already late.

'Right, okay.' I nod, still not understanding. 'So, you're checking if I'll look after the girls? Of course.'

'No.' He clears his throat, avoiding my eye line. It's strangely adorable how awkward he's being. 'Actually, my work colleague normally comes with me and she's had to cancel.'

'Riiiight?' Am I missing something here? Why is he being so weird?

'I was wondering...' He coughs, clearing his throat. 'If you'd be able to come with me instead?'

I stare back at him, mouth gaping open. He wants me to be his date? Go with him to a function as something more than a nanny?

'Sorry...' I just want to clarify. Check I'm not getting the wrong end of the stick. 'You're asking me to go to a function with you?'

I'm aware I sound like a dumbass repeating myself, but I'm speechless. Surely, he has a list of eager females in his black book he could call on.

'Yes.' He nods, biting his lip. 'It's too late to get anyone else and besides, I don't want anyone to get the wrong idea and think I'm dating them.'

Oh, so it's definitely not a date then. Not that I thought it was. Not even for a minute.

'Yeah, gee, you wouldn't want a female thinking that. Clingy little things that we are,' I say.

He rolls his eyes but graces me with a rare smile. They're so rare that I find myself getting giddy with glee when I get one. It scares me how much I'd be willing to do in order to get one.

'Look, I'll get you a huge TV for your room if you come?'

Resorting to bribing. He must be desperate. I look over at the small fifteen inch television I'm using right now. I could really do with another one and I'd never bother buying one myself, especially with me leaving soon. But I hate that he thinks he can buy me.

I pretend to mull it over some more, to really make him worry I'm turning him down. 'I mean, I really should be getting on with the costumes for the parade.'

Is he starting to sweat? I love having the power to make him jittery.

'But... okay, you've got yourself a deal.'

He nods without smiling. Wait, what the hell am I going to wear? I'm guessing with his penguin suit it's a fancy affair.

'Oh, but I don't have a formal dress.' You don't normally need one with a nanny job.

He frowns, his eyes darting from side to side. 'Ah. That could be a problem.' I nod. 'Actually, I might have an idea.'

He takes my hand and leads me out of my room. He keeps hold of it up the two sets of stairs and into his top floor bedroom, pulling me along behind him. It feels so strange to be holding his hand. Being in his bedroom is weird too. I haven't seen it before, and it feels strangely intimate. It's all very tranquil, whites and pale blues.

He leads me into a dressing room. The kind of thing you see on Pinterest and pin just in case one day you win the lottery. All wooden doors and glossy mirrors that look like they've never been touched. Mrs Dumfy must be an amazing cleaner.

He opens one of the doors to reveal a treasure's chest of evening gowns. Wow. They must be his wife's gowns.

'I never had the heart to throw any of her clothes out,' he admits, dropping my hand.

I smile at him, wanting nothing more than to take his hand and give it a squeeze, but I know he wouldn't like me to.

'Are you sure you don't mind me wearing one of these? Aren't they kind of precious to you?' I don't want to overstep.

Knowing me I'll drop my wine down it. It's a lot of pressure.

He sighs, looking at them with fondness. It's like every

memory of her wearing them goes through his head until he's clearing his throat, choosing to hide the emotion.

'Yes, but they're just going to waste in here. You might as well borrow one.'

'Okay.' I flick through them, taffeta, silk, lace. They're all stunning but I choose a floor length chiffon lavender dress with a sweetheart neckline and cap sleeves. It's simple with a cinched in waist, the fabric flowing to the floor. It's the most stunning dress I've ever seen in my life. I'd never get a chance to wear this in my world.

I take it down to my bedroom and quickly curl my hair and apply make-up. Thank god I showered and shaved this morning. I put the dress on, but need help zipping it up. It doesn't matter how much I contort my arms; I just can't get to it. I check myself in the mirror and you can see my black knickers. I can't ask him to help me with this. Damn.

I tangle my arms as far around as I can, trying to get it up to at least a respectable height. I'm still trying when he knocks on my door. Dammit.

I quickly open the door, still trying to grapple with it. He freezes and just stares at me, eyes wide. So much so that I worry there's something on my face. Or that I've sneezed and smudged my mascara under my eyes.

'What?' I ask, feeling around my face.

'Sorry.' He shakes his head as if only just coming back to reality. 'Nothing. It's just that you look...' He clears his throat and straightens his spine. 'Fine. You look fine.'

I roll my eyes. 'Gee, thanks for the amazing confidence boost.'

He smiles and shakes his head, his brown eyes meeting mine. They hold an intensity I've never seen before. Flipping flamingos, if he keeps looking at me like that my knickers will full on combust.

'Come on, you know you look good.'

'Ooh, from fine to good,' I joke. 'My confidence has gone through the roof! I don't know if I'll be able to fit my head out of the door at this rate.'

His eyes roll to the ceiling. 'Do you need help with the zip?'

I stop trying and turn around for him to help me.

'Marge!' he calls, making me nearly jump out of my skin.

I turn around to face him. 'Are you serious?' Is he scared of me or something? 'Just be a man and do it yourself.'

He huffs, like it's really putting him out, but eventually relents and does me up. Not all slow and sexy like it is in the movies. Nope, he zips it up so quickly I'm surprised he hasn't caught my skin in it.

He claps his hands together. 'We're late. Let's go.'

I snort. 'And they say chivalry is dead.'

'After you.'

CHAPTER 20

Ruby

I'm thrumming my hands nervously on the inside of the cab as it hurries through the streets of London.

'Stop doing that,' he snaps, his voice never raising. 'You're annoying me.'

I sigh. He's such an arsehole. I'm always irritating him.

'Well, *sorry*. Remember you're the one that's ruined my night. I could be at home binge watching Netflix in my pyjamas right now.'

His eyes widen and his mouth turns in disgust. 'Some women would find it a treat to be taken to a fancy hotel and treated to champagne and canapes.'

I raise my eyebrows at him. 'Yeah, well I'm not most women.'

'You can say that again,' he mutters under his breath, looking out of the window.

It's so hard to say whether he truly finds me a pain in the arse or actually ever so slightly amusing to have around. I feel like I'm constantly walking a tight rope between them both.

The black cab comes to a stop outside The Landmark hotel. Oh God, this looks posh. I hope it's not full of pretentious arse-holes. I swallow, my throat suddenly dry. I'm used to always being in the background of posh people. This has me suddenly worrying if I'll stand out like a sore thumb.

'Show time,' Barclay says, jumping out and offering me his hand.

I take it to get out and then he offers me his arm to link onto. I take it, glad for the emotional support. He must know I'm nervous. Either that or wants to treat me like a little trophy.

We walk into the foyer. I'd like to think I've been to a fair few hotels in my time, but never have I seen anything like this. It's all cream marble with enormous palm trees in plant pots. Around them are what look like holiday apartments. It's very bizarre.

He leads me into a room with high ceilings, stunning huge chandeliers and round tables set up with white tablecloths, people chatting around them. Luckily, we're not so late that people stop what they're doing and stare at us. He guides me over to a table just as they're serving the starters.

Everyone says their hellos to Barclay.

'May I introduce Ruby Campbell.'

I smile awkwardly. 'Like the soup.' Then I snort a laugh.

Jesus, alive! What the hell is wrong with me?

Barclay raises his eyebrows, as if warning me to at least appear normal to others. He quickly introduces them, one by one. I forget their names as soon as I'm told them.

Some cheese and walnuts are placed down in front of me.

He leans over to whisper in my ear. 'Sorry, these are Queenie's choices.'

The feel of his breath against my skin does funny things to me. I look at my arms and yep, I've got goosepimples. Must get a grip, Ruby. This is not a date.

Queenie? Hang on, isn't that the woman I caught him making out with the other night? She's his work colleague too? Talk about dipping his end in the company ink.

I grimace and whisper back. 'Yeah...I don't like cheese.'

He stops dead and stares at me like I just told him I have six nipples and moo at the moon.

'Sorry? You don't like *cheese?* What kind of person doesn't like cheese?' He seems genuinely pissed.

I put my hand up. 'This kind of person.'

I mean, I'll have it melted on a pizza, but I can't stomach it on its own. He's probably been brought up with goat's cheese fountains being the norm and he has the audacity to call me out as the weirdo.

'Champagne, madam?' A waiter asks me.

'Oh.' I stop him pouring and beckon him closer. 'Do you have any prosecco?' I whisper conspiratorially. I've never liked champagne. Too sharp.

He purses his lips to try and hide a smile. Obviously not used to women refusing champagne in favour of the cheaper stuff. Riff raff that I am.

'Of course, madam. I'll go arrange that for you.'

'Thank you!' I whisper, giving him a thumbs up.

I push around the cheese on my plate, at least trying to look like I'm enjoying it. Every now and then Barclay takes a bit from my and eats it. Thank God. I don't know if he's doing it to be sweet, so I don't get embarrassed or because he doesn't want me showing him up.

The waiter brings back a glass of prosecco and I smile my thank you.

'What did you ask for?' Barclay questions, giving me a suspicious smile, one eyebrow quirked.

'Prosecco,' I admit my face scrunching with a cringe. I don't know why. I'm not embarrassed. 'I hate champagne. It gives me a headache.'

He smiles and shakes his head. Like *'only you.'* Plenty of people prefer prosecco, thank you very much, *you pompous arse*.

I take the walnut in my hand and attempt to crack it open. Barclay discreetly takes my hand and hides it under the table. When I look up at him, he's still talking to someone, never missing a beat. He ever so discreetly shakes his head and removes the walnut from my hand.

Bloody spoil sport. Maybe I'll try to do it again. I like it when he touches me. Well my body does at least. My skin is still tingling from his touch.

Next its chicken breast with potato and green beans. Finally, something I recognise. I munch away, happily tuning out the boring chit chat they're all droning on about. Nothing of it interests me and I doubt he brought me along to hear my scintillating conversation about playground politics or the latest Peppa Pig episode.

'You happy?' he asks, biting his lips to try and hide a smile, watching me enjoying my food.

'I am now,' I nod, doing my happy food dance. What can I say? When I'm eating something yummy my body can't help but dance in celebration.

Dessert is even better. A pear baked with chocolate cream and vanilla sauce. I nearly orgasm right there at the table.

When I'm done, I keep looking around, trying to find my waiter guy to top up my glass. I suppose I'll have to go to the makeshift bar in the next room.

'Just going to the ladies,' I lie to Barclay, excusing myself. I don't want him to have an excuse to take the piss out of me again.

I go straight to the long table they're using as the bar. I hide behind a huge burgundy flower arrangement, just in case Barclay sees me. I smile at a barman and request my prosecco.

'I'm sure I can find some for you,' he smiles, going off in search of it. I'd probably have more fun with the waiters. More my kind of people.

I check my phone just in case Mrs Dumfy has been trying to reach me. I hate the idea of the girls waking up and neither me nor Barclay being there.

'Barclay!' Someone exclaims, in a ridiculously posh voice, the other side of the flower. 'How are you? It's been a long time.'

'Too long,' Barclay agrees.

I shrink down, desperate to be hidden. If he finds me at the bar, he'll think he's brought a right lush.

'Who's that hot totty you brought with you? New plaything?'

My eyes widen in horror. Do people really talk like this? It's like an episode of *Made in Chelsea*.

'No, no, nothing like that,' he says with a chuckle. 'She's just the kids' nanny.'

I feel like I've been kicked in the stomach. *Just* the kids' nanny? I shouldn't be offended by that. It is, after all, what I am. But it's the way he said *just*. Just as if being a nanny is a low down derogatory job. Like I'd definitely be in the basement in Downton abbey.

'Mind if I take a crack at it then?' his pig of a friend asks. *Ugh. Just try it fuck face*, I'll knee you in the balls so quick.

Barclay laughs. Actually laughs. The traitorous bastard. They're talking about me like I'm some cheap tart.

Just then the waiter comes walking towards me. 'Found the prosecco!' he says loudly.

Shit, loud enough for anyone to hear.

CHAPTER 21

Ruby

I grab the glass off him, mumble a thanks and high tail it out of there. Only, I have to pass Barclay and his friend to go back into the main room. I do with my head down, but Barclay is already watching me with trepidation written all over his face. He probably knew it was me the minute they mentioned prosecco, common little thing that I am. I'm mortified.

I see him race after me in my proverbial vision, but I don't stop until I'm back in the main room. I back myself into a corner and down the prosecco, some dribbling down my face. Real classy, Rubes.

'Ruby,' Barclay says, not noticing my fuck off vibes. And my vibes are *strong*.

'Don't Barclay,' I stop him, my palms up. 'I'm going home.'

I pick up the front of my dress and high tail it out of there. There's a line of black cabs outside, thank god. I jump in one the doorman directs me to.

'Wait!' I hear him shout.

The doorman holds the door open for him and he jumps in next to me. Ugh, idiot.

I give the driver our address and attempt to stare out of the window, ignoring him. Nothing he can say will make me feel less of a disposable human being. It's started to rain. It fits my mood perfectly. I feel like Gabrielle in that music video.

'How much of that did you hear?' he asks carefully. Ugh, I hate how he's trying to manage me right now.

I turn to face him, a heavy sigh leaving my lungs. 'Enough, Barclay.'

I don't know if I'm more disappointed in myself for giving him the benefit of the doubt.

'Listen,' he starts, fidgeting with his coat button.

'No,' I interrupt. I'm sick of this shit. 'I'm really tired right now, Barclay. I just want to go home to bed.'

I turn to stare out of the window, wishing the driver would get us there quicker.

As soon as we're home, I jump out, leaving him to pay. It's the very least he can do.

Instead of heading for the main front door I instead go downstairs to the door of my basement flat, the keys already in my hand.

I'm about to shut the door when he runs in and forces himself in past me. If it wasn't his house, I'd tell him to fuck off.

'I'm sorry, Ruby, but we're not going to bed until we talk

about this.' He stares stubbornly at me, his beautiful bastard lips pursed.

I sigh. For fucks sakes. He must want to purge his conscience before bed. Selfish arsehole. I cross my arms over my chest and lean back against the door, ready for his bullshit excuses.

He starts pacing, his hands clasped behind his back. 'I assume you heard all of that, so I'm guessing you're pissed because of how he talked about you. I know I laughed when he asked if he could he have a shot at you. Honest to God though, Ruby, I was just about to tell him that you weren't to be touched by his filthy hands when I saw the barman bringing over the prosecco. I knew instantly it was you.'

'Of course, you did,' I scoff. 'Commoner that I am.'

'I never said you were common,' he snaps, his face furious. 'I would have punched him in the face if he wasn't the son of one of our board members.'

I roll my eyes. 'Whatever. That's not even what really upset me.' I kick off my heels, already aching to get into my comfy fleece pyjamas.

He frowns at me, staring intently. 'So, what upset you so much?'

Now that I have to say it out loud, I feel kind of pathetic for having thrown such a tantrum. He doesn't owe me anything. I'm just staff to him and here I am acting like a child.

'Come on,' he encourages; his brown eyes kind. He steps closer to me. 'Tell me.'

His job is to charm people, I remind myself. He's only being nice because he wants to know. Pure curiosity.

'It's stupid,' I insist, trying to undo the dress myself.

He sighs. The kind of sigh that reminds me what a huge inconvenience I am.

'Ruby, how am I supposed to apologise when I don't know what you're upset over.'

Ugh, men and their rational points. So irritating.

I huff. 'Fine!' I shout. 'It was when you said I was just the nanny.'

He stares back, his forehead pinched.

'I know I *am* just the nanny, don't get me wrong. But it was just the way that you said it. Like it was such an inconsequential job. I love what I do and I'm helping to shape the young minds of the future and I'd hardly call it inconsequential.'

Jesus, Ruby. A bit of prosecco and I'm rant city.

'Neither would I,' he agrees, his voice serious, eyeing me intensely. 'In fact, I'd say it's the most important job in the world to me.'

Well, I definitely didn't expect him to say that.

'You're looking after my children. The most precious things in my life. Please don't think that I'd just allow any old idiot to do the job. I went through your resume. I called your references. They all spoke so highly of you.'

'Really?' I just assumed that Mrs Dumfy handled all of that.

He nods, stepping forward again, this time to tuck a stray bit of hair behind my ear. It makes me shiver, goose bumps appearing up and down my arms.

'You are *so* much more than just a nanny.'

He looks at me, his eyes having now taken on a more devilish glint. It's as if I'm an edible dessert he has every intention of resisting but wants nothing more than to eat all up. Where has this come from? I have no idea. Maybe he's drunk.

I can't help but gaze into those longing brown eyes, my chest panting in anticipation. I want nothing more right now than for him to kiss me. But I know he won't.

If someone asked me right now if I wanted world peace or his lips on mine, I know which one I'd choose. Wars could erupt right beside me and I wouldn't notice.

Please kiss me, I beg silently.

His chest is panting too, like holding himself back is pure agony. I inch ever so slightly closer to him, gazing at his perfect plump crimson lips. He stays completely still, as a statue. Damn it, he's not going to kiss me. I don't know what I was thinking. I feel like such a fool. This is what happens when I drink prosecco. Slutty Ruby comes out to play.

I'm just about to officially give up when he takes my face in his hands and plants an urgent kiss on my lips. My eyes spring open in disbelief. I quickly let them flutter closed and let out a sigh of relief through my nose. It comes out more as a moan. I sound like a horn dog.

He kisses me softly, his hands working into my scalp. God, it feels heavenly. Did he work at a hairdresser when he was younger? Because with how skilled he is I wouldn't be surprised. He teases at my mouth with his tongue. Our tongues tangle together, as if they were made to dance. As if I've been waiting my whole life to be kissed by him, only him.

His tongue eventually slips out and his kisses slow to closed lips. He pecks at my lips a few times, then kisses my nose, making my heart melt into a puddle of goo on the floor.

I open my eyes, unsure of whether I'm going to find myself in my bed, having dreamt it all. He smiles down at me, his own eyes looking love drunk, his lips red and swollen.

We both pant, our breaths the only sound in the room. What the hell just happened?

Our breathing finally calms down enough for us to be able to speak. Not that I know what the hell to say to him. I don't think I could form a single word if I tried.

'I'm sorry,' he says, his forehead wrinkled.

I blink. Did he seriously just say that? Just apologise for giving me the best kiss of my life? Wait...does he regret it?

'Don't be,' I mumble, lifting my fingers up to touch my bruised lips.

He steps back and clears his throat. I see it happen, see his mask go back on. His walls built straight back up. It's over.

'That was terribly unprofessional of me. I'm sorry, Ruby.'

'Don't be sorry. I wanted it too.' God, I sound pathetic. What I really want to do is to cling onto his leg and beg him to kiss me again.

He shakes his head. 'That can't happen again. I'm sorry.'

He turns and walks out.

Well, that's that then, I suppose. Only, how the hell can you taste a bit of heaven and then just go about your normal life. I know I can't.

CHAPTER 22

Monday 16th December

Ruby

I wake up in the morning still in the dress from the night before. I never could take it off without the assistance of anyone else. I'll have to ask Jessica to help. I don't think I even took my make up off. Just threw myself face down on the bed, the most sexually frustrated as I've ever been. I'm not ashamed to say I pulled out Vinnie the Vibrator to help me get off to sleep.

I glance at the clock. Eight am. Shit, we're late. I must have forgotten to set my alarm. I race up the two flights of stairs; nearly giving myself a heart attack, to find the two girls still sleeping peacefully. If I was this rich, I'd invest in a lift.

'Girls! Wake up. We're late for school.' I throw Jessica's

curtains back, not that it brings in much light, the dreary London weather making it seem more like early evening than morning.

Jessica rubs her eyes, stretches and curls back into a ball. Lottie stumbles in with her bunny, jumps up onto Jessica's bed and snuggles in next to her.

'Morning, baby,' I say, with a smile I can't help but show. They're so adorable when they're sleepy. 'We need to get going if we're not going to be late.'

Lottie reaches out her injured plastered arm. 'Cuddle.'

I look down at those big hazel eyes; so similar to Barclays. I can't refuse her. I crawl into bed with them and snuggle up. Who cares if we're late? I've learnt never to turn these opportunities down. These are the things you remember when they're all grown up.

Lottie pushes her cheek against mine and the sweet smell of her baby soft skin has me feeling like I couldn't move even if I wanted to. I wrap my arm around Jessica and she slowly opens her dreamy blue eyes, a tired smile greeting me.

'Morning baby.'

She yawns again. 'How late are we?' Her voice is all cute and husky.

'Well, if we get up now, we can just about make it to the school bell.'

She looks me over and crumples her forehead. She looks so like Barclay in that moment. It hurts my heart to even think of him.

'Why are you wearing an evening gown?'

I snort a laugh. 'Long story.'

See, these are my people. Not those snobby people from last night sipping on champagne and taking bollocks. Innocent kids who say exactly what they think. They're the people whose opinions I value.

They help me out of the dress, and we rush around in order to get out of the door. I had to substitute myself for them to look well turned out. Don't get me wrong, I don't normally bother with make-up, preferring just a slick of lip balm and maybe if I'm feeling crazy some mascara. But today my hair is scraped up on top of my head like a demented pineapple and my blotchy 'night after alcohol' skin is free for the world to judge. I grabbed some sweatpants and a comfy jumper and completed the outfit with my fake Ugg boots. Yep, a real *I don't care* outfit.

To say I look disgusting is an understatement. I haven't even washed my face, just brushed my teeth and threw on some deodorant. I decided they were the two most important things to do if I was going to see people.

The bell rings just as we run into the school. I say goodbye to Jessica, handing over her book and lunch bag. Next is Lottie at the nursery door. In the short space of time I've been with her she's already showing an improvement in her confidence. Instead of clinging onto me she gives me a quick kiss, hug and then walks in, turning to wave every two seconds with her poor little broken arm. I wave back with a thumbs up until I can't see her anymore.

'Well, would you look what the cat dragged in,' someone says behind me.

I turn, sure they weren't talking to me, to find Clementine looking at me smugly.

'Excuse me?' I ask with a fake smile.

'I heard you were out with Barclay last night.' Jesus, news travels fast around here. 'I didn't realise nannies offered those services too.'

Oh no she didn't.

'Excuse me?' I bark, hand on my hip. Did she really just insinuate that I'm acting as an escort? A sort of hooker?

She eyes me bitchily, taking in my admittingly shit clothes.

'Plenty of women around here have been trying to get into Barclay's pants since Claire died. I really fail to see what is so special about you. Please enlighten me?'

I lean on one hip, ready for this fight she's intent on having. She's had it in for me since I joined the PTA. She doesn't realise I haven't had my morning coffee yet. It's like starting a fight with a wild animal.

'First of all, I'm not getting into Barclay's pants. Second, I'm not even trying. I accompanied him because his business partner couldn't make it. As simple as that.'

'Really?' she says with a huge shit eating grin. One I'd like to smack off her face. 'And why on earth should I believe that?'

'Fine,' I shrug, attempting to act unbothered. 'Don't. But if I hear that you're spreading rumours about me I'll—'

'You'll what?' she interrupts stepping into my face, completely invading my space. Wow, this woman's a bully. She really has no shame. Her kid's gonna grow up to be such a shit.

I think quickly of something to scare her.

'I'll... I'll go after your husband,' I say lamely.

Her mouth drops open, hand shooting dramatically to her chest. 'Excuse me?'

Well, that's got her.

'You heard me.' I nod, faking confidence. 'I'll go after your husband. They all like a bit of rough. Imagine how many people will laugh when they hear how you didn't satisfy your husband enough, so he had to find comfort in the common nanny.'

She blinks rapidly. 'He'd *never* sleep with you,' she says, clearly not even believing herself.

I lean a bit into *her* space. 'But just think who people will believe. You'll have already told them what a slut I am. It will all make sense.'

She huffs, trying and failing to come back at me with something. Her over pumped lips opening and shutting frantically like a goldfish.

'You better watch yourself.' She turns, flicking her long brunette hair in my face and storms off.

I hope to God she doesn't make my life even harder on the PTA. I have enough to worry about without that cow bag making my life difficult.

Tuesday 17th December

Barclay

I cannot believe I kissed her last night. What the hell was I thinking? *That she looked pretty fucking perfect in that dress* my subconscious reminds me. Seeing her out of her baggy jumpers and in something that showed off her figure just shocked the living life out of me.

Then that jackass Aubyn talking about her as if she were a piece of meat. I would have knocked him out, had it not been some a prestigious event and his dad a board member. Seeing her feelings hurt like that, seeing her that vulnerable, it just got to me. Her heavy-hearted eyes penetrated my soul.

And I just... I jumped. I took the chance the moment it crossed my mind, not stopping for a second to talk myself out of it.

Only now I've put her in an impossible situation. I've taken advantage of my position of power and kissed my employee. Jesus, she could sue me for sexual harassment! I wouldn't even blame her.

Of course, she kissed me back. The poor thing was probably scared to death of her boss taking advantage of her. Scared I'd throw her out that very night.

I apologised but nothing I say will erase that kiss from my mind. Now that I've tasted her, felt her pressed up against me, I know that no woman will ever feel as good.

CHAPTER 23

Ruby

I still can't believe that bitch Clementine. Who the hell does she think she is? I hope the other mum's aren't talking about me. Not that I should care, but no one wants to be labelled the whoreish nanny, do they?

I'm over-reacting at every glance from a mum, sure they're whispering about me. Juliette has re-assured me that they're still talking about Fire Gate. Great. Not exactly re-assuring.

Barclay promised me a new TV if I came along last night. Although after the awkward kiss I'm not sure I can bring it up with him. Not that I've seen him since. I'd think he was avoiding me if he wasn't normally always out of the house.

Only, well now that I've put the kids to bed my TV has started to have two fuzzy lines running through it. It's basically unwatchable. Typical. Especially when I'm intent on finishing these parade outfits.

I go to the kitchen to find ice cream. That'll cheer me up. Marge is still cleaning up after dinner.

'What's up, Ruby?' she asks, sensing my mood.

I can't tell her the truth. Oh, you know, kissed the boss and all that.

'Just my TV on the fritz,' I admit, sounding like a spoilt brat as I search the freezer for ice cream.

'Why don't you go and watch in the sitting room?'

I look at her as if she's insane. 'In the *main house?* Are you nuts? What if Barclay finds me in there?'

She shrugs. 'He always goes straight to his office and then to bed. He's never in there.'

'Well, my TV *is* pretty busted.' Could I really risk it?

She grins and hands me a spoon for my ice cream. 'Enjoy.'

Damn bad influence. I run downstairs to get the costumes I'm still working on and walk like a naughty schoolgirl to the sitting room, open the door and peer in. The coast seems clear. Barclay hasn't even come home yet.

I've never actually been in this room before. It's different to the rest of the house. All black and gold. Overly glamorous and almost bachelor pad like.

I sit down onto the plush enormous crushed velvet sofa. Agh, it feels as comfy as a cloud. I find the remote and click on my favourite show, *Ru Paul's Drag Race. Ooh, surround sound.*

An hour later I'm spread out, having consumed most of the ice cream and finished my costumes, when I hear a noise. It's hard to know if it was just something from the surround sound or an actual outside noise.

The door opens and, as if in slow motion, Barclay walks in, catching me slumming it up on his sofa, my hair still in the demented pineapple from earlier this morning. I try to sink into it, but damn reality won't let it happen.

He stares right at me, the only light from the huge TV exposing his facial features. I'm expecting angry, but instead he looks like he's confining a laugh. He crosses his arms and leans against the door frame. Damn him to hell; he looks so sexy when he does that.

'Ruby, what are you doing in here?' he asks, with a grin.

'Sorry, Marge said you never come in here.' I hurry up and collect my ice cream pot, spoon and costumes.

'Were you... waiting up for me?'

Huh? Oh God, he thinks I'm acting like a lovestruck puppy. Trying to seduce him after last night. Mate, if I wanted to do that, I'd be wearing something sexier than sweats.

'God, no! I honestly thought you wouldn't notice. I'm sorry. I'm gonna go.' I can feel my cheeks burning. All the embarrassment from last night comes rushing to the surface.

I go to walk past him, only he blocks my path.

'Ruby.' I look up into his dark brown eyes, a clear mistake. 'You're more than welcome to spend time in my sitting room. You're welcome anytime.'

Why does that feel like more than just an average invitation. I avoid his penetrating stare, scoot past him and run as fast as I can back to the safety of my flat. I don't know what's happening between us, but it feels weird and I don't have time for weird right now.

Ruby

I get a text around 6.30pm from Barclay saying he's going to be late. It's the first time he's ever bothered to tell me. The girls were really hoping to see Daddy tonight, especially as they were bored to tears while I had their friends try on their outfits and pin them accordingly. I know they're going to be disappointed to not see him.

'What time will Daddy be home?' Jessica asks, as if reading my mind.

I'm starting to think she does actually have the gift. My Grandma's sister did. She predicted the week I'd start my periods. Now don't tell me that's a weird thing to predict and get right.

I stroke her hair. 'I'm afraid he's going to be late, sweetheart.'

Her little face drops, her eyes growing despondent.

'Daddy's always late,' Lottie says folding her arms in front of her, her bottom lip jutted out.

I have to think of something to take their mind off it. Cheer them up.

'I know!' They both look up at my exclamation. 'Why don't we toast some marshmallows?'

Jessica scoffs. She can be so like her father. 'We don't have a bonfire.'

Good point.

'No, but we have the fire in the main sitting room. That'll do.'

Their eyes light up. 'Let's do it!' Jessica shouts punching the air.

We gather the supplies, handily finding everything in the pantry, I swear to God Marge stocks absolutely everything in this house, and head into the main sitting room loaded with snacks.

'We never come in here,' Jessica says, sounding unsure, looking round apprehensively. 'Are you sure we're allowed?'

I raise my eyebrows. 'Jessica, do you honestly think I would sneak in here if we weren't allowed? Your daddy only told me last night that I was allowed in here. Plus, this is *your* house.' It's so strange how they feel like they're not welcome in their own sitting room.

'Okay,' she says, clearly not believing me.

I turn the fire on with the click of a button and stick the marshmallows on the long stick prongs I found in the kitchen. I hand them over to the girls.

'Now you have to be *really* careful girls,' I stress. 'I'm trusting you to only hold the marshmallows above the fire. If you go too low, you'll set the stick on fire.'

I think of Fire Gate. I'll be called a fire maniac if this goes wrong. I could be committed.

I keep a close eye on Lottie. With her cast it makes it trickier for her, but she still manages. From what I've learnt over the years, children love when you give them a bit of responsibility, but that doesn't mean you shouldn't still keep a close eye on them.

They get on great, toasting the marshmallows and then, after them cooling down picking off the goo with their fingers and eating it.

It goes so well we start again with some more. I look down at their chubby little fingers holding onto the sticks so carefully. God they're adorable. I'm going to miss them so much.

'What the HELL is going on here?' someone bellows from behind me.

I jump, my heart escaping into my throat. I turn around to see Barclay staring open mouthed in complete disbelief at us. Like he just walked into us shooting up heroin.

The girls startle and tense behind me. I hate that he can install fear in them so young, especially with everything they've been through.

'Let's take this outside,' I insist, quickly grabbing his elbow and dragging him to the door. I turn back to the girls. 'Put down the sticks and sit safely on the sofa.' I watch them do it.

I drag him out to the hallway. 'You really need to calm down in front of the girls. Can't you see they're scared of you?'

He scrunches his face up in distaste. 'Don't be ridiculous.'

How can he not see it? How can this be the same man I let kiss me less than 48 hours ago?

'I'm not. I feel their little bodies tense up beside me when you arrive. They should be running into your arms, not running from you.'

His face is thunder. 'How dare you try to lecture me on how *my* children are feeling.'

I open my mouth to snap back, but we're both stopped with an ear piercing scream. We exchange horrified glances before turning towards the sitting room and running in.

To my absolute terror Lottie's ignored my instructions and obviously taken the stick and somehow in the commotion caught it on fire. She must have thrown it at the curtains as they're now ablaze. That's right, on fucking *fire*. I am the fire monster.

'Lottie!' I shriek, sprinting over to her. Jessica's trying to drag her away from it.

'My marshmallow!' she cries, bursting into tears, obviously completely unaware of the danger she just put herself in. Shit, the danger I put her in by turning my back for a second. I should know better.

Barclay swoops in, takes the curtain rail off the wall, flings it to the floor and stamps on it until the flames are completely put out. He runs, scoops Lottie up as if she weighs nothing than a bag of sugar and sits on the sofa, checking her all over.

'Are you okay?' he asks her over and over; his hands trembling.

Jessica cries and clings to me, obviously shaken from the whole experience. I hug her close. Well done Ruby. You've fucked it up again.

Lottie finally stops crying. 'Can I have another marshmallow?' she asks me with wide innocent eyes.

Barclay glares at me.

'No, baby,' I say, smiling through the choking fear still clinging to my neck. 'I think it best we leave the marshmallows for tonight.'

'What the hell were you thinking?' Barclay shouts, placing Lottie carefully on the sofa. 'She could have suffered third degree burns! Are you completely psycho?'

Jessica cries louder. 'Daddy, it wasn't her fault! She was trying to do something nice for us. Please stop shouting at her.'

He grits his teeth. 'It is my duty to keep you safe. It's as simple as that.'

'But Ruby keeps us safe! I don't want you to shout at her,' she pleads.

He sighs, running his hands through his hair. 'This is something I will discuss with Ruby later. Take your sister up and I'll put you to bed.'

She begrudgingly takes Lottie's hand and leads her out of the room, leaving us alone.

He glares at me. 'I'll see you in my study after I've put the girls down.'

I nod. Might as well get it done with as soon as possible.

CHAPTER 24

Ruby

J wait in his study, pacing the floors. I'm surprised I haven't worn out these floorboards by now. I swear he's taking his sweet time just so I sweat it. Sadistic bastard. Just when I think he's growing a heart he turns and reminds me who he really is.

He's going to tell me to pack up and leave tonight. I just know it. If he doesn't give me a chance to say goodbye to them, I'll scream bloody murder.

Finally, I hear footsteps. Let's get this shit show on the road. He opens the door and goes straight to sit behind his desk. I've come to realise he definitely does it this enforce his power over me. Like I said, sadistic. God, this man infuriates me.

'Ruby, what you did was reckless. You willingly put my

daughters in front of a fire and gave them a fucking stick. I mean, what were you actually thinking?'

I sigh, collapsing into the chair across from him. 'I was thinking that you were late home, *again,* and the girls needed a distraction from how much they missed you.'

He raises his eyebrows. 'And you couldn't have just stuck on a DVD or something similar? *Anything* other than fire.'

I sigh. 'No, I stupidly thought it was a good idea. From what I've learnt from children, they love when you give them a bit of responsibility. Especially when it's something dangerous. I was honest to god watching them every second. You shouting just caught me unawares. It caught us all unaware, which is why she ended up with a fire stick!'

He stands up, so quickly, I jump up and back away. 'The reason she had a fire stick was because you handed it over to her.' He creeps towards me, his eye ablaze with rage. *'You* are the reason, Ruby.'

He backs me into the wall, so close now that he's in my face, smelling amazingly delicious. He places his hands on the wall, either side of my head. 'You're the reason my calm household has been turned upside down.'

His troubled brown eyes stare at me, his laboured minty breath touching my face. I'm panting too. What the hell is wrong with me? Why do I find his cruel words sexy? It's his face. His beautiful, glorious, bastard face.

'What is it about you, Ruby?' he asks, his voice quieter as he searches over my face, as if expecting to find the answer on a Post It. 'Why is it you drive me so crazy?' I can see his genuine confusion over his conflicting feelings.

I look down at his lips. He's going to kiss me; I just know he is. And I want it. I want those plump lips on mine so bad it hurts my heart. My eyes flutter, so lightheaded I feel I might pass out.

He edges his head closer, his lips already a whisper on mine. When the door opens.

We jump apart guiltily as Lottie walks in rubbing her eyes.

'Ruby, I need you to kiss me goodnight,' she says in the sweetest little gravelly voice.

I smile guiltily back at Barclay before scooping her up.

'Come on then. I'll put you back to bed. I missed our good-night kiss too.'

I walk up the stairs and tuck her in, giving her a kiss on her cheek. 'Night, baby.'

'Daddy wasn't too mad at you, was he?' she asks, clinging onto bunny.

I push the hair from her face. 'He was only upset because he loves you and doesn't want you hurt.'

She holds sleepily onto my face. 'I'm only hurt if you're hurt.'

How can a three-year-old be so bloody profound?

Wednesday 18th December

Ruby

I have no idea what's going on between me and Barclay. How

191

he can seem to despise me one minute and the next be almost kissing me.

Either way I'm still trying to make up for yet another fire incident. They're gonna call me the pyromaniac. So, I decide to suggest a Christmas inspired activity. Something to take all our minds off it. Mostly to take my mind off Barclay and the weird vibe between us.

'So, would you girls like to do something Christmassy this weekend?' I ask as energetically as I can over breakfast.

'Like what?' Jessica asks with a shrug. It still makes me sad how she's not excited about Christmas. Her stupid father is taking all the fun out of everything.

'Like maybe ice skating?' I knew to be prepared with ideas. Their lack of imagination still astounds me.

'Ice skating!' Lottie shrieks jumping up and down on the spot. 'Yes! Let's go ice skating. Can we ask Daddy?'

Jessica smiles at her, but it doesn't reach her eyes. As if she already knows Daddy won't be able to make it. How sad to be six years old and already have no faith in your Father.

'Of course, we can ask Daddy,' I reply enthusiastically. 'I know what would get him coming with us. Why don't we write him letters after school? That way I can give it to him later when he comes in and he'll see how much it would mean to you both.'

Jessica smiles, her little nose crinkling. 'That could actually work.'

'Of course, it will,' I grin, shaking her jokingly with her arms. 'It was my idea and I only come up with the best of them.'

Lottie goes running towards their craft corner.

'*After* school,' I remind her. 'And after yoga.'

'Can we use sprinkles and glitter?'

I grin. 'Is the pope a Catholic?' I snort sarcastically. They stare back at me blankly. Oh, I suppose they wouldn't know that. 'Of course, we can!'

'You promise you'll give him our letters?' Jessica asks as I tuck her in later that night. Her hope and excitement are addictive. I just bloody hope he can come now.

I nod. 'Of course, I will. I was hoping he'd be home on time, but he must have to work late.'

'He always has to work late,' she says with her eyes fixed on the ceiling.

I push her silky blonde hair back from her forehead. 'Your daddy works very hard so that you and your sister can have a good life. He does it because he loves you.'

She sighs as if the weight of the world is on her little shoulders.

'Well, please tell him we'd much prefer him to come home earlier.'

How do you explain to a six year old that they've probably got a huge mortgage on this house and he has to work damn hard to keep it? Except I know that's only part of it. He can't bear to be around them sometimes, because his love for his girls also hurts him; a constant reminder of his wife.

'I'll mention that to him too, then.' I give her a kiss on her squishy little cheek, taking a cheeky sniff of her beautiful baby lotion scent.

She pulls the cover up to her cheek. 'Promise?'

'Of course.'

She beams back at me, her eyes sleepy. 'You aren't scared of him, like the other nannies.'

I just smile. *That's because the other nannies didn't love you like I do*, I think to myself.

'See you later, alligator.'

'In a while, crocodile,' she replies through a yawn.

CHAPTER 25

Ruby

*W*hen I walk down the stairs, I find him just walking in, putting his keys on the side table.

'Oh hi,' I squeal, sounding a little hyperactive. 'I have something to give you.'

He smiles back at me, clearly entertained. His eyes are tired yet again, as if getting through the day is taking it out of him.

I rush to the playroom and pick up their letters, still wet and tacky from the glue and glitter. I blow on it desperately as I run back up to he's pouring himself a whiskey in his study.

I hand them over. I open my mouth to explain when he holds them away from him, horrified.

'Ugh, these are still wet. And they're full of glitter. Do you know how much this suit costs?'

I steel my jaw and try to count to ten, but I'm pretty mad.

To dismiss their beautiful creations like this... Well it pisses me off.

'I'll hold them while you get changed into some tracky bottoms then.' I stand on one hip to show him I mean business.

He narrows his eyes at me. 'I think we both know that I don't own tracksuit bottoms.'

The idea of him lounging around in them amuses me. I don't think he'd even know how to relax if he tried.

'Whatever. Your daughters have taken the time and care to write and decorate these fabulous letters. The very least you can do is read them.'

He sighs, rubbing at his eyebrows. 'Ruby, I've just got in the door.'

'Precisely my point,' I growl. 'The girls have no way to communicate with you, seen as you're always at work. They've had to resort to writing a letter.'

'Excuse me?' he grunts, his eyebrows raised, as if he really wants to say, '*I beg your fucking pardon?*'

'You heard me.' I square my shoulders, ready for a show down. 'The girls are getting older and they're starting to notice that you're not around. Jessica told me tonight that she'd much rather you be around than live in a big, fancy house.'

'I have to work.'

Bullshit.

'No, you *like* to escape to work.'

He rolls his eyes, pushing past me towards the kitchen.

'Please don't try and analyse me. I pay you to play with my daughters, not try to fix me while you're here.'

Play with his daughters? Could he belittle me anymore? Arrogant arsehole.

I follow him, not letting this go.

'Part of me *'playing'* with your girls,' I snarl. 'Is to talk to them and to look out for their welfare. And they miss their father, they've already lost their mother, don't let them lose you too.'

His nostrils flare with rage he's trying desperately to keep inside.

'You're way out of line,' he spits through gritted teeth.

I shrug. I can't hold back my opinions anymore. He needs to hear the hard cold truth.

'Maybe, but I think it's very rare that anyone in your life actually tells you the truth.'

'Oh really?' he snarls, leaning into me. A normal woman would be scared, but I'm not afraid of him.

'Yes, really.'

He keeps his glare on me for three whole seconds before releasing some pent up breath.

'I'm just stressed, Ruby. Jesus, can't you just leave me alone?' He stares down into his glass of whiskey.

'Alright!' I snap back, palms up, knowing I've pushed him enough for tonight.

Calm down, Ruby. Don't let this man get to you. Try to kill him with kindness.

'It's just that...' I really can't stop myself. 'You know, a problem halved and all that.'

He rolls his eyes. 'Jesus, am I honestly not going to get rid of you until I tell you why I'm stressed?'

I cross my arms over my chest and raise my eyebrows, challenging him.

'Ugh,' he shouts, like a moody teenager. 'Fine, I'm just a little bit fucking sick of my life.'

Well that's a statement and a half.

'Have to be a bit more specific there, Barclay boy.'

He raises his eyebrows at my nickname. I just can't help myself. He's so easy to wind up.

'Maybe I'm sick of this whole stuck up society that I live in. Maybe I'm stressed to fuck in a job I don't enjoy so I can pay my huge mortgage. Maybe I wish my dad would get off my arse occasionally.'

Wow. He really is hassled.

I shrug. 'So, sell up, move out to the country.'

He raises his eyebrows and scoffs a laugh.

'Ruby, don't be ridiculous. It's not that easy in the real world.'

Why must he always treat me like some fanciful fairy that lives in woods made out of make believe?

'Are you implying that I don't live in the real world?' I challenge, daring him to confirm it. With the way I'm feeling right now I'd stab him with a glitter pen.

He sighs heavily. 'What I mean, is that I have commitments here. My mother and father are here. I grew up here. The family business is here.'

'Hang on. Didn't you just say that you don't enjoy your job?'

He drags his hand through his hair. 'That doesn't mean I want to quit.'

Oh, what a complicated man he is.

'Why not?'

'Because I'm just being a brat,' he admits, his shoulders slouched. 'The truth is that I do love my job, well, I do when I don't have my father breathing down my neck.'

'So, your dad owns the company?'

'Exactly.' He nods. 'He keeps pressurising me to start taking the reins of it. Wants to retire soon so I can be the big boss.'

Being your own boss of a company actually sounds pretty good.

'Surely when you're your own boss you won't have him stressing you out?'

He shakes his head. 'Wrong. He'll still chair on the board. Everything will still have to go through him. All of the fun from event planning will disappear and be replaced with budgets and schmoozing clients.'

I grin. He must hate having to be nice to people as a job.

'Well that's a shocker. You not being good at schmoozing clients. You seem such a charmer.' I can't help but throw my head back and chuckle.

'Ha ha,' he deadpans, the hint of a smile on his lips. 'Yes, I hate talking crap with clients. And it's not even clients, its big CEO's of companies. Not the actual people organising the event.'

I suppose now I actually listen to him it does sound a bit shit. My parents were always supportive of whatever I wanted to do. Back then I had a list that included astronaut, nurse, rockstar and ballerina. Never once did they make me feel like I couldn't achieve any dream I had.

'So, can't you just tell him you like your job the way it is and don't want to take over?'

He looks at me with raised eyebrows, as if I'm mental.

'No Ruby. I can't just turn my father down. I either make partner or I'll have to leave, and then he'll probably never speak to me again.'

Jesus, what kind of father would do that? I'm starting to understand him a bit more now if he was raised by a man like that.

'Surely he wouldn't sever your entire relationship over a business?'

He chuckles. 'It's very apparent you haven't met my father.'

Apparently, I never want to either.

I chew on my lip. 'Could you not talk to your mum?' She seems lovely and reasonable.

'Please, Ruby,' he says stopping me with the palm of his hand. 'I don't want to involve her. I shouldn't have even told you any of this.'

'Hey, it's good to unload sometimes.' I touch his arm before I think it through. 'Even if there isn't a solution to the problem.'

He smiles but his troubles are weighing him down.

'Thanks, Ruby. It has helped to say it all out loud. I'm off to bed.'

Dammit, he made me forget about the letters.

'Oh, but wait. The girls want you to come ice skating with us on Saturday. Hence the letters.'

His face drops and his eyes darken. Shit, does he have a phobia of ice skating or something? This guy gets weirder by the second.

'Can't they do something else?' he asks with a frown, choosing instead to look at the floor, as if needing time to compose himself.

'Ice skating is perfectly safe and besides, they chose it.' I square my shoulders, tired of his moods. 'Can you come or not?'

He takes his phone out of his pocket and scrolls through it. So long I actually wonder if he's forgotten whether I'm here or not.

'Fine,' he eventually agrees. 'Book it. One o'clock at Somerset House.'

'Great,' I smile, glad I've got my way. The girls will be ecstatic. I turn to walk away but have an idea. I spin back round.

'You know, it would go a long way if you'd write a letter back to the girls accepting their invitation.'

He doesn't turn to acknowledge me, but I know he heard. Stubborn bastard that he is.

'Oh, and don't forget tomorrow night is the wine and cheese thing for the PTA,' I quickly slip in before turning away.

'What?' I hear him yell after me.

'Sweet dreams, goodnight, don't let the bed bugs bite,' I sing.

'God, you can be annoying, Ruby.'

Yeah, yeah, *didn't stop you kissing me though, did it*.

Barclay

I know it's ridiculous, but I actually do feel a little better for sharing with Ruby. I mean, I know she lives in club cuckoo land where every problem can be fixed with glitter, but it was still nice to offload. The sad thing is that I don't actually have any friends these days.

When Claire was alive, we had lots of couple friends, but I didn't want to hang out with them once she'd passed. Don't get me wrong, they offered lots of pity dates where I'd be the only single guy there. I wasn't going to go and be gawked at and be given the sad little head tilt whenever anyone asks how I'm doing. No thank you.

So that brings me to the present with not a soul I can really speak to. It's easier with Ruby, even if she doesn't understand. At least I know she'll be on mine and the girl's side. She strikes me as a good friend, someone who would fight for you, not have anyone talk about you behind your back. That kind of loyalty is rare these days, especially around here.

But... the ice skating. She might as well have stabbed me in the stomach. When Claire was pregnant with Charlotte, she was so excited that Jessica was going to have a sibling. With me and her both being only children she was insistent on it. We always talked of having a completed family and us going on family days out together. She always loved Christmas and said one year, when the girls were old enough, we'd go to Somerset house and ice skate.

It was one of the things she cried about towards the end. When I held her frail body in my arms and let her sob about the unfairness of it all. How she wouldn't get to see our daughters grow up, watch them graduate, get married, have children of their own. I was thinking all the same things, but I had to be the strong one for both of us.

Going without her somehow feels disloyal, like I'm betraying her. Living her dream when she can only watch on. But I also know that she'd tell me to do absolutely anything to keep those girls happy. If that means ice skating through my heart ache, that's just what I'll have to do.

I grab a pen from the drawer and decide to take Ruby's advice. A little letter might go a long way.

CHAPTER 26

Thursday 19th December

Ruby

The next morning I'm delighted to see there's a letter addressed to the girls in the kitchen. I can't actually believe he listened to me. He might be the most infuriating man on the planet, but with some guidance he can be less of a pig. I just hope my replacement, whoever they may be, are able to get through to him.

'Look girls!' I say with glee. 'Daddy wrote you a letter!'

Their mouths drop open and then we all dance round the kitchen, even grabbing Marge who's cooking their porridge and forcing her to dance the conga. She complains, but I think she secretly loves it. I see that smile she's trying to hide.

'Let me read it,' Lottie says, the first to exit the conga line.

'No, Lottie,' Jessica moans, 'I'm the one that can read.'

I hand the letter to Jessica, shrugging apologetically to Lottie.

She clears her throat. *'Dear Girls, thank you so much for your invitation to ice skating. I would love to join you. Ruby is going to book us in for Saturday. I have something in the morning, but I'll meet you there at 1pm. Love Daddy.'*

She clutches it to her chest. 'He's coming! He's really coming,' she says, verging on tears.

'Of course he is.' I nod. 'With awesome letters like that, how could he possibly refuse?'

Lottie nods. 'It was the glitter. *Definitely* the glitter.'

Well tonight is the dreaded wine and cheese evening for the PTA. Barclay said he would be out this evening at an event so at least I don't have him hovering around making me even more uneasy. Marge sorted me out by ordering some amazing cheeses and wine.

I've styled them out on the table in the kitchen/diner and dressed myself in some smart jeans and a plain black top. A quick brush of the hair, some lip gloss and I'm presentable, drumming my fingers on the table as I anxiously await their arrival.

It's only two minutes past eight but I'm already wondering if this was all just some elaborate joke and they're not going to turn up at all. I'm sick to my stomach. It reminds me of all the mean girls at school. That's why I always stuck to my close friend Georgie. Only with me nannying and her moving to America with her new husband we lost touch.

The doorbell rings. I gulp down the bile attempting to rise up my throat. You can do this, Ruby. You can chat shit to these women and actually try and pretend to be one of them. It's just for the evening and you're doing this for Jessica.

I open the door to find all the women on the doorstep, obviously with Clementine in the middle holding a red bottle of wine. Did they all get a minibus here together? Weirdos.

Clementine is the first to walk in, thrusting the bottle of wine into my chest. I almost stumble backwards from the force.

'I brought this. Wasn't sure whether you'd have any decent wine.'

Oh, because a meagre Nanny like me has no idea of what wines are good. I mean, I don't, but I resent the judgement.

Coats are taken off and thrown at me. Juliette helps me to hang them all up. We walk into the kitchen to find they've all made themselves at home, helping themselves to the cheese and wine.

'Lovely house you have here,' Clementine says with a smug little smile, knowing full well it's not mine.

I roll my eyes. 'Obviously it's not mine, it's Mr Rothchesters. But he's kindly let us host this little evening tonight.'

'Hmm, where is he?' she asks between a mouthful of cheese. So, she does eat. With how skinny she is I did wonder.

'Out tonight, working.' I fake a sad smile.

Her face drops, disappointment written all over it. Ah, so that's definitely why she wanted it here. She wanted her grubby little hands on Barclay, even though she's supposedly happily married. I doubt she is, especially with how she paled when I mentioned trying it on with him. No-one with that much bitchiness is getting laid regularly. A few orgasms would chill her the fuck out, surely?

'So, are you going to give us a tour?' one of the friendlier women asks, smiling hopefully.

'No,' I shake my head. 'Like I said, it's not my house. Plus, the girls are asleep.'

Juliette smiles at me and mouths, *'calm down.'* It's nice knowing *someone's* on my side.

I have to endure an hour of them all talking over and around me, unless of course Clementine finds a way to put me down in some little way. Juliette tries to involve me, bless her, but they're all just so different to me. The only thing I can join in with is talk of the parade tomorrow, but even then, Clementine reminds me the costumes are not finished. They're basically done. Jessica was so excited it was hard getting her off to sleep.

I'm just wishing away my life when I hear the front door close. That can't be Barclay. He's normally out all night at an event.

'Ooh, is Barclay home?' Clementine coos, practically running into the hallway. 'Barclay, how the devil are you? Long time!' I hear her boom at him, the red wine making her louder than usual.

I can almost imagine his cringe and discomfort from here. No one wants to come home to a Clementine in your face. I'm sure even her husband doesn't.

He walks into the kitchen, after saying a very formal, 'Hello, Clementine.'

'Sorry,' I quickly apologise with a cringe. 'I thought you'd be out all night.'

He shrugs. 'The event was well taken care of.' He throws his keys down onto the kitchen island. 'Plus, I'll admit that I forgot this.' He gestures at the room. 'Was this evening.'

I sink my head into my shoulders.

'Sorry.'

He gives me an amused smile and leans in to whisper, 'Something tells me you've suffered enough punishment already.'

Just the feel of his hot breath on my ear has my spine tingling. God, what I'd do to have that mouth somewhere else.

I grin back, almost dizzy. 'You're right.'

He says his most polite hellos to the ladies.

'Maybe you should wait it out in the lounge. I'm hoping it won't be too much longer until they leave,' I suggest.

I walk him out of the kitchen, but we both stop dead in our tracks when Clementine shouts 'FREEZE!'

Everyone turns to look at her.

A devilish smile takes over her face. 'You're under the mistletoe,' she says.

We both actually look behind us, expecting two of the mums to be under it, ready for Clementine to force them to kiss. I wouldn't put it past her.

But no, she's talking to us. We both glance upwards and low and behold, there hangs a tiny little bit of mistletoe. What the hell? I never put this here. And the girls couldn't have reached, even with the help of a chair. Could Clementine have hung it here, especially for this excruciating moment?

Barclay chuckles, but I know it's an awkward one.

'I don't think it would be very professional, for me to kiss my employee,' he explains with a polite smile.

I nod frantically. So frantically I look like one of those nodding dogs. Chill the fuck out, Ruby. Way to look unbothered by it all. This is basically telling everyone I have a humungous crush on him. I can feel my cheeks burning. I hope it doesn't show.

I quickly duck out from it and decide to fill up everyone's wine glasses. Not that they need it, they're all already looking a bit worse for wear, lipsticks smudged, and eyeliners run. Barclay walks into the sitting room.

'Ooh, bit of an awkward one for you there,' Clementine says, looking like the cat who got the cream. 'I might offer Barclay some wine.' She grabs a bottle and a fresh glass and sashays away towards the lounge.

Stay away from him, you skanky bitch, I want to scream. Why am I so jealous? *Because he's mine.* No, he's not, Ruby. Instead I just watch her, hoping to God Barclay tells her to fuck off.

I wait for fifteen agonizing minutes for her to return. When she finally does, I just can't read whether something happened. She's always got that bitchy obnoxious smile on her face.

Another hour later they all finally start saying their good-byes and going home. Clementine is the last to leave. Of course she is. She doesn't say thanks, just that she was impressed I actually stocked some decent wines, then laughed and said I must have had help.

It annoys me that it's true.

I really don't know why I let her bother me so much, but every time she speaks, I just want to crash something into her skull.

I knock on the lounge room door, peeking my head through. He's propped up on the sofa, his tie loosened round his neck in that delicious way he does.

'They've gone. Just wanted to tell you the coast is clear.' Any excuse to spend time with him.

'Thanks.' He smiles and the glare from the television lights up his handsome square jaw.

I point around the room, wanting any excuse to spend more time with him.

'Can I ask, why is this room so different to the rest of the house?'

He smiles sadly. 'I let my mother redecorate it for me. It reminded me too much of Claire.'

'Oh.' I nod. 'Did it help?'

'Tonight, is the second time I've ever been in it. Turns out memories stay with you, no matter how many times you re-wallpaper.

I smile sadly.

Grabbing his wine glass, he follows me out into the kitchen, silently helping me to clear up, loading the glasses into the dish-washer and corking the wine. Well, after we've both taken a few cheeky swigs. It makes me feel like we're mischievous teenagers, not boss and employee.

'Well, I better get to bed,' I say with an awkward smile, before turning and leaving. I can't stand the awkwardness.

I'm just entering the hall when my hand is pulled. I glance

at it to find Barclay's hand engulfed in mine. I look up into his eyes, now alight with lust. My mouth turns slack as I forget how how to move anything at all.

Next thing I know his lips are moving towards mine and then my eyes are shut, his lips on mine.

I'm too flabbergasted to do anything really. My mouth is still partly open. He takes that as an invitation and sticks his tongue into my mouth. I'm so surprised that my eyes spring open. His are closed, his hands coming up to cup my jaw with his fingers. I close mine, letting myself enjoy it for a moment.

Enjoy his tongue caressing mine. Before all the doubts and sensible thoughts start to infiltrate my brain.

Then he pulls away, letting my face go. He smiles mischievously.

'Can't let the tradition not be adhered to.' He grins, pointing up at the hanging mistletoe.

'Uh-humm,' I answer. Jesus, I can't even speak.

I quickly turn my body away from him and scuttle away, down to my room where I can scream into my pillow in peace.

CHAPTER 27

Friday 20th December

Ruby

*W*hy must he keep kissing me? It's playing with my bloody emotions. The more I kiss him the more it feels like the most natural thing in the world for us to do. I just don't know if he's using me for a quick kiss, just like that Queenie, or if he does actually like me.

It almost feels like we hate each other, but some cosmic force is constantly pushing us together. I just can't help but be drawn to him. I'm starting to wonder if it's down to my limited experience of relationships. Maybe a normal person would be cool with it and I'm just bugging out wondering if it actually means something.

Anyway, I don't have time to mull it over today as it's the

parade. I've just got all the costumes done in time. It was really down to the wire, especially with Clementine sending abusive texts every ten minutes. Giving me *incentives* as she called them. I cannot wait to quit.

They're letting them out of school early so everything can be ready for 2pm. I imagine the kids not doing it are equally as ecstatic. Jessica's been smoothing down her fire officer costume for a while now. She has no reason to be scared. She looks awesome, if I do say so myself. This year they're all dressed as service jobs. I think Clementine took advantage of my sewing skills.

'Are you nervous, sweetie?' I ask leaning down to her level.

She gulps. 'A little,' she admits, not properly meeting my eyes and biting her lip.

Damn it, all this work I've done and now she's afraid.

'You don't have to do it if you don't want to, you know.' Although with everything I've been through I hope she does.

She chews her lip further. 'I'd be letting everyone down.' Her voice wobbles. I can tell she's on the verge of tears.

I shrug. 'Who cares?'

'I do.' She shakes her head. 'I'm fine. I'm going to do it.' She has a new steely determination on her face. 'I'm going to do it and I'm going to have fun.'

I give her a cuddle. This girl. She's come such a long way in such a short time.

'You're amazing, Jess. Just remember that.'

She beams back at me. Then she shoos me off.

I watch as she passes me and Lottie on the float. She's waving like a Disney princess, like she had no worries about today at all. She catches our eyes and waves like crazy. I manage to get it on video. I just hope I didn't record the little sob that escaped from my mouth. Especially as I plan to forward it onto Barclay.

Barclay, who I now have an undeniable crush on.

'Oh, Ruby!' I hear from behind me.

I know that voice by now. I hear that voice in my nightmares. The bitch Clementine is walking towards me. Damn it, why does she always seem to appear whenever I'm trying to have a pleasant moment? And how is she not hungover after all that wine she sank last night? She probably drinks the blood of virgins first thing.

'Ruby, I need you to do the expenses.' She attempts to dump a large folder, overflowing with receipts into my arms. I dodge it like the plague.

'Don't you have a treasurer for that?'

She rolls her eyes. 'Bloody Antoinette has come down with the flu. I told her she wouldn't have got the flu if she wasn't so overweight, but by then she was so high on the medication, she ended up shouting abuse at me.'

Or she did that because you told the woman she was overweight, you horrid bitch.

I shake my head, deciding to stand my ground. 'Whatever, I'm not doing these expenses.'

She shakes her head, as if not believing I dare to speak up to her.

'*Excuse* me?' There's no doubt that she heard me. She should have said '*I beg your fucking pardon.*'

'I said I'm not doing this. In fact, I quit the PTA.'

I only joined to help Jessica out and little do they know I'll be gone by the new year.

Her eyes flare with rage, her mouth contorting. Ha, take that bitch!

She turns and starts running towards the float.

'Take Jessica off the float!' she screams after them.

Oh my god. She can't seriously be trying to take my child off the float mid parade. She is. She actually is!

I grab her by the hair, yank her back against my front, and cover her mouth with my hand. I'm surprised at the strength in me, but it turns out, yet again, I'll do anything for Jessica.

Plus, I've done so much work to get her to this parade. I'm not having this bitch ruining it now at the last hurdle.

I look around at the other ladies in the crowd. They see, I know they do, but they all turn a blind eye. All no doubt been burnt at some point in the past by Clementine. Clementine, meet karma. She's a bitch like you.

When the float rounds the corner to finish, I loosen my grip on her. She chooses that moment to elbow me in the ribs.

'Fuck!' I gasp, bent over, winded from the pain.

Lottie looks up at me in horror, obviously wondering who I've become in the last few minutes. I really shouldn't be swearing in front of her either, but it was a natural reaction to being elbowed in the ribs! Damn they hurt.

'How fucking dare you, Ruby!' She glares at me with such intensity I'm shocked I'm not bursting into flames. 'I don't know *who* you think you are, but you are going to be *very* sorry you ever crossed me.'

I really try to care, but I just can't. I'm too happy for Jessica.

'She's a mean lady,' Lottie says, eyes wide.

'You can say that again, sweetheart.'

I thought that was the last I'd hear of Clementine over the weekend, but I should never have under-estimated her.

For once Barclay is home in time for dinner. I can't help but fantasize that he rushed home to see me. Pathetic, I know, but a girl can dream.

We've barely finished when there's a knock at the door. Barclay looks towards it, his forehead furrowed.

'Are you expecting someone, Ruby?' he asks, as if put out.

God forbid I have any life around these girls.

I shake my head. 'No, but I'll get it.'

I run up to the door and swing it open to find two uniformed police officers. Oh God, has there been a break in down the road or something?

'Hi, can I help you?' I ask, attempting to discreetly look down the road to see if anywhere has been cordoned off. I hope it's not a brutal murder.

'Ruby Campbell?' the taller policeman asks.

'Yes,' I nod with a gulp. What the hell do they want with me?

'Can we come in?'

CHAPTER 28

Ruby

'Err...' I look back into the kitchen at the table with the girls and Barclay. 'Yeah, why don't you come down to my flat so we can talk privately.' I look back at Barclay. 'Back in a minute.'

I grab a set of keys, knowing my spare is on there. I run down and let them into my flat, picking up discarded clothes from the floor. Of course, I have two sets of dirty knickers sprawled out. I'm clearly an animal. I quickly kick them underneath the bed.

'So, what is this about?' I ask, crossing my arms over my chest.

I already know it's something to do with Clementine. That spiteful bitch just couldn't let this go.

'You've been accused of an assault of a Mrs Clementine Allerton.'

Oh my God. I knew it. She rang the police on me. That little rat. Hasn't she heard that snitches get stitches? I wish I was strong and brave enough to knock her out, but I'd probably just break my hand.

'An assault?' I attempt a scoff, but it comes out as a hysterical tinny laugh. *Way to look innocent, Ruby.* 'I don't know what you're talking about.'

'Mrs Allerton claims that you hit her, restrained her and attempted to shut off her air supply.'

I roll my eyes. Don't tempt me.

'Yeah, I don't think so!' I laugh, attempting to appear carefree and innocent.

I take a breath, ready to go into my side of events when my internal door suddenly opens. I turn to see Barclay walking in. He takes in the two police officers, his forehead wrinkled in concern. Well this doesn't look good.

'Ruby, what's going on?' He doesn't sound angry, more worried on my behalf. It actually warms my heart. Maybe he does like me a little.

'Um... I've been accused of assault,' I admit begrudgingly, looking to the floor and spotting yet another pair of knickers. Damn it, Ruby! I quickly kick them out of view.

He stands by my side. It's a simple act of solidarity, but it means the world to me.

'You can't be serious. Do we need a lawyer?'

I love that he referred to us as a *we*. For a second I imagine us as a couple, raising the girls together. I quickly shake those thoughts away. I'm clearly getting hysterical.

The policeman grimaces. 'I'm afraid that you might, sir. We don't have enough evidence to take Miss Campbell in, but any help with our enquiries at the station would be appreciated.'

I'm about to offer to go down there to clear this all up when Barclay stops me with a hand on my arm. It causes goosepimples to appear all over my body. Damn it, this man has no idea what he does to me.

'As she's not under arrest you can ask any questions you'd like to here, with me present.'

The policeman steels his jaw, obviously pissed he knows what he's talking about. I have no idea how. He must watch a lot of crime dramas.

'Very well.' He turns to me. 'Can you please tell me, in your own words, what happened?' He gets out a pen and little black note pad.

I swallow, a lump suddenly in my throat. 'Well, I was watching the girls in the parade and she came over asking me to do a load of filing for the PTA. After being her lackey for the best part of two weeks, I refused. Then she started trying to stop the float to get our Jessica off it.'

'You can't be serious?' Barclay asks, his jaw ever so slightly open.

I nod, glad he's just as outraged as I was.

'So, I just...well I tried to stop her.' I pull at my cardigan, suddenly hot.

'Did that involve choking her?' the policeman asks with an accusing stare.

'Please don't put words in her mouth,' Barclay snaps.

Him sticking up for me is making me feel all kinds of inappropriately hot for him. I'm tingling in places I shouldn't be.

'No, I just... pulled on her arm so she couldn't stop the parade. Jessica would have been devastated. But I at *no point* tried to choke her or shut off her air supply.'

A little white lie won't hurt, right?

'Can't you see how this is just a big misunderstanding?' Barclay offers with a tight smile. 'Just some PTA matters gone wrong.'

He nods, closing his notebook. 'We have to investigate any claims, you understand. I'll speak to the list of witnesses, but as long as they're singing from the same hymn sheet, we should have no problems dismissing her claims.'

Shit. The PTA women. They're bound to take her side.

'Great,' Barclay smiles, squeezing me on the shoulder, obviously thinking this is over. This is *so* far from over.

He shows the policeman to the door, thanking him for understanding.

What the hell am I going to do? Will I be charged with it? That'll stay on my record. Damn it. I'll never work again.

As soon as the door is shut Barclay walks over to me. Do I see the hint of amusement from the creases of his eyes? Or is he cross? It's so hard to tell.

'Now, do you want to tell me the *real* story?'

I roll my eyes, cross my arms and sit down on the edge of my bed like a stroppy teenager.

'Fine, I may have... been more... persuasive than I first described.'

He raises his eyebrows, sitting down next to me.

'But I didn't choke her,' I quickly add. 'She's just being dramatic.'

He smirks. 'Well, I want to thank you for sticking up for Jessica. Not many people would go to those....' His mouth twists with a smile. 'Extremes, to protect her.'

I push his shoulder with mine like a juvenile.

'Yeah, yeah, I'm a thug. But at least I was a thug for Jessica.'

'Exactly.' He nods.

He glances down at my lips, as if distracted by them. I don't know why, they're nothing special. Shit, is he thinking about kissing me? Our bodies are so close. I can feel the heat from his chest. God, how I want to rub my fingertips down it, feel his heart beating beneath them.

'I didn't choose the thug life, the thug life chose me,' I whisper, trying to be funny but instead it comes out strangely sexual; my voice husky, me panting for him.

He leans in at the same time as I do.

It's happening again. It's happening and I'm not strong enough to stop it.

'Ruby!'

We both turn our heads to find Jessica and Lottie barrelling through the door.

'What happened? Why were the police here?'

Well, it looks like our almost moment is gone. Yet again.

Barclay

What the fuck am I doing? I was mere centimetres away from her lips. If the girls hadn't had run in, I'd have kissed her. Again. But damn, hearing her go crazy protecting Jessica just had me thinking crazy for a moment.

What is it about Ruby that just makes all rational thoughts go rushing from my head? Maybe it's because I know I've already fired her, that she's already leaving. I've always wanted what I can't have. There's no prospect of it actually going anywhere.

Yeah, that must be it. It must be. God knows I'm not emotionally available enough for a real relationship. I'm still in love with Claire.

I need to stop. I'm confusing myself and Ruby by letting my teenage hormones take control. I'm a man and my dick needs to listen up; this can never happen.

I go up to my bedroom, needing space away from everyone. Just give me a second to myself. Even then I'm hoping Ruby follows me up.

'Barclay.'

Shit, I nearly jump out of my skin. Mrs Dumfy is behind me folding laundry.

'You nearly scared the life out of me.' I put my hand to my chest, my heart beating erratically. 'What are you doing here?'

'Just doing the laundry,' she smiles. 'Actually, I did want to talk to you. About Ruby.'

'Oh?' Jesus, what has she done now? Upset Mrs Dumfy. She must have really gone to town to do that. The woman is so even tempered. It's the only way she's managed to put up with me all these years.

'What's going on between the two of you?' she asks with a quirked eyebrow.

'Nothing,' I quickly reply. Far too quickly.

She looks at me with one raised eyebrow, as if to say pull the other one.

'Don't lie to me, Barclay. I would have thought after all these years you'd at least afford me the truth.'

I sigh. Why is it everywhere I go in this house there are feisty females wanting something from me?

'The truth is, I have no idea what is happening between us. I just know that nothing can ever come from it. She's my employee and I'm her boss, end of story.'

She leaves the laundry and walks to stand in front of me.

'Don't let a simple thing like that get in your way. I can tell she likes you too, so why not?'

She wants a reason why Ruby and I can't be together? Is she actually serious right now?

'Why not? I'll tell you exactly why not. Because I'm in love with Claire and I will be forever. Because the last time I let myself love someone she went and died. Because I don't want to feel that kind of happiness again, even if I could.'

'Oh, Barclay.' She smiles kindly. 'Don't let what's happened to you make you hard. Don't let the pain make you hate. Don't let the bitterness of what's happened to you steal your sweetness.'

I drop my head. Yet again she's called me out on my bull-shit, just like Ruby does, albeit with far kinder words. She forces me into a hug, patting me on the back.

'Just think about it, Barclay, hmm?'

Little does she know I've fired her and she's leaving. We all need to get used to it; Ruby will be leaving after Christmas and that's final.

CHAPTER 29

Saturday 21st December

Ruby

We've been so busy with school stuff and buying Christmas presents that Saturday comes around far quicker than I'd have liked. God knows I've been avoiding Barclay. I have no idea why I turn into a lustful bimbo around him. It's so annoying, but it's not like it's completely one sided. I'm starting to think he just likes teasing me. It's all a moot point anyway because I'm leaving, and he hasn't asked me to stay. I need to get my life together and contact the agency. See if I can still get that South of France position.

I've half been expecting to find myself arrested. I mean, surely the policeman would have spoken to the other PTA mums by now? I would have thought they would have dobbed me in, scared of Clementine's repercussions. I'm flinching at every knock of the door.

I'm scrabbling round trying to find clothes both warm enough as well as sturdy enough for ice skating after swimming. I don't want them hurting themselves if they go over. Lottie's already at a disadvantage with her broken wrist.

She's also a little hard to get into jeans and prefers pretty dresses. She insists on wearing her pink glitter tutu over jeans, teaming it with her purple wellies. She looks like a crazy child, but I've realised that if you fight her, she digs her heels in more. To think she was the scared, clingy child when I first arrived and now she's bossing me around.

We stand outside of Somerset House looking around for Daddy, bouncing from foot to foot to try and keep ourselves warm. It's so cold every time the wind hits my face it's like a slap to the cheek. Well I won't miss this in the South of France.

It's three minutes past one and I'm already worried they're going to give our booking away. It's packed. If he lets them down, I might have to murder him.

Still, the thought of seeing him, having to spend a day with him has my stomach doing somersaults. I really need to get over this crush. Barclay clearly just likes playing with my emotions. I'm nothing but a toy to him, I remind myself. My heart begs with me not to listen to my head.

'Do you think Daddy is coming?' Lottie asks, looking up at me with those huge almond shaped hazel eyes.

'Probably not,' Jessica says, kicking a stone on the floor,

trying to appear unbothered. 'Probably got called away with a work thing.'

Bless her, it's as if she's resigned to the fact, he's going to let her down. I suppose she doesn't want to raise her hopes for them just to be dashed.

'He wouldn't do that, would he, Ruby?' Lottie asks looking up at me, her eyes filled with unshed tears.

I look away, desperately clawing for any better excuse when I spot him hurrying down the road. I can't help it, my face lights up as soon as I see him. He made it. He kept his promise to the girls.

'He's here!' I shout, pointing towards him.

They break away from my hands and run towards him, practically rugby tackling him. My heart swells in my chest. He kept his promise.

He walks over, carrying Lottie, Jessica clinging to his leg.

'Sorry I'm late,' he apologises to me with a shy smile.

For a second he actually looks like a bashful little boy. I suppose it *is* awkward with us having kissed twice and almost kissed another two times. At least it's not just me feeling weird. He does have a heart, even if it is buried deep behind his heartache.

'No worries,' I shrug, like the most laid back person in the world. Not someone who a minute ago was planning his murder.

We queue up and finally get our skates. They ask if we'd like instructors for the girls. We thank them, but insist we'll be fine, but we do get a polar bear stabiliser thing for Lottie, so she doesn't fall down. Jessica insists she's too grown up for it.

We have a few falls, a few tears, but after about thirty minutes we've found our groove and we're having fun. It isn't the clear blue skied day I was hoping for. It's quite grey and already seems a bit dark, but it somehow makes it the more magical. The fairy lights are having their chance to shine.

I skate a bit ahead of them, having skated every Christmas since I can remember I've got the edge on speed, and turn to pull my phone out. I take a few snaps before they even realise.

'Are you taking our photo?' Jessica asks with a pout and frown. 'I *hate* photos.'

Six-year-olds can be such divas.

'Since when?' Barclay asks with the same identical frown as her. God they're cuties.

'Since you hate them,' she answers with a shrug.

He raises his eyebrows at me before leaning down to her, almost toppling over.

'I don't hate photos, sweetheart. Why do you think that?'

She shrugs, not meeting his eyes. 'Because you don't have any up anymore. You took them all down.'

He looks to me, obviously embarrassed to be having to discuss this with me around. Just a common nanny. I look away, deciding to keep a close eye on Lottie instead.

'That's not because I hate photos, baby. I just...' He swallows, his Adams apple bobbing up and down. 'I get sad sometimes looking at photos of Mummy. I thought it was easier if I put them away.'

'Well, I love photos,' Lottie says, posing for my phone. I can't believe I ever thought she was shy.

'Maybe you can put the ones of mummy in my room?" Jessica suggests, avoiding his eye contact, scared of the rejection.

He looks to me, his eyes full of vulnerability. I see every ounce of hurt and fear he holds so close to his chest.

He pulls her into a hug. 'We'll sort it out.'

He looks up at me, clearly worried. He's probably already thinking she needs to go to therapy; drama queen that he is.

'Okay,' I interject, wanting to lighten the mood. 'So now we can agree we all like photos, let's take some.'

The girls start pulling funny faces and posing. The people skating past looks over and smile. It's obvious they find them adorable. Any breathing being would. I wonder if to anyone else we look like a normal family, me being the mum. Nah, I'm sure they can sniff out my Primark leopard print coat from a mile off. I've got so used to little kids wearing designers next to my high street, I barely notice anymore.

Barclay skates over and takes my phone from me. You can tell he's not used to people saying no to him.

'Let me take some of you and the girls,' he offers with a kind smile. His dark eyes are still cautious around me, but I appreciate him trying.

'Really?' I can't help but blush. I suppose he wants them to have some to remember me by. 'Okay.'

Families never want me in the pictures. They like to pretend I don't exist in real life.

I skate over to the girls and teach them how to do Madonna's vogue. They giggle hysterically.

'Who's Madonna?' Jessica giggles.

Barclay raises an eyebrow over the phone, and we share a secret smile. Way to make us feel ancient.

'An amazing singer. She had this one song...' I can't help myself, knowing it'll wind Barclay up, 'It went, *'like a viiiirrrgin.'*

Barclay pulls the camera from his face sharpish, his face like thunder. 'Ruby!'

I can't help it. I just love annoying him. It's too easy.

'Like a viiiiirrrgin,' Lottie sings back, giggling. 'Wait, what's a virgin?'

He glares at me. 'Just someone that hasn't done something before,' he explains quickly.

Jessica giggles, her hand up to her mouth. 'Before today I was a skating virgin!' she shouts for everyone to hear.

'Sssh!' we both hiss.

I meet his eyes and we both crack up laughing, but I want to poke the bear. He's too easy to wind up.

'Excuse me,' he asks, flagging down another skater. 'Do you mind taking one of all of us?'

He wants one of *all* of us? Why? I don't get it. He's already got some of me and the girls.

'Yay!' the girls sing, cuddling up to me.

He skates up to us effortlessly, puts one hand on my lower back and the other around the girls. My skin tingles from his touch.

'Cheese!' we all sing, for one split second the picture perfect family.

I know I should be happy, but I can't help but let the anguish creep in. He only wants a picture to remember me by.

He knows soon enough I'll be gone. Knows he can tolerate me and any of the weird sexual tension between us until then.

The thought of leaving these girls has my heart clenching so tight it feels as if I can't breathe. What the hell am I doing to myself?

CHAPTER 30

Ruby

*W*e both put them to bed that evening, the girls completely shattered from the fun of the afternoon. They would have been happy with just ice skating, but Barclay said we should get the bus to a cafe he knows that does the best hot chocolate in London. The girls were over the moon to go on a regular bus. It's as if Barclay forgot they've had a far more sheltered life than most kids their age.

Then he insisted on going to Harrods, regardless of us going recently. They had so much fun playing with all the toys, then watching all the pets get pampered on the top floor. Except it backfired when they asked for a puppy. Barclay said a very firm no. Lottie's asked me to work on him.

We're just walking down the stairs from their bedrooms when Barclay starts fidgeting.

'Do you fancy watching a film?' he asks, almost shyly, his hands in his jean pockets.

He seems so awkward that I chuckle. *So* awkward that I can't let him down and make my excuses. It would just be cruel.

'Yeah, go on then. But only if it can be a Christmas movie.'

He rolls his eyes but graces me with one of those rare smiles. 'Jesus, what is it with you and Christmas?'

I shrug, unable to hide my Christmas cheer.

'It's just my favourite time of the year.' He's such a scrooge.

He smiles, his eyes playful. 'You're like a little elf.'

I stop at the bottom of the stairs and turn to stare up at him.

'Are you calling me short?' I hate that I have to look up to ask him.

He towers over me. 'Of course not. It's your pointy ears you have to worry about.'

I smile, shoving him in the chest like a teenager at school. He brings out the real idiot in me.

'Just for that, I get to choose the snacks too.'

I run ahead into the kitchen, far too excited for someone who reasoned with herself earlier that I was only a plaything to him. But when he looks at me like that, well, it's like he casts a spell over me. I can't physically say no.

I brew the kettle, deciding to make us hot chocolates. One can never have too much in December. Who says you're ever too old for them? They always remind me of my dad. He served nothing but hot chocolate as soon as it was December and Mum carried on the tradition after he'd died. Drinking it always makes me feel closer to him.

I rummage through the cupboards, hating how I don't know

where anything is. I finally find some popcorn which I shove in the microwave. I finish our hot chocolates with some Baileys and marshmallows.

I put everything onto a tray and bring it into the living room. Going into this room always feels like I'm sneaking into my parents' room. So forbidden.

He raises his eyebrow. 'Hot chocolate again. Really?'

I smile, secretly loving it when he teases me. 'Hey, it has Baileys in it. Totally a grown-up drink.'

He smiles, pointing over at the huge collection of DVD's hidden behind a cabinet.

'Your choice.'

'Wow, you know you can stream stuff nowadays, right?' I chuckle. He's so old school.

'Hey, I'm not that old! I just like having the DVD's.'

'Control freak,' I mutter under my breath. I realise I'm right when I see they're alphabetised.

'What was that?' he asks, a cheeky smile on his face.

'Oh, nothing, Mr Rothchester,' I joke back. 'How old are you anyway?'

'I'm forty three.'

Shit, I'd never have guessed that old. Thirteen years older than me. Another reason we'd never work.

'So, what do you fancy?' he asks, his eyes wandering down to my lips.

Jesus, don't ask, Barclay, *don't ask*. Nope, I'm not letting that happen again. I'm only here because I have nothing better to do on a Saturday night. Not because I have complicated feelings for him, at all.

I browse the titles. There's a lot of romantic comedies here that must have been his wife's. I can imagine them snuggled up in here. He must have felt such a shock of loneliness when she died. No wonder he busies himself with work.

'What about Home Alone?' It's the least romantic film I can think of. I don't want him getting any ideas.

'Home Alone?' He laughs, his eyebrows almost touching his hair line. 'Are you serious? You spend all day with kids and then you want to watch a kid's film in your spare time?'

I shake my head. 'Home Alone is not a kids movie. Trust me. It's all about bad guys breaking into a kid's house. I've learnt the hard way that it gives little kids nightmares.' I remember the boys being up all night, convinced someone was coming for them.

I'm always too busy wondering what Macaulay Culkin's dad did to be able to afford that giant house.

'Okay.' He shrugs taking it out of its case and slotting it into the DVD player.

I grab my hot chocolate and snuggle into the enormous sofa. I can feel the tension radiating between us, but both of us ignore it. He sits next to me taking a sip of his drink.

'Shit, Ruby, this is strong!' he exclaims, almost choking on it. 'Are you trying to get me drunk?'

I snort. Real attractive, Ruby. 'You *wish*. Sounds like you'd be a cheap date if I did.'

He grins back. I tear my eyes away from him, forcing myself to focus on the film and not his beautiful face.

As I hoped he joins me in laughing over the hilarious stunts little Macaulay Culkin pulls on these guys. Seems he does have a sense of humour.

'How old were you when you first watched this?' he asks me towards the end.

'I was eight,' I answer immediately, remembering it well.

'Good memory,' he nods on a pout, impressed. He seems to pout whenever he's pleased by something. Not that I'm looking at his lips. No way.

My heart aches at the memory of me and my mum laughing and crying through it.

'I only remember because it was the first Christmas after my dad died.'

His face falls, his jaw going slack. 'Shit, sorry I didn't know you'd lost your dad young.'

I shrug. 'Yeah.' My throat clogs whenever I think of him. 'Well, anyway it was the first time me and my mum truly laughed after he'd died. We needed it; you know?'

He nods in silence. Of all people he'd know, of course. Not that he laughs much, ever. I'd bet he's laughed more, *at* me, in the last few weeks than he has in the last few years.

'That's sort of why I wanted you to come today. To remember that having fun isn't betraying the memory of Claire,' I admit shyly.

'And I did.' He sighs, as he always does when I'm around and I force him to think. 'If I'm honest, the real reason I was worried about going was that it was one of the things me and Claire talked about when she was pregnant with Charlotte. She'd always had this vision of the four of us ice skating when the girls were old enough. But then... well, you know the rest.' He looks into his lap, unable to meet my eyes.

'I'm so sorry.' I rest my arm on his bicep. The slut in me wants to gasp at how defined it is. 'I know all of this is hard for you, but... well, even though my dad passed early December we still had a great Christmas. Well, the first one was a struggle, admittedly. But the good thing was that my mum kept his memory alive in her stories.'

He nods, as if understanding what I've been trying to do. Encouraging him to keep Claire alive too.

'I was actually wondering if you had anymore spare photos of Claire and the girls?'

'Why?' he asks suspiciously. Damn it, every time I feel I'm getting somewhere I push him too far and he creeps back into his shell again.

'Remember I told you about the Christmas tree baubles that you can put photos in?' He hasn't mentioned it since so I'm assuming, he's forgotten. 'I think the girls would love a picture of them with their mummy on the tree. Something to see every year they get the decorations down.' *Something they'll still get out once I'm long gone.*

He sighs, running his hands through his hair. 'I suppose it makes sense now.' I frown, confused. 'I mean, why you care so much. You've been there.'

I nod. 'It's still different.' I smile at him. The same sad smile that I used to hate receiving whenever anyone would ask how I was doing in school.

'What about your mum? Doesn't she miss you? Doing this job, you mustn't get to see her much.'

'Actually, she passed the day after I turned eighteen.'

His face falls. 'Jesus, Ruby. How are you so happy all the time when you've been through so much tragedy?'

I shrug. 'I guess I just know they'd hate to see me waste my life moping. I'm still here so I kind of have to live for them, you know?'

He chews on his lips, seeming thoughtful. 'I'm starting to,' he admits.

He stares at me and, without saying a word, he pours his heart out to me. I feel every ounce of the pain he experienced, and he still holds in his heart every day. I want to heal him. I want to carry some small part of the pain for him, but I know that I can't. I shouldn't.

I'm his employee and I'm fired. I'll be gone in a matter of days. Although I've still delayed calling the agency; some small part of me clinging onto the hope that he'll ask me to stay.

'You know, it's funny,' he says with a bashful smile. 'I've ended up liking you far more than I originally planned.'

That's probably the nicest thing he's ever said to me. Which should be weird in itself.

'It just took you to fire me for you to realise it,' I say with a smile. He smiles back but doesn't ask me to stay.

'I should get to bed.' I jump up, collecting the mugs and popcorn bowl, despite us not having finished the movie. I need to get away from him before I do something stupid.

'Ruby?'

I turn, almost at the door.

'Yes?' My voice sounds hopeful. Pathetic that I'm still hoping he ask me to stay.

'Thank you. For today.' He smiles wistfully.

I smile back, feeling the undeniable pull towards him. I want nothing more than to wrap him in my arms and cuddle away the pain. God, I'm in trouble. I need to get away from him before I start tearing up.

'Actually,' he begins, looking hopeful. Oh God, don't give me the hopeful eyes. I can't cope.

'Yes?' I ask far too eagerly. *Keep it together, Ruby.* He's probably just asking you to load the dishwasher.

'I'll walk you to your door.'

I laugh. 'In case the boogie man jumps out on the way downstairs?'

He grins back, his eyes alight with mischief. 'You can never be too careful.'

Oh Jesus, what are we doing? Why do I insist on walking this dangerous line with him when I know it's a bad idea? I'm acting like a dumbass. But damn, when he gets that mischievous look, I'll do just about anything.

CHAPTER 31

Ruby

I dump the stuff in the kitchen. Now is not the time to clean. We walk down to my room, our hands so close every few seconds our knuckles brush each other. I feel like an inexperienced teenager. My pulse is quickening, wondering if he'd dare kiss me again. I hope so. I shouldn't but I do.

I don't know why, but this man is quickly becoming irresistible to me. I mean, I *know* why. He's fucking gorgeous, but so emotionally unavailable. Not my usual type at all. Not that I really have a type. I never have time to date. He's the one man I definitely shouldn't want, but do so badly, it hurts.

I open my door, close to him in the narrow corridor. The fairy lights from the playroom twinkle a romantic glow over us.

'This is me.' I grin, stupidly acting like he's just walked me home from a date.

I look up at him, his dark eyes brooding down at me from the shadows.

His chest heaves. My chest heaves. I can feel my nipples straining against my bra. No nipples, we are *not* getting some.

'Goodnight then,' he says, his voice husky, his pupils dilated.

I gulp. Shit, it's going to happen again. Why is it going to happen again? Stop it, Ruby. Stop it.

'Goodnight.'

I should go into my room. Right now. Listen to the sensible part of my brain.

Only... in a crazed moment of confidence I go up on my tip toes and peck him a quick kiss beside his mouth. Not his cheek, not his mouth, more the corner of his lips. It's not well thought out and the minute I do it I regret it, feeling like I've crossed a line.

Slutty Ruby. *Bad,* slutty Ruby.

My tip toes start retracting, dread and embarrassment weighing them down, when he grabs my face with both of his hands. He plunges his lips onto mine and pushes me back into my door. I almost fall flat on my back from the impact, but he catches me, his hands securing me, holding me tight against him.

I kiss him back with everything I've got, pouring all my muddled feelings into this one kiss. If this is all I ever get, I want him to remember it. To know how I feel before I go, even if I can't voice it in words. My body is willing to help bridge the gap of communication.

He pushes me into the room, kicking the door shut behind

us. His hands travel down my spine, causing every vertebra to shiver, until they're cupping my arse and I'm moaning into him. I'd be embarrassed if I wasn't so into it.

I unbutton two shirt buttons and press my hand in to feel his chest. His skin is hot, like I've imagined, peppered with the briefest of hair. I want to wrap my whole body around him just so I can feel his warmth on me.

One of his hands travels round to cup my breast through my black tank top. It feels tiny in his enormous hand. I groan again despite myself. I'm tempted to strip myself naked to let him know exactly where I want this to lead, but my thoughts are broken by him speaking.

'We shouldn't be doing this,' he says during urgent kisses that line down my neck.

I groan, my whole body tingling. 'Please, Barclay, for once just shut up, will you?'

He chuckles against my throat. I grab the bottom of my vest top and tug it over my head. His eyes widen, taking in the view. I don't stop for a second. I know if I do one of us will realise what a giant mistake this is.

Instead we both fumble to tear off his shirt. As soon as his skin is released, I bury myself into him. I want to feel the heat of him pressed up against my nipples. He quickly unclasps my bra, allowing me to finally feel him skin to skin. I haven't got the largest boobs, but what I have is at least pert.

I cuddle myself to him, sliding my palms up and down his bare muscled back. I bet if I looked right now, he'd have the same sexy back of Patrick Swayze in Dirty Dancing. His whole body is beautiful. A work of art.

I lean back for him to kiss me again, but he's already pushing us back towards my bed. He sucks a nipple into his mouth, his erection pressing against my stomach. It feels better than I've ever felt anything before. Not that previous boyfriends had even a smidgen of Barclay's sex appeal. Or size for that matter.

I tug on my jeggings and drag them down my legs while Barclay does the same with his jeans. I shamelessly reach into his boxer shorts and feel the beautiful soft length of him. Damn, he's big; I knew he had big dick energy. I tug off his boxers with the heels of my feet.

His thumbs tuck into the sides of my knickers, thankfully not the huge granny kind, and pulls them off. He dips one finger inside me. It's embarrassing how wet I am.

'Jesus, Ruby, you're soaking,' he gasps with surprise.

I grimace. 'Please just shut up and give it to me.'

He sits back for a second. Oops, have I scared him by being too eager? The heat disappearing is enough to make me cry out.

'I don't have a condom,' he admits, his face fallen.

It actually turns me on more that he's not walking around with a condom, expecting to get lucky any second. Except I don't have one either. You're not usually caught out doing the dirty in this job.

'Me either,' I admit on a pained growl.

He kisses me on the lips, this time softly, bringing this to an end.

The thought of this stopping, of not feeling him inside of me, well it has me feeling stupid things. Stupid, reckless thoughts that no sensible woman would ever consider.

'Oh, fuck it. Do it anyway.' I don't even recognise my own husky voice or its careless instructions.

'Are you sure?' he asks, joining a second finger inside me. *Jesus.* I never noticed how long his fingers are. How is anyone supposed to think rationally when just the man's fingers have me feeling this giddy?

'I mean, you're clean, right?' I ask, embarrassed, but wanting the reassurance.

He nods. 'I've only ever slept with... one woman.'

It's clear he was about to say his wife's name. I'm glad he didn't. It might have broken the spell he has me under.

'Okay, well I've only ever done it with a condom. Plus, I'm on the pill,' I explain quickly, thrusting my hips up, so I can get some much needed friction from his fingers.

His eyebrows raise. Oh God, that makes me sound like a slut. No one likes a slutty nanny.

'Just for my periods, that kind of thing,' I add quickly.

Oh Jesus, why am I talking about menstruation? A sure fire way to get rid of his erection.

'If you're sure,' he whispers in my ear, already nudging at my entrance.

I've never wanted another dick like this in my life. Not that there's been lots. Only two other men. I spread my legs wider, welcoming him in. I lick my lips, just the anticipation enough to kill me.

He thrusts inside me furiously, all the way to the hilt. I can't help but cry out. Shit, it feels like he's going to come up my throat any minute. The man is ridiculously large, and he's given me no chance to acclimatise to him. Bastard that he is.

Then he reminds me that he can be so sweet sometimes and kisses my neck, stroking my hair back off my face and maintaining eye contact. It's the longest he's ever looked at me, which is weird considering the guy is inside me. Those brown eyes are just hypnotising.

He makes me feel cherished, staring into my eyes as if I'm the most beautiful woman in the world. It's hard knowing his heart actually belongs to his wife and is only on loan to me tonight. It crushes my spirit a little, but I keep reprimanding my own thoughts, concentrating on the pleasure zinging up my spine and back again all the way to the tips of my toes.

A pressure starts building up from the bottom of my stomach, warming me from the inside out. The tension builds until I feel like I might explode. I almost ask him to stop. That's if I could speak at all between the relentless thrusts. That is until I do actually explode all around him, my eyes rolling to the back of my head. Oh my *god*.

I lay panting; my hair a mess, stunned by the amazing sex I just experienced with my boss. How can one man be such an amazing lover? How can he have only slept with one person? I push the intrusive thought from my mind. He won't have lied to you.

He rolls to his side, pushing my hair out of my face.

'You're so beautiful.'

I roll onto my side, so we're face to face. 'You're not so bad yourself.'

I don't think I could be any happier than right now in this moment, him looking at me with that softness in his eyes.

He kisses the end of my nose. I'm just about to snuggle into him when he stretches and sits up, reaching for his shirt.

What the hell is he doing?

He's putting his shirt on. He's... leaving?

'Are you not staying?' I ask like a clingy little bitch. But hell, the man was just inside me two seconds ago. Is it too much to ask for a little snuggle?

He stands, putting on his boxer shorts.

'I don't want the girls to find me here in the morning.'

'Oh. Of course.' I can't keep the disappointment from my voice.

That's understandable, I suppose. Of course, that would be inappropriate. He's only thinking of the girls. But come on, a little bit of pillow talk isn't too much to ask, right? I bunch the cover up around my boobs, suddenly feeling self-conscious.

'I'll see you tomorrow.' He takes my chin, kisses me briefly and then leaves without a second thought.

And I can't shake the sensation I've just been used.

CHAPTER 32

Sunday 22nd December

Barclay

I can't believe I did that. Slept with Ruby. What the hell was I thinking? I totally abused my power of being her employer. I'm pretty sure she could sue me for what we did. But... God, just looking into those pale green eyes; it was like they hypnotised me into just thinking about myself. Not my girls. About what *I* wanted in that moment. For once what I just wanted.

And it felt wonderful to be selfish, while it lasted at least. The minute it was over, and I was lying next to her every intrusive thought I'd been holding back came jumping to the forefront.

Had I just cheated on my wife? Why was I sleeping with my

kids' nanny? The nanny I had in fact fired and knew was leaving in a matter of days.

Maybe that's why. Because I know she isn't staying. That it can't last.

Then I started comparing her to Claire. Every time we made love came rushing to the forefront of my mind. I had to run. I wasn't ready.

I escaped out of the house early this morning and went to work out at the gym. I didn't even want to shower after, instead wanting the sweet smell of her to stay clinging to me. I grabbed breakfast and went to the event to help set up. Something I never normally do, but I had time to burn and I couldn't even consider facing Ruby. Especially if she's hurt, knowing I did that to her. She doesn't deserve that. She trusted me and I left her all alone after she gave herself over to me.

All I know is that the more alcohol I drink the less I think and that's exactly where I want to be right now. If I don't think I don't have the crushing guilt weighing heavily on my heart. That's how I've found myself drunk during a client's Christmas do we've organised. Drunk by 10 p.m. What a lame arse.

I never normally let myself get drunk, let alone at a work event, but it's been the only way to cope with the onslaught of emotions Ruby brings out of me. One minute I want to throttle her, the next I want to kiss her; to protect her, to get her to stay. But I can't and I know that I shouldn't. I can't promise her anything and it wouldn't be fair to her or the girls to pretend like I can.

'You're totally smashed,' Queenie says, helping me into the

house a few hours later. I've tried to tell her I was fine, but she won't listen.

'I'm perfectly fwine,' I chuckle, tripping over my own foot.

Okay, maybe I am a bit plastered.

'Come on. Let me help you to bed.'

I chuckle. 'Oi, oi, matron.'

She helps me up all the stairs and into my bedroom. It's not easy with me falling down every few steps. I keep telling her to shush, so we don't wake the girls up. Or worse, Ruby. God, my delicious Ruby, probably fast asleep downstairs. Her freckles. I really love her freckles.

She throws me on the bed, just as the room starts to spin.

'Ugh, I feel sick,' I announce before my eyes, heavy and weary, close on their own accord.

Monday 23rd December

Ruby

The good news is, that by realising Barclay is in fact a lying, selfish playboy bastard it's made me leaving far easier. That's the conclusion I came to after crying all night and berating myself for being such an idiot, ruled by my stupid emotions.

I've decided to accept the job in the South of France. I feel awful for abandoning the girls, but I can't stay here now. Any clinging to the hope that Barclay would ask me to stay have been trodden on.

Every time I even *think* of Saturday night, I feel dirty. He used me, just because I was convenient and for that I will hate him forever. Using my kind nature and my weakness towards him; the wanker.

This will be better for the girls in the long run. It'll be awful for them to have to survive around our toxic atmosphere. I'm sure they can already sense something is wrong, despite him sneaking out early and staying out all night. The coward.

I'm ringing the agency as soon as the girls are at school. I just hope that job is still available.

I yawn, dragging myself up to the girl's bedroom first thing. I can't wait for them to break up for the Christmas holidays today. Although what kind of school breaks up on a Monday? Bloody ridiculous if you ask me.

Still, I'm excited for not getting up this ridiculously early for a while, although it's just another reminder that my days with the girls are numbered.

My foot hits the last creaky floorboard on the landing when footsteps creep down from Barclay's level. I quickly crack a smile, ready to greet him in a professional manner. The first time I've seen him since we had sex the other night. I plan on acting unbothered by him running away. I'm embarrassed to admit I put on a bit more make up this morning. I just want to feel my best while having to deal with him.

Only the foot that steps into view is a woman's.

I look up to see Queenie, his slutty work colleague creeping out, still in her evening gown, clutching her high heels. My jaw hits the floor, my stomach in my knickers.

She spots me and quickly tries to dart back up, but it's too late. We've seen each other. She cringes, having clearly been caught out.

'Sorry,' she says, wincing. 'I was trying to creep out before the girls woke up.'

I can't speak. Words literally escape me right now. He slept with Queenie? The very night after me? There was me thinking he was sweet for not carrying around condoms, but it was clearly because he had just run out! Or maybe once he slept with me, he couldn't wait to get back on the horse.

'Oh... yeah... yeah...' I stutter, my tongue flopping around uselessly in my mouth.

Nice one, Ruby. Show her how stupid you are by your lack of putting a whole sentence together.

You should be asking her what you're thinking. *Did you just sleep with Barclay? Have you been sleeping with Barclay? For how long? Did he bullshit when he told me he'd only slept with one other person? Or did he mean since his wife had passed? Or was I just a practise run so that he could end up banging you? Someone he really sees a future with? Someone from his world.*

'Anyway, thanks for being so discreet.' She sidles past me and trots down the stairs. Trots because she's still a horse.

I can't move. I look up towards his room, my heart shattering into a million pieces. Why must I be such a fool? Did I really think for a second that I'd ever be more than a plaything for a man like Barclay? Rich and powerful men like him don't go for women like me. Maybe they sleep with us for a quick bunk up. But they date and eventually marry women like Queenie.

I've been such a bloody fool. I've never felt so stupid or inconsequential. It seems despite my pep talk in the mirror this morning I've still been clinging onto a fragment of hope. I watch too many damn Disney films.

Lottie comes out of her room rubbing her eyes.

'Ruby?' she asks, with her adorable husky morning voice.

I lift her up, needing a cuddle right now.

'Morning, sweetheart.' I quickly wipe away the tears falling down my cheeks. 'Let's go wake up your sister.'

I go into nanny mode, on complete auto pilot while my heart breaks piece by piece inside my chest, each jagged edge turning around to stab me again. I'm surprised I'm able to continue breathing while enduring so much pain. My mum dying of a broken heart suddenly makes so much more sense.

I get the girls up and go feed them breakfast. Halfway through their porridge Barclay comes running into the kitchen, still doing up his shirt buttons.

'Jesus, why didn't anyone wake me?' he asks, grabbing a slice of my toast. The bastard.

I'm not his personal assistant. I don't have to answer to him.

'Sorry, Mr Rothchester,' Marge apologises, looking flustered. 'I didn't realise you wanted to be woken today.'

'No, it's fine,' he dismisses quickly, still not even looking at me. 'It's my fault I slept in.'

She's already running around putting coffee into a travel mug.

'Must have been one hell of a night,' I can't help but comment bitchily, not able to look him in his beautiful bastard face. I know if I do, I'll break. Either that or try to stab him with the butter knife.

I notice him frown in my peripheral vision. Probably

wondering how I knew that. *I know everything you dirty, lying prick.*

'I've got to run. Have a good day girls.'

He smiles at me. I look away. I'll let his bit of stuff fill him in at work.

CHAPTER 33

Barclay

*W*aking up still fully clothed was a relief. Thank God I hadn't done something with Queenie.

I'm hungover to fuck, but the worst feeling of all? Seeing Ruby this morning. Seeing how cold she was towards me. I can normally always count on her for a smile, but she only made a weird comment about it being a wild kind of night. Nothing about how I had sex with her and then ran a mile. God, just remembering how vulnerable she looked as I left her lying in that bed. I'm such a bastard.

'Knock knock!' My mother sings, walking into my office. Ugh, just what I need.

'You know saying knock knock doesn't give you the right to just barge in,' I bark at her.

She smiles. 'Oh Barclay, are you especially moody this morning, darling?'

I sigh, rubbing at my sore eyes. 'You could say that.'

She perches herself on the edge of my desk. 'What is it darling?'

I sigh. 'Nothing, Mum, it's fine.'

She smiles knowingly at me. 'It's that nanny, Ruby, isn't it?'

Shit, how the hell does she know that?

'What makes you think that?' I ask carefully, swallowing down the lump of guilt in my throat. I feel bad enough, I don't want to be berated by my mother.

She shakes her head. 'Honestly, Barclay, you really think I don't know you, don't you?'

Well yeah, my nanny raised me. Mum was always too busy helping my father advance his career.

'The minute she came on the scene I could tell she was different. That you were affected by her.'

I roll my eyes. 'You got that from my whinging did you?'

'You might think that I wasn't all that present while you were younger, but I still know my baby boy. I'm around now. Why don't you tell me what you've done wrong?'

I scoff. 'Why is it you assume *I'm* the one to have done something wrong?'

She grins. 'Because I've met Ruby. I know how special she is. Tell me, have you fallen in love with her?'

'Mum!' I'm aware I sound like a moody teenage boy, but I don't want to discuss my love life with my mother.

'Barclay Rothchester,' she snaps sternly, her eyes now hard.

She's not going to give in. 'Stop being such a pig headed man and tell me the truth.'

'Ugh.' I throw my head onto the table. I need at least four coffees before I can have this conversation.

'Fuck, I don't know.'

'You don't know if you love her?' she asks, one eyebrow raised.

God, love? I haven't even considered that.

'I don't know if it's possible for me to love anyone anymore,' I admit. 'Not after Claire.' It actually feels good to voice it out loud.

'Darling.' She walks round the desk and takes my hands in hers. 'It is possible to love more than one person at a time, you know.'

I roll my eyes. 'Really, mother.'

What the hell does she know? She just wants me married off again, so she doesn't have to worry

'Yes, really. You know.' She pauses, considering if she's going to tell me. 'Before I married your father, I was in love with a boy that grew up down the road from me.'

Shit. I just assumed Dad had been her first love.

'I would have married him too, if he'd have asked me, but he decided to take a job in America. Then shortly after I met your father.'

Wow, Dad was second best. I wonder if he knows. Is that why he's such a miserable bastard?

'I still think of him now. If I'm brutally honest with myself, I don't think I've ever stopped loving him.'

'Jesus, Mother!' I don't want to hear this; that she doesn't love my dad.

'But,' she interrupts, 'I also love your father. Even if he can be an incredible shit sometimes. Which is how I know it's possible to love two people.'

I suppose she does have a point. But how could I ever let myself love Ruby? How could I let her be second best? It's not fair to her. She deserves to be someone's entire universe.

'Darling, don't let your love for Claire stop your love for Ruby. She'd want you to be happy, you know that.'

I know she would. She was the kindest woman on the planet, which is why it hurt all the more when she was taken from me.

Who knew? My mother has actually given me something to think about.

'Thanks Mum. You've actually helped.'

She smiles, seeming just as surprised as me.

She beams back at me. 'See. I am useful occasionally.'

Ruby

I got a text from a PTA mum this morning, shortly after finding horse girl Queenie sneaking out, asking me to be at the same address as before, tonight at 8pm. It's obviously some kind of planned show down with Clementine.

Whatever, I'm going and I'm ready to stand up for myself.

I'm never going to see these bitches again anyway, so I couldn't care less.

The agency couriered the new contract over this afternoon. It's all signed and back with them. No backing out now.

As I approach the door, I'm half expecting them to be in black capes ready to offer me up to the pagan gods as a sacrifice. Honestly, nothing would shock me anymore.

I try to remind myself that I've told Mrs Dumfy where I am, and they therefore can't get away with my murder. I knock on the door, my hands still trembling slightly.

'Ruby!' Clarissa says, swinging the door open, already holding a glass of wine. No cape. So far so good. 'Our guest of honour!' She engulfs me in a hug, shocking the life out of me.

What the hell is happening here?

I follow her down to the basement kitchen where the others have congregated.

'She's here!' she sings.

I'm expecting them to turn around with pitch forks ready for my public execution. Instead they beam lipsticked smiles at me.

I look around for Clementine, but I can't seem to find her.

'Sorry, but... why are you all smiling at me? Where is Clementine?'

They laugh. 'You mean you haven't heard?'

I shake my head. Are they messing with me?

'She's resigned from the PTA!' Clarissa shouts triumphantly raising her wine in the air.

My mouth almost touches the floor. 'Are you serious?'

'Yes.' They all nod, their smiles wider than I've ever seen them.

'What the hell happened?' I can't even begin to process this.

'Well, the police were keen to speak to all of us,' Juliette explains. 'Find out what happened at the parade.'

I nod, waiting for them to continue. 'And?' I ask desperately.

'And we all told them that we saw nothing. When the police told her they had exhausted their enquiries, and had no evidence to charge you with, she went ballistic. Asked us why we hadn't told them the truth. None of us had an answer for her, so she threw a tantrum and said she was done with the PTA.'

'Wow.' I broke the head bitch.

I didn't think she'd ever leave the PTA. They're her power-house, but little did I know they've always secretly hated her. They're immediately more relatable to me.

Someone hands me a glass of wine.

'So, cheers to you, Ruby Campbell! Ding dong, the witch is dead!'

CHAPTER 34

Ruby

*B*arclay comes in at around eleven thirty. I've been waiting for him in the kitchen, like a complete psycho, needing some kind of closure. Well, that's what I decided after all the wine I've drunk. He comes in and spots me.

'Hey,' he says, coolly, loosening his tie, avoiding my eye line. I'm glad to see he's not drunk.

'Hey.' I nod, avoiding eye contact.

He grabs a water from the fridge. 'Man, what a day.'

'I bet.' I nod again, wanting to make a bitchy comment but managing to hold my tongue. Probably had a quickie with Queenie in the toilets. 'Anyway, I just wanted to tell you that I've accepted another job and my last day here will be Christmas Day.'

His face drops. Obviously been planning on having a few more shags before I left. Well this fun bun is closed, jack arse.

'I won't let on to the girls until Boxing Day morning,' I continue in a rush. 'I don't want to ruin their Christmas.'

He looks sombre, his eyes suddenly weary.

'They're going to miss you terribly.'

Yep. *They're* going to miss me terribly. Not him. Not *I'm* going to miss you terribly.

I nod, physical pain clutching at my throat. 'I'm really going to miss them too.' Shame *he* won't miss me. 'But I've arranged for Louise Enterland to come meet you. She's a nanny I recommend. I'd feel happy knowing they're being looked after by someone I know and trust.'

He nods again. His lips press together in thought.

'Okay. Sure, I'll meet her.'

'Great.' I nod, staying professional.

I stand, spin on my heel and walk out of the room.

'Ruby?' he calls after me.

Damn it. Him just saying my name has my already battered heart throbbing in fresh agony. I begrudgingly turn around.

'Yes?' I meet his face. Wrinkles mar his forehead.

'Am I missing something?' he dares ask.

I snort out a laugh. Is he fucking joking?

'Excuse me?'

He seems serious. 'Have I done something to upset you?'

Does he honestly think I wouldn't mind being used and abused like that? Or maybe his bunk up buddy didn't tell him I ran into her. He still thinks he's getting away with it.

I shake my head. 'Of course not. Just trying to get this back to what it should be. A *professional* relationship.'

He gulps, visibly wounded. 'Right.'

I turn just in time for him to miss the traitorous tears spilling from my eyes.

Barclay

Fuck. How could that have gone so terribly wrong? Yes, I know I shouldn't have run away after sleeping with her and then sneaking out the next day, but I was hoping tonight we could talk about it.

I couldn't stop thinking about what mum said earlier. After basically doing no work and considering it all day I was going to ask her what she thought about us giving it a go. Quietly of course. I wouldn't want the girls to know right away, not until we worked out if our relationship was going to progress and be solid. I didn't want to raise their hopes.

I was feeling brave until I saw her. The minute I laid eyes on her hard face I knew I was too late. She'd moved on. I thought I might at least have another week to try and win her round, but no. She's going boxing day. Jesus.

I know I shouldn't have got so drunk at that work party. I should have just come home and talked to her then, not left it too late. Instead I got bladdered and can barely remember getting home.

I need to just let her go. I'd be no good for her anyway. I'm too fucked up and she needs someone with no baggage that can give her the life she's dreamed of. The Disney fairy tale she deserves.

It guts me to already see how much I've hurt her. I can't promise not to fuck up again and how can I even really try when I'm still so in love with Claire?

No nanny will ever compare to Ruby. No one will love the girls as much as I know she does, but I have to look forward.

How is it I finally find a nanny well suited to us and I go and ruin it? The girls are going to hate me forever for this. *I'm* going to hate myself for this.

But it's too late now. We had a second chance of happiness, but I had to go and ruin it.

Christmas Eve

Ruby

There's never a good time to have a broken heart, but it sucks extra hard when it's at Christmas and you have to live with the guy. Having to put a brave face on in front of the girls is torture. Especially when I already miss them.

I've already considered staying just for them again, several times, but I know that I can't do that to myself. It would be too much of a sacrifice. To have to watch Barclay get a girlfriend, eventually marry her. Have her as my boss and a step-mum to the girls. It's too much to consider while my heart is shattering inside my chest.

I'm such an idiot to have fallen for him. It's Nanny 101. Never fall for your boss. I used to laugh when nanny friends told me they had crushes on the dads. I used to find it so pathetic and strange how they couldn't separate their work life from their personal life. Now look at me.

It's always hard. We do merge our lives with the family, but I've never minded before. Seeing my mum lose her soul mate made me never want that kind of overpowering love that has the ability to break you. I was just happy to make the children's lives happier and be part of a family. But now I've gone and screwed everything up; been shown something I want but can't have.

Barclay's meeting the nanny Louise I suggested today. Thank God she agreed to the interview. I met her a few years back and she seems very loving and affectionate. The children she was looking after at the time looked at her like she was the best thing in the world. These girls only deserve the best.

And now I'm going to cry again.

The thought of her getting to see them grown up to be the kick arse women I know they'll be has my eyes stinging.

I find myself pacing outside of his office, waiting for her.

Mrs Dumfy comes around the corner, her chin high and her eyes tight. *Uh-oh.*

'So, you're leaving?' she asks, cutting the small talk and going straight to the point.

She's about as subtle as a brick.

'Barclay told you?'

She nods. 'Yes and I saw your suitcases out.'

'You were in my room?' I can't help but sound like a teenager.

She huffs. 'Calm down, I'm in there all the time. I do your washing, remember.' Her stare turns pained, her skin bunching around the eyes. 'I really thought you were going to be the one to stay.'

I hate that she's disappointed in me. It really is the icing on the heartbreak cake.

'Look, it's a lot more complicated than that. Me and Barclay, we have... different ideas. Things are... complicated.'

She sighs and clenches her jaw. 'You've fallen for him, haven't you?'

Shit, how does she know that? Do I have *dickhead that's fallen for her boss* tattooed across my forehead?

She reaches out and rubs my shoulder. 'I've seen the way you look at each other, when you don't think anyone is watching.'

So, she sees it too. It makes me feel less stupid actually, knowing she's noticed his interest in me. It hasn't just been me throwing myself at him all the time.

'So, what's happened to make you want to leave? And don't give me a rubbish excuse.'

She's such a hard arse when she wants to be.

I motion for her to follow me into the kitchen and sit down around the table. I don't want Barclay to overhear me.

'Look, I thought it was happening, but then he slept with that stupid horse woman, Queenie. I can forgive a lot of things, but I can't forgive that.'

She frowns, aghast. 'That doesn't sound like Barclay. He's never cheated before.'

Like she'd know.

'Well, we're not even together properly, so I suppose he's a free agent,' I shrug, trying to act cavalier. Instead my chin wobbles. 'It's just that I really thought we might have something.'

She smiles, reaching across to touch my hand. 'I know you love those girls, but do you love Barclay?'

I force a lifeless laugh. 'God, who knows? I've never been in love before.'

Her eyes widen. 'Never?'

'Never,' I nod. 'I mean, I've only ever dated two men and it wasn't anything special. In this job you never really have the time for a relationship. Maybe I'm incapable of loving someone.'

She frowns. 'Why on earth would you be incapable of loving someone?' she asks, studying me with curious eyes. 'You're the most loving person I know.'

I think back to the love my mum and dad shared. The love that basically broke her when he died.

'I guess I've always been kind of afraid to fall for someone. To give them that sort of power over me.'

'What makes you say that?'

I sigh. 'My mum and dad were madly in love. It destroyed her when he died. I don't want that to happen to me. It's happened to Barclay and look how it's left him; a broken man, incapable of feelings.'

She smiles sadly. 'Ruby, you can't go through life being afraid of love. Love is the greatest emotion there is.'

I sob. 'Then why is it that it also comes hand and hand with potential ruin and heartbreak?'

She smiles. 'Because, my darling, the greatest risks in life carry the biggest rewards. Do you think your mum wished she'd never met your dad? Never felt such strong love towards him if she knew she'd lose him some day?'

I think about it. I suppose I hadn't ever thought of it like that. I know, without a doubt, she would have taken that heartache twice over if it meant she still got those precious years with my dad.

'What really is life, if we live it without love?' she pushes.

I think of Barclay. Do I love him? I've only ever thought it was a pathetic crush up until now, but I do already feel bereaved for leaving him.

'I know that I love those girls,' I say, a fresh well of emotion threatening to creep up my throat. God, I love them so much.

'I know you do.' She smiles kindly. 'That's why I'm shocked you're going.'

'Even after I told you he slept with that bitch, Queenie?' I can't help but sound hurt.

She sighs. 'Just think about it for a minute. Why are you so hurt that he did that?'

Jesus, Mrs Dumfy.

'Because he's a bastard and he's led me on. Using me as a little plaything. And worse than that he's never asked me to stay.'

She frowns, thinking for a moment. 'Maybe he's been waiting for you to offer. Barclay is an incredibly proud, stubborn man. He won't ask for help.'

You don't have to tell me.

'My question is, regardless of Queenie or his actions, deep down in your heart, do you love him?'

Yes, my heart answers for me.

It's true. I've been trying to be realistic this whole time, to think with my head, but my stupid heart has fallen head over heels in love with the stupid man.

'I've signed a contract,' is all I can utter through the veil of tears. 'I'm leaving.'

'A contract might seem binding to you. But nothing binds you to something like the heart does. Trust me. The cost of not following your heart is spending the rest of your life wishing you had.'

Damn, Mrs Dumfy. This woman is profound.

She stands up. 'Just think about it.'

She leaves me to wrestle with my own feelings. Could I put myself out there? Tell Barclay how I feel, risking the potential and likely rejection? I just don't know if I can put myself through that.

CHAPTER 35

Ruby

I don't have time to consider it right now as I hear Louise emerge from his office. I quickly wipe away the tears and run to greet her in the hallway.

I raise my eyebrows. 'How did it go?' I whisper so Barclay can't hear me.

She huffs out a breath. 'He's a handful,' she says with a half-smile.

You have no bloody idea.

I nod. 'He is,' I agree. 'The girls are worth it though.'

One eyebrow shoots up to her eyeline. 'That's why you're leaving, is it?'

My cheeks heat up. Well she's got me there. I obviously didn't tell her the whole story. I didn't know I loved the man myself until about two minutes ago.

'The reason I'm leaving has nothing to do with the girls.'

She nods. 'The agency warned me about his reputation. I'll give it a go, see what it's like before I commit to a full contract.'

Oh, that's not what I wanted to hear. I wanted her to say she was here to stay, regardless of how hard work Barclay is. What if the girls go through another stream of nannies? I could never forgive myself.

I say my goodbyes and then start pacing outside his office again. I can't work out if I want to go in or not.

'Ruby?' he calls from inside.

I poke my head through. 'Yes?'

'Is there a reason you're pacing in front of my office?' The bastard has the cheek to ask, looking smug and amused. He has no right to smile. The heart breaking wanker.

I pull the rest of my body in and fold my arms across my chest. Keep your cool, Ruby. Do not snatch his letter opener and stab him in the chest with it.

'I just wanted to know how your interview went? If you think she'll be a good fit?'

He sighs, rubbing his forehead. 'She's not you, Ruby.'

My eyes shoot up to his. Did he really just say that? What the hell does that mean? Is he giving me a compliment?

'You mean she'll follow the rules?' I offer, trying to lighten the mood.

He smiles sadly. If I didn't know better, I'd think his eyes were sombre. 'I've booked a table for us all tomorrow at Le Traite De Beau.'

'French food?' I can't help but shriek. On Christmas day?

Just when I think I love the man he goes and does something so utterly ridiculous.

'Oh, you know it?' he asks, impressed.

It pisses me off that he assumes I don't know of it. I've walked past it a few times and thought about the pompous arses that must eat in there. And now he wants me to be one of them. On Christmas bloody day of all days!

'You can't have French food on Christmas day! It's supposed to be turkey.'

He clenches his jaw. 'Well I can't exactly tell Marge that she can't have Christmas day off.'

'Then *I'll* cook,' I shrug. 'Part of the fun of Christmas day is that you get back from the pub and get changed into your pjs and start playing with your toys.'

'The pub?' he shouts in disbelief. 'On Christmas day?'

This man really must have been born on the moon.

I roll my eyes. 'Yes, the bloody pub. It's a well-known British tradition.'

He rolls his eyes. 'Honestly, Ruby. Bringing the girls to a pub on Christmas day. You can't be serious.'

'I'm deadly serious,' I insist, leaning aggressively on one hip. Apparently, my last Christmas with the Rothchesters has to be traditional. 'Look, just relax and let me organise it will you?

At least that way I'll know it'll be done right. I can't let those girls down.

'Okay,' he begrudgingly agrees with tight lips. 'I suppose I'll indulge you, being as it'll be your last day.' *Indulge me.* What a prick.

I nod, my throat suddenly thick. 'Think of it as my going

away party,' I manage, sounding defiant but feeling all the while like my world is falling apart.

But I don't have time for that. Right now, I need to find a turkey on Christmas eve.

I asked Marge where the best place to get a turkey this last minute was. All she did was laugh in my face. Nice, *real* nice.

So, I gathered the girls and now we're trying to park in Tesco. We tried the local Waitrose, who also laughed in our faces. But I'm thinking this is a huge Tesco, so they're bound to have loads of them.

I hurry the girls in with a confident smile on my face.

'We're headed to the meat section,' I say with a determination I've never heard in my own voice before.

As soon as we round the corner of the aisle, I see a man dressed in a butcher's outfit stood in front of the desk. People are firing questions at him, but it's easy to see from here that there's no turkeys left. Damn it.

That's when I have an idea. I can get a frozen turkey. I remember my mum used to get them frozen all those years ago. We run to the freezer department. I look for the poultry section and find one frozen turkey left. I look down at it in wonder. I knew it.

I grab it and lift it out of the freezer, needing both hands, but all of a sudden it is pulled away. I look up to see some old dear with a walking stick clutching on the other end of the frozen turkey. What the hell?

'I saw it first,' she has the audacity to say.

I bark a harsh laugh in her face. 'Don't be ridiculous. I'm the one who opened the freezer. This is my turkey.'

If I have to take this old lady out I will. I'm here to save Christmas, damn it.

'It's mine,' she croaks, pulling it towards her so hard I go along with it, but manage to keep a hold on its frozen body. 'You'd do well to remember your manners and respect your elders.'

I look back at the girls, their wide eyes glued on us.

'That doesn't mean you let them get away with murder. I believe in justice. And justice is what's going to get me this turkey.' I look to the girls. 'Call someone from the tills, girls.'

They scurry off. Damn, I really shouldn't be sending two young girls off on their own in a crowded supermarket. What the hell am I thinking? I'm about to go after them when I feel a kick to my leg. I look down to see she's whacked me with her walking stick. Jesus, woman! Have some self-respect.

'How dare you hit me! That's abuse!' I shriek. 'I should call the police on you.'

She laughs. 'I'll be long gone by then. Along with my turkey.'

The girls quickly re-appear with someone who looks like he's already over working this nightmare shift.

'Ah finally!' I smile, glad we can get this sorted out.

'Young man,' old dear begins, 'this yob has been abusing me, both physically and verbally since I got hold of my turkey.'

I roll my eyes. I can tell the supermarket clerk wants to too. He sighs heavily instead.

'Come on ladies. It *is* Christmas. Can't we come to some sort of arrangement?'

I huff. 'Go back and watch the CCTV if you like. I had my hands on this turkey first.'

'Age before beauty!' the old lady shrieks.

'I'm saving Christmas for these girls!' I yell, looking to them both. Lottie's eyes appear glassy. Shit, she's about to cry. What the hell am I doing?

I immediately drop the turkey and go to her. I scoop her up in my arms.

'It's okay baby. I'm sorry I'm acting crazy.'

'You shouldn't have let go,' Jessica humphs, her hands on her hips. The little fighter.

The old lady is already walking off with a smug smile. Merry Christmas you miserable old bitch. I hope you slip on a banana skin and break a hip. Shit. Where did that come from? I've turned into a monster.

The supermarket clerk shuffles awkwardly on his feet.

'Look, I could get fired for this, but...' he lowers his voice to a whisper, 'I might know a guy you can get a turkey from.'

I almost drop Lottie in excitement.

'Really?' I ask, far too eagerly. 'Who? Where?'

CHAPTER 36

Ruby

So that's how I find myself waiting in a dodgy car park behind a butcher's shop later that day. I feel like I'm doing a drug deal, not trying to purchase a turkey. He told me it would be sold for a premium, but that's fine. I've been to the cash point and took out the whole limit of three hundred pounds. I'm sure he won't want that much, but I'd rather be prepared.

A small blue fiat pulls into the car park, spins round and parks across from me. I twiddle my keys in my pocket nervously. The things I'll do to save Christmas. Santa Claus better write me a personalised thank you letter. It's the least I deserve.

A short stocky guy in his twenties gets out, chewing gum and carrying a black sack. Shit, he's not going to murder me, is he? I get out of the car, trembling with trepidation.

'You the lady after the turkey?' he asks with a nod of his head.

Being called a lady makes me feel about sixty.

'Yep, that's me.' I do an awkward wave. 'Have you got one?'

'Right here,' he nods. 'Frozen one though. Not sure if it'll thaw out properly in time for tomorrow.'

'It'll be fine,' I nod, quickly looking inside the bag. Make sure it's not a cabbage in there. 'How much?'

'Two fifty.'

'Bah!' I balk. 'Are you serious? For a turkey?'

He rolls his eyes. 'A turkey on Christmas eve, love. You won't get it anywhere else. But no skin off my nose.' He turns to walk away.

'No, wait! I'll have it.'

I begrudgingly count out the cash and hand it over.

'Ta. Merry Christmas,' he has the cheek to say.

It'll be a very bloody Merry Christmas for him this year, but the main thing is that I have my turkey. I'm saving Christmas. These girls are going to have a great Christmas day if it kills me.

Christmas Day

Ruby

Christmas Eve ended a lot calmer than it started. Well, after I'd called Marge and pleaded down the phone for her to tell me how to defrost a turkey. I put him in a hot bath to thaw out. I remember my mum doing it one year.

Then it was Christmas PJs, a themed story book and hot cocoa with marshmallows. I managed to busy myself with the girls and avoid any eye contact with Barclay. I hurried off to bed as soon as I put them down.

Christmas morning the girls and Barclay wake me up at 06.30. The girl's excited squeals are the first thing I hear before Lottie's snuggled her way into my arms and Jessica's jumping on the bed. In fact, they're so excited that they don't seem to notice the partially packed suitcases on the floor.

'Ruby, what's this?' Jessica asks holding up my vibrator.

My mouth drops open. I look to Barclay and find him staring at me with the biggest grin on his face.

I quickly get up and usher them out.

'Just my... turkey baster,' I quickly lie. Barclay barks a laugh. 'Coffee?'

I nod. 'Yes please.' I've never needed it more.

We go into the kitchen where the huge tree is; presents from Santa adorning it. At least he got that right.

'Can you believe how many presents we have?' Jessica shrieks in delight, her face completely lit up.

This is what I love about them, they might be rich, but they aren't spoilt.

'It's because you're such good girls.'

They start ripping them open and shrieking in joy when they find out they've got what they wanted.

Barclay hands me a coffee. He doesn't mention the vibrator

and I'm grateful. We both watch them storming through the presents until they get to mine.

'Ooh, this one is from you, Ruby,' Jessica says, shaking at it excitedly.

'Wait, Jess. Make sure you and Lottie open them at the same time. And remember, its only something small from me.'

Lottie finds her present and sits eagerly next to Jess, her gummy smile beaming up at me.

'Go!' I shout, watching as they rip it apart to reveal a box.

They pull out the personalised Christmas decorations I had made for them. Baubles with pictures of their mum in them. Jessica reads the back of hers out loud.

'Jessica, always in my heart, Ruby.'

They both stop and look at me with so much love and adoration I have to stop and look away. I can't bear seeing their devotion, knowing I'm abandoning them tomorrow.

I clear my throat. 'Oh, let me give you yours, Barclay.'

He seems surprised as I hand over the silly present. I bought it before everything went completely tits up so I thought I might as well give it to him.

'Wow. Thank you.'

I debated not giving him anything, but I couldn't resist this.

'You haven't opened it yet,' I grin, trying to contain my laughter. I can't wait to see his face.

He breaks open the paper to reveal the most embarrassing Christmas jumper I could find. It actually lights up.

'Oh my god,' he says, his mouth completely turned into a smile.

I love getting that smile from him. It's such a challenge, but all the more rewarding for it. Not that I get to keep it. I try to lock it into my memory.

'You have to wear it today,' Lottie says, clapping her hands in front of her.

He rolls his eyes but reaches behind the tree. 'I got you something too.'

He bothered to get me a present? Or should I say, he got his assistant to buy something for me on the way home yesterday. Oh well, look pleased with the insincere box of smellies.

I unwrap the ribbon and pull the paper away to find a black photo album that has felt wording on the front spelling out *Ruby's Christmas*. He's made me a photo album?

I open it up, wondering if he's put any photos in it. Not just one but loads greet me. All the photos I've What's App'd to him over the last month. He's even got the skating tickets stuck in. Next to some pictures Jessica has written something saying why she loved that day and how I make her feel special and loved.

My eyes fill with tears. He did this, for me.

As a farewell, I have to remind myself. He's being nice, knowing I'm gone tomorrow; no longer his problem. But still, having something to mark my stay with them feels so special.

'Thank you, girls, so much.' I grab them and squeeze them for a cuddle, a few tears streaming down my cheeks.

I look to Barclay. He seems sad but doesn't say anything. If only he'd say something. Anything at all. I'm sure I'd find a way to stay.

Barclay

She's going. There was my chance to say how I really felt, to ask her to stay and I couldn't. Maybe it's for the best. Not the best for the girls, I know that, but best for me. Best for me to move on and carry on with my life without any complications of romance. Look what it's brought me. Nothing but heartache my whole life. Some people just aren't meant to get their happy ever after. And I'm one of them.

CHAPTER 37

Ruby

We came back from the pub to find my turkey was a bit burnt. Oops, turns out I totally timed it wrong. I cut off the burnt bits and still served it to their horrified faces.

'Ruby,' Barclay says as he swallows. 'Why does this turkey taste like chicken?'

I frown back at him, putting a forkful in my own mouth. It's obviously dry and burnt, but he's right. This does taste like chicken.

'Maybe because I burnt it?' I offer, not really having any idea.

'Where did you buy this from?' he asks suspiciously.

Oh god. The girls look at each other with secret smiles.

'Um... just at the supermarket.'

That bastard in the parking lot sold me a chicken. I paid two-hundred and fifty quid for a bloody chicken!

Lottie starts giggling. I raise my eyebrows, hoping she understands the universal look of please shut up.

'Well, I think you bought a chicken,' he continues. 'You must have bought it from the wrong freezer department.'

I couldn't feel more of an idiot.

So, we ended up eating a roast chicken dinner after all that stress. It wasn't that bad, but I could have hit Barclay with his smug little grin. I can actually cook, it's just that I'm not used to their oven. Anyway, the girls didn't seem to care.

We're all changed into our pyjamas now. Barclay tried to get out of it, but of course the girls bought him some cringe worthy Christmas pyjamas that match theirs. They're all elves. He hates it but has let me take some photos.

The girls are playing with their toys in the living room while we sip our hot chocolates, heavily dosed with Baileys. The fire crackles, *It's a Wonderful Life* on in the background. It's a perfect moment, one that I feel I belong to deep within my soul. I have to remind myself that this is not my family. Not my man. Not my future.

I'll learn to open up my heart again and find my own person to have a family of my own with one day. One no-one can ever take away from me. If nothing else me falling in love with Barclay has shown me that I'm capable of giving up my heart to someone. Sure, it's gone wrong this time, but I'll find someone I can be happy with. Happy enough.

But I know whatever my future holds I'll always remember these girls and this moment. Oh, who am I kidding? And I'll remember Barclay. Screwed up, confusing as fuck, sexy as sin, Barclay.

'We didn't get a white Christmas then,' he says turning to look out of the window.

I shake my head. What I really want to say is that he's just like snow, beautiful but cold.

He turns to look at me, his eyes dark.

'You could always stay, you know,' he whispers, so the girls can't hear.

I nearly spit out my hot chocolate. 'Stay?' I shriek. He's waiting until the night before to broach this?

'Stay working here.' He nods, his face serious. 'If that's what you want.'

He says it so detached, as if I'm just any other employee to him. If it's what *I* want. What I want is for him to beg me to stay, to tell me that *he* wants me to stay. To stay as his equal, as his partner, not just the nanny. But I know that's never going to happen. Not with a heart as closed off as his.

'What do *you* want?' I can't help but ask, desperate to get a response out of him. Something, anything, to show he wants what I want, or could possibly want it one day in the future.

He looks down at his lap. 'I just want you to be happy. Wherever that may be.'

My heart sinks.

'Well, then thanks, but I think it's time for me to move on.'

Boxing Day

Ruby

When I put the girls to bed last night, I couldn't help for a few tears slip out. They asked me what was wrong, but I just said I'd had too much baileys in my hot chocolate and was feeling silly. As soon as their doors were shut, I allowed myself to burst into tears.

I practically ran to my flat and let all of the grief and despair take over. I allowed myself some time to wallow face down in my bed. But then I got organised. I packed up all my things apart from the stuff I'd need in the morning.

I barely slept a wink but did go into a deep sleep around 6am. I'm woken by the girls at 08.30. The questions are almost immediate.

'Why are there suitcases?'

'Where's all your stuff?'

'Are you going somewhere?'

I look into their frightened eyes and pull them close.

'I'm so sorry girls, but I'm leaving.'

'Why?' Jessica shouts, pushing me off her and standing up. She's chosen to go with anger being her leading emotion.

'Did we do something bad?' Lottie asks, her eyes teary. I start crying again.

'Of course, you haven't,' I say between sobs. 'You're the best girls in the world.'

'She's lying!' Jessica shouts to Lottie, her arms crossed over her chest. 'If we were the best girls in the world, she wouldn't be leaving us, just like the rest of them did.' She sits to turn away from me.

My heart shatters all the more. This is why it's so hard. The girls don't deserve this. They deserve the world.

'Is it because of Daddy?' Lottie asks clinging onto my pyjama top. She's turning back into the clingy koala bear I met when I first arrived. All my hard work has disappeared in seconds. 'Is it?'

Jeez, what a loaded question. Especially from a three-year-old.

'No. I just have to go.' I sniff, deciding it's easier for them to be angry at me. 'There's some boys and girls out there that need me more. You've got your daddy and he loves you more than anything.'

Jessica crosses her arms across her chest.

'Come on, Lottie. Let's go upstairs. We need to get used to being without her.'

Ouch.

Lottie looks at me sadly before turning and following her out of the room. I throw my head down onto my pillow and sob.

Barclay

Seeing the girls faces and hearing them cry was too much. I was expecting it, sure, but trying to comfort them while attempting to hold my own heart together is too much for me to bear. I excuse myself from the girls and go for a walk, knowing she'll be leaving soon.

This is when I should be there for the girls, but I can barely keep it together myself. I'll be no good to them until I can get my head on straight.

I walk past the shops and carry on until I stop in front of Hole of Glory. The doughnut place Ruby took the girls after Jessica's nativity. It feels like a lifetime ago. So much has happened since. So much that has changed forever.

What the hell am I doing? When Claire died, I told myself that I'd never experience love again. And here I am, being offered it by someone who is not only adored by my daughters but someone that lights that spark in my chest again. The one I thought died long ago with Claire.

I can live with the guilt, the guilt of being happy when Claire isn't around to see it, if it means the chance of some happiness. She'd want me to be happy to fight for her. At that very second a feather falls in front of me. I look around to see where it came from, but there's nothing around. I look above. *Is that you Claire?* Giving me your blessing? A snowflake drops on my nose, followed by several more. Somehow, I know it's a sign.

I'm stopping her. I'm telling her she's mine and she's not going anywhere.

I just have to pop into one more shop first.

CHAPTER 38

Ruby

I can't believe Barclay isn't here to say goodbye to me. It hardens my heart just enough to make leaving bearable. Thankfully Marge and Mrs Dumfy are here for the girls.

Jessica is still angry with me, but I can see from her reddened eyes she's been crying. I bend down and sit on my knees in front of her. She refuses to look me in the eye.

'Jessica, I know you're angry with me right now, but eventually you'll see that this is for the best. I promise you your new nanny is lovely. I used to work near her, and I chose her specifically because I know she'll love you just as hard as I have.'

'If you love me so much, why are you going?' she challenges, her chin high in defiance.

I burst into tears. I can't help it. I love these girls. Seeing

Jessica's guard back up has made me lose it. I so wanted to be strong in front of them.

'Baby, I wish more than anything in the world that I could stay. That I could give up my life for you both, but I know that I can't. I have to be selfish for the first time in my life. Just know that it's killing me to do it to you.'

Lottie throws her arms around me and I laugh through my tears.

'I'm going to miss these cuddles.' I press her squidgy cheek against mine and squeeze her so hard I worry I'll hurt her. I close my eyes and try to embed her smell into my memory.

I look to Jessica. 'I know you're upset, but you might regret not saying goodbye properly later.'

A single tear falls down her porcelain face. She moves Lottie over and puts herself into the group hug.

'I love you, Ruby.'

I squeeze her hard, my chest shaking from my sobs. 'I love you both so much.'

'See you later alligator,' Jessica says. It nearly breaks my heart straight in half.

'In a while, crocodile,' I choke out.

I force myself to pull away and smile at Mrs Dumfy through the tears.

'Thanks for everything. Please look after them for me.'

She smiles back. 'I will. I feel like I never stopped looking after Barclay.'

I sniff, confused. 'What do you mean?'

She smiles as if she's been hiding a secret. 'I mean I was his nanny when he was younger. At least, I was the one who stuck around. Been looking out for the man since.'

No way. Mrs Dumfy was the amazing nanny Barclay talked about? That actually makes a lot of sense. The way he trusts her so implicitly. I thought it was just because she'd been working for them a while, but all along she's been his constant. She stayed.

'I'm so sorry I can't stay,' I say with a deep, chest aching sob.

She pulls me into a hug, patting me on the back. I pull myself away, wanting to at least appear slightly strong in front of the girls. I give Marge a quick squeeze. I turn and lug my suitcases down the stairs towards the waiting car. A snowflake falls in front of me. I smile up at the sky. At least they got one of their wishes. It's going to snow.

The girls stand with Mrs Dumfy on the doorstep, tears streaming down their faces, not even excited at the snow settling on the pavement. I take one final look at what I'm leaving behind before getting in the car and telling him to drive away as fast as he can.

Barclay

I turn the corner to see a car pulling away. I walk faster to see the girls crying at the door. Shit, I've missed her. I run, shouting after the car, skidding on the already snow covered road, but it's already too far away.

I turn, my head in my hands, to see the girls depressed faces.

I walk up the steps. 'She left early?'

Mrs Dumfy doesn't even answer me, she just turns and disappears in disgust. I've let her down. My own nanny, the only nanny that I've ever really trusted, being so disappointed in me, has my gut twisting.

'She's gone, Daddy,' Charlotte says through snot bubbles.

'She's gone and it's all your fault,' Jessica snaps, hitting me in the stomach.

'I know, I know sweetheart,' I admit, taking the punches. I know I deserve them.

I get my phone out and dial her number. It rings behind us in the hallway. She left her work phone. Shit, I don't have her other number.

'I'm going after her,' I announce, searching the street for my car. I can't remember the last time I drove it.

'Yes!' Charlotte yells, punching the air.

'*We're* going after her,' Jessica informs me, her face lit up with determination.

I find my keys and eventually the car. The girls get in behind me and plug in their seat belts.

'Hold on girls. I'm going to try and cut them off.'

I know she's headed for the airport, but which one? London City? Heathrow? There are a few different ways there, but I'm really hoping the driver goes with the route I have in my head. If I speed and break every speeding law out there, I should be able to cut them off.

The girls squeal in delight as I turn corners like a mad man, completely unsafe in this snow, all the while hoping and praying that it's not too late. I'm not too late. That I haven't lost Ruby forever.

I pull out without looking and a car screeches to a stop behind me. I turn to see it's my usual driver. I've done it. I've stopped her car.

'You two, stay in the car. Do you understand?' I shout. 'Under *no* circumstances leave this car.'

'Yes, Daddy,' they both say quickly.

I run out of the car just as she's stepping out, obviously wondering what's happening.

Ruby stares at me. 'Barclay?' she utters in disbelief. 'What the hell are you doing?'

'I can't believe you left,' I blurt out, walking towards her, so agitated I'm barely able to say anything else. My blood is singing in my veins.

Her already wet eyes pour fresh tears. 'You never asked me to stay.'

I take a deep breath. 'Well I know I'm late, but please, stay,' I beg, all pride out of the window.

'What?' She starts walking towards me, like an angel surrounded by falling snow.

'Stay. Don't go. The girls need you,' I blurt out, hoping to God it's not too late.

She smiles sadly, stopping in front of me. 'I'm sorry, but that's not enough for me.'

Shit, she thinks I just want her as the nanny.

'No.' I shake my head. 'You don't understand.' I take her hands in mine. 'Don't stay as the nanny, stay as my wife.'

Her eyes widen to twice the size. 'Your *wife*?'

I squeeze her hands with my own sweaty palms. 'Look, I know I'm shit at this, but I'm in love with you.'

Her wide eyes nearly pop out of their sockets. 'What? How can you say that when you slept with Queenie the very next night after we were together? People in love don't do that, Barclay.'

'Queenie?' I shout. 'What the hell are you talking about? Nothing happened with Queenie.'

She rolls her eyes, dropping my hands. 'Barclay, I caught her sneaking out the very next morning. She asked me if I could be discreet. Don't try and bullshit me.'

Queenie asked her to be discreet. That damn bitch made it look like something had happened.

'Ruby, I swear on the girl's lives, nothing happened with Queenie. She put me to bed because I was so ridiculously drunk, trying to run from my feelings for you. Nothing's happened with anyone since you've become the one person in my life I can't live without. You're the only mother I want for my kids, the only woman I trust with my battered and bruised, fucked up heart.'

She smiles, her eyes glassy. 'Seriously?'

'Seriously.' I nod, wrapping my arms around her waist. 'Yes, you might annoy me more than anyone ever has, but I want to spend every bothersome minute with you, for the rest of my life.'

She raises her eyebrows, but she can't hide that giant smile from me.

'Say yes!' We both turn to see the girls, having taken the sunroof down, jumping up and down on the leather seats.

We both laugh. Of course, they want to be involved.

'But...' I start.

'But?' Yeah, it's hardly the type of thing you want to hear from a man wanting to marry you.

I take a deep breath, needing all doubts to be squashed. 'But only stay if you love me too. I don't want you to stay for the girls or because you pity me. I want you to stay for me and you. Even though I can act like a right dick sometimes.'

She grins. 'You do, but I'm pretty sure I love you anyway.'

She throws herself into my arms.

I kiss her like my life depends on it, like she is truly leaving, and this is the last thing I give her to remember me by.

The girls are doing a victory dance behind us while other cars beep their horns in annoyance. I couldn't care less. Time has stopped for me. Everything ends with Ruby.

I take the small velvet box out of my inner coat pocket, remove the ruby engagement ring and slide it onto her finger. It fits perfectly. I kiss her ring finger.

'You're mine now. You're not going anywhere without me ever again.'

'Thank God.' She presses her lips onto mine.

With the girls going crazy and the horns getting longer I can't help but dramatically dip her for a kiss for all to see.

She breaks the kiss to smile up at me. 'I finally got the family I always wanted.'

I can't hide the grin from my face. 'Really?'

She nods. 'It was my Christmas wish. My wish-mas come true.'

EPILOGUE

18 months later

Ruby

I pin the last of the washing up on the line, baby George asleep in my sling. I wave over at the girls sat on a blanket on the grass blowing bubbles. Life has changed a lot in the last year and a half. Ever since that Christmas that I went to live with the Rothchesters.

We had a long chat that Christmas and decided to sell up and buy in the suburbs. We're now in Bagshot, Surrey. Still within an hour commute of London but embracing the relaxing village life.

I insisted on putting my savings into the sale, much to his annoyance. Why change the habit of a lifetime? He couldn't believe how much I'd saved over the years.

I look lovingly at the four bedroom detached character property we ended up buying. It's on the most beautiful corner plot in a quiet cul-de-sac with the most charming Aga in the kitchen, brick open fireplace in the sitting room.

But the thing that really sealed the deal for us was the garden. With it being a corner plot its huge, actually a third of an acre, with more than enough room for our vegetable garden. It's also so enclosed by mature shrubs and trees that you feel like you're completely private.

The girls have settled in so well to their new school and made loads of friends. I have too, with the help of little George being a great conversation starter. Talking of the little devil, he decided to make an appearance on that pregnancy test only a few short weeks after Christmas. That one unprotected night. I couldn't believe I was pregnant, with me taking my pill religiously, but it seemed that the gods had decided regardless of me leaving, I would always be bound to this man.

It made us take stock of what we wanted. Within a month we'd decided to move and delay the wedding. I couldn't cope with all that stress together. We're planning a small garden wedding next year.

Barclay stood up to his dad and resigned. He now works from home as a freelance event planner. He's in London two to three days a week and it seems to be the perfect work/home balance for us. With no huge mortgage hanging over his head he's a completely changed person, only taking on events he wants. He's done a lot for non-profit charities.

His relationship with his father all but ended when he announced he was leaving the company and striking out on his own. Luckily his mum, Freda, is a constant visitor. She even insisted we got a sofa bed in the lounge so she could stay over. *Rough it* she called.

Mrs Dumfy decided to move with us and bought a little maisonette a few roads away. The girls were over the moon. She still helps with cleaning three times a week, but more than anything she's a member of our family. Even if she does still insist we call her Mrs Dumfy. She's been dating a local man for the past six months and seems very happy. I bet she doesn't get him to call her Mrs Dumfy.

Well, Barclay's still the pig-headed stubborn man I fell in love with, but he's a lot calmer. Or maybe he's just got used to me, who knows. All I know is that I'm happy and I got my Christmas wish; a family of my own.

THE END

Sign up for Laura's newsletter so you don't miss out on her next book – eepurl.com/bpR2ar

www.laurabarnardbooks.co.uk

ACKNOWLEDGMENTS

Firstly, thank you so much for reading my book! I would absolutely love if you'd take the time to write a quick review on amazon/goodreads. They really do help us spread the word.

I'd like to thank my long-suffering husband, who by now should be used to talking to me and me just saying *yeah* while completely engulfed in a work in progress.

What can I say about my Mum? Well, the poor woman keeps me alive! If it wasn't for her coming round, helping with all of the housework and feeding me I don't know where I'd be. Probably dead!

To my auntie Mad, your continued love and faith means the world to me. Knowing you always have my back is such a safe feeling.

To my Barn-Hards! I love our group. It's a safe place I can go to moan, post a hilarious and inappropriate meme and get the encouragement or kick up the arse I sometimes need. You ladies work so hard to help spread the word and I treasure each and every one of you. Big shout out to Vicki Roberts for coming up with the beautiful name of the book.

Massive thanks to the bloggers and bookstagrammers that have helped spread the news, whether it be in a cover reveal or a full review. You guys take the time out of your day to help make my dreams come true. It means so much that you'd help little old me.

To my Indie Girls support group – you girls are like a loyal sister hood. I'm never embarrassed to act a tit and ask a question I'm sure sounds stupid. Without your joint knowledge I know I'd be way behind with all of this marketing jazz we have to do.

Tammy Clarke – thank god you were introduced to me through Andie M Long. The cover for this is a one of a kind thanks to you. You know what I want even before I know myself! Your formatting is also super quick and thanks for not whinging about my constant changes.

Bare Naked Words – Thank you for taking me on at one of your busiest times of year and holding my needy hand while I asked a million questions and generally panicked all around you.

Anna Bloom you beautiful woman! Thank you for your editing genius and for telling me off for all of those adverbs ;-) I'm sorry I made you cry twice. I lie – give me your tears! But seriously, your comments helped shape the book.

CHECK OUT LAURA'S OTHER TITLES

Debt & Doormat Series
The Debt & the Doormat
The Baby & the Bride
Porn Money & Wannabe Mummy

Babes of Brighton Series
Excess Baggage
Love Uncovered
Bagging Alice

One Month Til I Do Series
Adventurous Proposal
Marrying Mr Valentine

Standalones

Tequila and Tea Bags
Dopey Women
Heath, Cliffs & Wandering Hearts
Road Trip
Sex, Snow & Mistletoe

Lightning Source UK Ltd.
Milton Keynes UK
UKHW020955221019
352062UK00006B/147/P

9 781916 273405